Zelda West-Meads has been a counsellor and psycho-sexual-therapist for Relate, the former National Marriage Guidance Council, for more than twenty years. As Relate's former spokeswoman she put counselling on the map, making it accessible and acceptable instead of an embarrassment to admit to. She broadcasts frequently and has a regular weekly advice column in YOU magazine. She is married with two children and lives near Hampton Court.

The Trouble With You

How Men and Women Can Learn to Understand Each Other

Zelda West-Meads

Hodder & Stoughton

Copyright © Zelda West-Meads 1995

The right of Zelda West-Meads to be identified as the Author of
the Work has been asserted by her in accordance with the
Copyright, Designs and Patents Act 1988.

First published in Great Britain in 1995 by Hodder & Stoughton
A division of Hodder Headline PLC
First published in paperback in 1996 by
Hodder and Stoughton

10 9 8 7 6 5 4 3 2 1

British Library Cataloguing in Publication Data

West-Meads. Zelda
Trouble with You: How Men and Women Can
Learn to Understand Each Other
I. Title
306.7

ISBN 0 340 65455 4

Printed and bound in Great Britain by
Cox & Wyman Ltd, Reading, Berkshire

Hodder and Stoughton
A division of Hodder Headline PLC
338 Euston Road
London NW1 3BH

For Roger, Tim and Caroline

Let me not to the marriage of true minds
Admit impediments. Love is not love
Which alters when it alteration finds,
Or bends with the remover to remove:
O, no! it is an ever-fixed mark,
That looks on tempests and is never shaken;
It is the star to every wandering bark,
Whose worth's unknown, although his height be taken.
Love's not Time's fool, though rosy lips and cheeks
Within his bending sickle's compass come;
Love alters not with his brief hours and weeks,
But bears it out even to the edge of doom.
If this be error, and upon me prov'd,
I never writ, nor no man ever lov'd.

William Shakespeare, 1609

ACKNOWLEDGEMENTS

I would like to thank the many men and women who have, in many years of counselling, shared with me the trauma, pain and joys of their lives and helped me learn so much. I have tremendous admiration for the remarkable degree of courage they have shown in struggling to cope with so many difficult and complicated problems.

I know also that I could never have written this book without the love, support and encouragement of my family and many friends. Tim and Caroline, my children, who when I thought I had lost a chapter or was panicking because one of the cats had leapt onto the keyboard causing chaos, patiently and calmly restored my sanity by instructing me on the telephone or rushing home to sort out me and my computer. My mother for her loving enthusiasm and endless encouragement. To Sarah Litvinoff and Fiona Newton for their belief in me, their time, and invaluable help. To Charlie Crowther Smith who introduced me to the totally mysterious and unknown world of word processors and computers. I am very grateful for the wonderful support from all the counsellors, appointment secretaries and receptionists Marion, Fleur, Pat, Evès, Gillian and Eileen and the manager Bridget Robinson at my Relate centre in Elmbridge. To Jan Clark and Caroline Buchanan, Sidde and Patricia Shirman and many other friends who have all been so warm and generous to me in the writing of this book.

I would also like to thank my agent Anthony Goff, of David Higham Associates, for the opportunities he has opened up for me, his humour and his faith in me. And Rowena Webb my editor at Hodder and Stoughton who has been so wonderfully good to work with.

Above all I would like to thank my husband Roger who not only gave endless encouragement, particularly in times of lost confidence, but who was also wonderfully patient and extremely helpful with his constructive criticism and insight, and to whom I am deeply grateful.

CONTENTS

FOREWORD

Professor Cary L. Cooper
University of Manchester Institute of Science & Technology

Goethe once wrote that, 'If you treat people as they are, you will be instrumental in keeping them as they are. If you treat them as they could be, you will help them become what they ought to be.' But to help men and women be as 'they could be', one has to get them to better understand the nature of their own behaviour and relationships, and that is the primary purpose of this most readable and down-to-earth book. It explores the way in which men and women behave in their relationships on a day-to-day basis, in the home, in their sexual relations, as parents, in dealing with relatives, and in juggling the demands of work and home. It's all about self knowledge, finding out about ourselves and how we relate to the most important people in our lives, in order to resolve differences and make our relationships last. When Alice finds herself in Wonderland, everything starts to change so rapidly, she doesn't know where or who she is any more, 'Let me think: was I the same when I got up this morning? I almost think I can remember feeling a little different. But if I'm not the same, the next question is "who in the world am I?" Ah, that's the great puzzle.'

Zelda West-Meads' book helps to better understand the pieces of that puzzle, which should enable men and women to begin to work together to create the complete picture, a more rounded relationship to endure the pressures of our times. It goes without saying that the immediate family context is often the greatest source of conflict as well as comfort, in our lives. In the delicate balance of human emotions which make up a love relationship, an extra weight – like financial pressures, problems with in-laws, juggling a dual career relationship, etc. – can easily upset our equilibrium. You will find this book invaluable in exploring the critical issues that affect close personal relationships, be it marriage or long-term partnerships. The scenarios created reflect many problems between men and women, and expose much of what we need to learn to 'make love work'. I strongly recommend this book for its direct and informative style, and for its profoundly helpful recommendations.

1

LEARNING EACH OTHER'S LANGUAGE

HOW MEN AND WOMEN CAN COMMUNICATE BETTER

Man's love is of man's life a thing apart,
'Tis woman's whole existence.
Lord Byron, poet, rake, misogynist

Stephen sat with his arms crossed, leaning away from Nicola. Staring angrily at her he said, in total exasperation, 'We've been over all this before. It's completely unimportant. We don't need to talk about it again.' Nicola, looking at him tearfully, replied, 'We *haven't* talked about it. You told me what you thought and how you see the situation, but you don't seem to understand what *I* feel about it.'

They had been married for about a year, and what they were discussing was the fact that Stephen had by chance met an old girlfriend of his, Lucy, and they had had a drink together. Stephen had not mentioned this to Nicola. She had only found out because Lucy had left a message on the answerphone, saying it had been nice to see him and wishing him goodbye as she was off to America to work for a year. Nicola felt there was more to it than Stephen was admitting – otherwise he would surely have mentioned it to her? But Stephen said she was getting things completely out of proportion: it had been a chance meeting, he no longer had the slightest sexual interest in Lucy, and he had intended to mention it but had been so busy that it had slipped his mind.

He felt he had explained the situation. In his view he and Nicola definitely had discussed it, and he was frustrated because she did not feel the same way. But Nicola thought the discussion had been all too brief. Stephen had not understood that she had felt hurt because he had not told her. She had also felt jealous, and what she was looking for was more reassurance from him that there was nothing to worry about and that he did not fancy Lucy any more.

A man's approach to a problem is often different from a woman's. He gives an explanation which he thinks is fair and logical, and allows little time for discussion. He may then be completely baffled when the woman wants to discuss it in greater detail, to talk not only about what she thinks but also about what she feels, and at much greater length than he thinks is necessary. For the woman, the brief exchange that men prefer makes her feel she has not been understood, and that the man has not listened to how she feels. This frustrates her because, for her, no conclusion has been reached and there are many things she has had to leave unsaid. The result of all this is that both partners end up feeling dissatisfied.

Two different languages

Lucinda, an attractive, outgoing, lively woman in her mid-forties, said to me: 'When I'm discussing things with my husband I sometimes feel he just doesn't understand me – it's as if we are both speaking a completely different language. Whereas if I talk about the same thing with a girlfriend she knows just what I am talking about.' And this is a couple who have a fairly good marriage.

Men and women often use language quite differently, which can lead to many misunderstandings. A woman may say, 'You never talk to me' (meaning 'You never talk about emotional matters and what is going on between us') but the man insists that he does (after all, he told her about Jones being fired, or complained about his shares going down).

Over the many years I have spent counselling men and women I have always been aware that, to achieve a happy marriage or a good relationship, it is vital to be able to communicate. So the more insight you can have about yourself and the way you relate to each other, the more you can avoid what men and women constantly say to each other: 'The trouble with you, darling, is you just don't understand me.' Nowadays, at last, couples who seek counselling are actually asking for help in learning how to communicate with each other better. They know it's important to know how to talk about their thoughts and feelings, as well as listening to and understanding what their partner is saying. They also recognize that it is important to be able to resolve arguments and to know how to negotiate. If you are unable to do this the relationship is in danger of crumbling: constant rows and arguments can drive you apart.

This book aims to show how men and women can learn to understand each other better as well as how to have loving and fulfilling relationships. It also explores why it can be so hard for the sexes to communicate. It looks at some of the danger points and bad habits that it is all too easy to fall into, and shows you how to avoid them.

Later chapters look at all aspects of men's and women's lives, and show how from earliest childhood boys and girls are brought up differently. It explores the different attitudes of men and women to falling in love, to sex, to affairs, to work and the family. It looks at how men and women relate to their children, their in-laws and their friends, as well as at who does what around the house. It shows you how you can learn to understand each other better, how to handle arguments, and how to transform negative interactions into positive ones. Most important of all, it shows you how to achieve real closeness and understanding as a couple, and how to make love last.

What he wants versus what she wants

When men and women fall in love, women more than men tend to want to minimize their differences and to be part of a couple, and they focus on developing intimacy. Most men desire this too, but, because of the way they are brought up and society's view of how men should behave, they often have difficulty in making the sort of intimate relationships that women want. And a woman frequently finds it hard to understand that the way she expresses her need to be close to the man she loves, spending time talking and being with him, can make him feel pressured.

Men are more used than women to establishing independence

and status in their relationships at work, and work is of prime importance to men. Above all it provides their sense of worth. So to make the shift to the intimate relationship that women are asking for does not come easily to them. Because women set a high value on intimate relationships the crucial part of their world consists of making relationships, and, even in the 1990s, work does not usually have the same priority.

The musical *My Fair Lady* includes a perfect example of the male attitude. Professor Higgins and Colonel Pickering congratulate themselves warmly on their success in turning Eliza Doolittle, the Cockney flower girl, into a lady by teaching her how to speak properly. They completely ignore Eliza and the effort she has put in. When she reacts to this – in their opinion over-emotionally – they are quite bewildered, and the following exchange takes place.

Professor Higgins:	Why can't a woman take after a man? Men are so pleasant, so easy to please, Whenever you're with them, you're always at ease. Would you be slighted if I didn't speak for hours?
Colonel Pickering:	Of course not.
Professor Higgins:	Would you be livid if I had a drink or two?
Colonel Pickering:	Nonsense.
Professor Higgins:	Would you be wounded if I never sent you flowers?
Colonel Pickering:	Never.
Professor Higgins:	Why can't a woman be more like *you*?

I think many men would empathise with these thoughts. If only women would be more reasonable they would be so much easier to live with, and life would be so much simpler!

All close relationships are about the struggle to combine the desire for intimacy with the need to be independent, and achieving that balance is not easy. In order to establish a close relationship with someone you have to get to know them very well, discover what you like about them, accept the aspects you don't care for, feel in tune with how they think and feel, learn to trust and respect them, believe in their value system, and be interested in many of the same things. A shared sense of humour is also an important element in any relationship. But you also need to remain an individual in your own right, with your own thoughts, opinions and beliefs. A relationship in which each of you encourages this in the other is one that enables you to grow as an individual as well as to develop as a couple. This is what makes for a healthy balance, but because of men's need for independence and women's need for intimacy a couple can often misinterpret each other's behaviour.

Harry was a member of a tennis club and tried to play at least twice a week, but it was a popular club and he had to book several weeks in advance. He always gave his wife the dates straightaway, but this annoyed her and she would say, 'How do you know we haven't got anything booked for those times?' His response was, 'Well, I'd look pretty silly if I had to come home to ask you every time if I was allowed to play.' What he had done was to turn that situation into one in which his wife was perceived as threatening his independence; what *she* thought was that he was just not thinking about her and her needs, and was ignoring the fact that maybe there was something they might like to do together which was now not possible. In addition, because she felt part of a couple she would always refer to Harry before making plans of her own, and resented the fact that he did not do the same.

When they realized they were coming to this situation from different perspectives, they agreed that before Harry went off to play tennis he would check diary dates with his wife and then try to make bookings at time that would also enable them to do things together. As a result Harry stopped feeling he was being controlled and she felt he was taking account of her needs. Balance and harmony were restored.

The changing role of men and women

Marriage has gone through considerable change in the last hundred years. For a start the concept itself has been turned completely upside down, and the sort of committed long-term unmarried partnership which many couples now have would have been socially beyond the pale not many decades ago. In most contexts the word 'marriage' in this book is also intended to cover the modern live-in partnership too.

Women in the twentieth century have changed much more, and faster, than many men. And that can cause problems for both sexes in the way they understand and learn to adjust to each other. Well into the nineteenth century men were legally allowed to beat their wives if they thought they had stepped out of line – so long as the man used a stick no thicker than the width of his thumb. When women married, their property became their husband's, by law. This took away women's independence and encouraged men to see a wife as their property, someone they owned. Although the bulk of these laws and attitudes changed during this century, small details lingered on. Until relatively recently a wife's unearned income (from shares, building society accounts and so on) was always taxed as though it belonged to the husband. And even today most women who choose to marry in church are 'given away' by their father or other male relative. And the old psychological attitudes still surface all too frequently.

Up until the 1960s men and women settled fairly unquestioningly into the traditional marriage. The man was the breadwinner and the wife the homemaker, whose main job was to look after her husband, children and the home. Marriage then was about falling in love – but it was also about security. A man provided, so that the woman was looked after financially. Marriage was about status, particularly where the woman was concerned. An unmarried woman above the age of twenty-five or so was not seen as she is nowadays – young, single and free – but as an old maid, a spinster. And as the years increased she was someone to be pitied slightly – the maiden aunt who was very useful to the rest of the family but who had not acquired a husband for herself.

Marriage today still has the romantic ideal of falling in love. But now what is being sought is very much more than love, security and status – now it is all about the search for the 'companionate marriage'. It is interesting that, despite the current high divorce rate, expectations of marriage have never been higher. The traditional roles have been overturned, and a woman's place is no longer in the home. What is perhaps most significant of all is that women insist on equality within marriage and relationships as well as in the workplace – and there's the minefield! Equality has created marvellous opportunities within relationships, but it has also thrown many men and women into complex and troubled waters.

Have we achieved equality?

Ask the average man if he has an equal relationship with his wife or partner, and nearly all of them will answer yes. Ask the average woman, and far fewer will agree. The struggle for equality is a battle that is fought on a daily basis in many households. It goes something like this:

'Michael,' Tricia calls out from the kitchen. 'Gemma's just been sick. I can't send her to school today. She isn't well enough.'

'No, of course you can't, darling. Maybe my mother could come over and look after her.'

'Don't be silly, Michael, you know your mother's away for a week,' replies Tricia. 'Oh, what am I going to do? I have to get to work. I've got an important meeting today which I really shouldn't miss.'

Michael, standing at the kitchen door, replies anxiously, 'So have I, darling, and I'm already late. You'll think of something. I must go now – I'm sorry darling, but we can't afford for me to lose my job. I really do have to go now.'

Michael, as he sees it, has tried to be sympathetic and to offer a solution. But when the chips are down he is still more likely to see his presence at work as vital. Although he knows Tricia's job is important, it's not quite up there with his job. And because he is under pressure, he is more likely to leave the sorting out to her.

Michael is still programmed into traditional role-playing. He probably thinks he has a marriage of equality with Tricia. After all, he has made great strides if he compares his approach with the way his father conducted his marriage. The trouble is, this may be far from what Tricia had been expecting when they embarked on their life together.

Equality in relationships is so much easier to achieve before children appear on the scene. That's when it is really put to the test. And couples who thought they had equality in their relationship find out that with the first baby things are not quite as equal as the women would like. Intellectually and emotionally, men support the idea of the 'new man'. They are all for equality in principle, but often find it very difficult putting the concept into practice. The reasons are that it involves extremely hard work, and the gains for them personally are less obvious than the losses.

Most men want women to have the same work opportunities that are available to them. They know it's fulfilling for the woman, and two salaries or wage packets mean that they can share the financial burden. But the crunch comes when men find they don't want to put up with the implications. The modern man is not being looked after the way his mother looked after his father. When his father came home from work, there was a meal on the table and slippers at the ready. When women were fighting for the vote in the early years of this century a suffragette called Hannah Mitchell commented wryly that 'men were more interested in whether there was going to be a meal on the table when they got home than if women got the vote'. The modern woman is not fetching and carrying the way her grandmother and even possibly her mother did, because she too has had a tough day at work and now there are the children to look after, the supper to get and the housework to do.

Men traditionally feel that it's all right for them to work long hours, to go away to conferences or to bring work home. But if a woman is doing too much of that many men start to resent her job and think it's making too many inroads into family life. The modelling they got from their own parents' more traditional marriage is hard to throw off. As one career woman said cynically: 'A man who works a twelve-hour day gets promotion, a woman who works a twelve-hour day gets divorced.'

Women, on the other hand, often confuse men by giving them mixed messages. Women want the sharing, caring new man who treats them as equals, but they also want the successful man who's got get-up-and-go, who achieves at work and who earns money. But then when he comes home at the end of the day she wants a man who spends time with her, who talks to her and who helps with the children and the house. She often thinks she would like a man who stays at home full-time and looks after the children, or cuts short his working day to get home and look after them – even though he might get overtaken in the promotion stakes. But then ambivalence creeps in and the woman may start to compare him unfavourably with the men she mixes with at work. Or she may find he is a little dreary to come home to, or regard his conversation as rather limited in comparison to her friends and her working life. This issue is one of the big dilemmas of the late twentieth century.

Where are men in this dilemma? Most men do want to work and be successful, but they would also like to spend more time with their wife (or partner) and children. So they too are often torn in different directions.

Women, like men, want to be able to choose whether they work or not, and they want equal opportunities in the workplace. It is good, and for many households essential, to have two incomes coming in, and most men would support this. On the other hand, the majority of men still prefer their wives to be there when they come home from work. A warm, friendly house is much nicer to return to than one that has been standing empty all day with the breakfast dishes still in the sink. It's nice to open the front door to a clean, tidy hall and the smell of supper cooking.

If they really had the choice, most men would prefer their wives not to work full time when the children are very young. It feels far better to most men if their children can be looked after by their mothers rather than a child-minder or au pair. Or perhaps what feels best of all is if they or their partner could work part-time, so that at least one parent can be with the children when they are young. Research shows that both men and women think that children are better in the care of at least one of their parents when very small – say, up to nursery school age. I share this feeling; of course I don't want to deny men and women an equal right to work when the children are young, but I am also very concerned about the long-term effect on a child of a continually changing supply of carers.

Equality for the working woman in the nineties may be much more stimulating, if not considerably more tiring, than for men; more of that later. But are women recognizing the new generation of latchkey husbands and partners who may not entirely share their enthusiasm for the modern marriage? The reality is that when men and women come home at the end of the day they *both* want time to relax and unwind. But surveys show that it tends to be the men who do more of this than the women – and that, of course, leads to arguments. When the woman comes in she puts aside her working life, attends to the children or moves into the kitchen to start the second shift. If the husband gets in first he may have a drink, he may potter in the garden, he may play with the children or he may turn on the television. But I am afraid he is less likely to peel the potatoes or cook the supper.

New pressures on marriage

Couples entering into marriage or long-term relationships nowadays have issues to tangle with that previous generations did not have to address. In the more traditional marriage a woman's role was fairly clearly defined and she did what was expected of her. But now the roles are much more interchangeable, so greater skills of understanding, discussion and negotiation are required.

A couple may share the same educational background and have jobs of similar status and earning capacity. Then the man is offered promotion which means moving to a different part of the country. For as long as it tends to be the man's job that takes priority, and the woman who moves to accommodate him, this situation will still cause trouble. The woman may well have a job that she does not want to give up, or the couple might lose their second income for a while at least.

When a baby is born it is still the woman who is more likely to stay at home and look after the newcomer. It may be what she wants, and it may be best for the child to have one parent at least at home. But it's a bad career move. And men are still fairly reluctant to take on this role.

If an elderly parent becomes ill and comes to live with the couple – even if it's *his* mother – it is much more likely to be the woman who does the main caring job or gives up work to look after them. Again this can cause a lot of resentment.

So most women are having to keep many more balls in the air than previous generations. Nowadays she might do some or all of the tasks mentioned above, and will very likely combine them with working and developing a life of her own. Of course she needs more understanding and help and support from her partner. So he too has to change and incorporate into his life some of what the woman is asking from him. It all means a lot more negotiation and give-and-take so that the distribution of labour can be differently balanced – and this is hard to achieve.

Men are changing in these areas, but maybe more slowly than

women would like. Of course, if the boot were on the other foot and men were wanting the massive changes that women are now demanding from men, women might not be quite so keen to change. But unless men and women learn to shift their roles around more flexibly it will continue to be the source of much conflict.

Communication is the key

The first essential in helping to resolve problems is better communication through better understanding. If men and women are going to learn how to understand each other, men need to acknowledge more that what women want most from them is closeness, intimacy and the ability and willingness to talk about his feelings as well as listen to hers. Women also need to understand and appreciate that talking about emotions does not come easily to many men. (I should add that it doesn't come easily to all women, either. In counselling I not infrequently see men who say their wives can't communicate and don't understand about close, loving relationships.)

At a party a group of men and women were talking about why they thought men were so bad at communicating their feelings. Nancy, a woman in her late forties, turned to me and said, pointing at her husband, 'I've got one of those. Nick's a hopeless communicator. He can't talk about his feelings at all.'

'She's absolutely right,' said Nick, smiling.

'Why can't you?' asked someone.

'I have absolutely no idea,' replied Nick, quite unperturbed.

'Well,' said his wife triumphantly. 'If he was able to talk about his feelings he'd be able to tell you.'

Time and time again in counselling women say to me, with desperation in their voice, 'Why won't he talk to me? I wish he would say what he really feels. If only he would listen to how I feel.'

Women are asking a lot from men nowadays. What they want from a man is a best friend, a good lover, a loving and involved father to their children – someone to share every aspect of their lives. Many men want this too, but often their needs are more focused on being looked after, on home being a good place to return to; and their need for emotional closeness is less than a woman's.

Men often don't realize until it is much too late the importance that women set on friendship and of having someone they can really talk to. A young woman said to me, 'I used to try telling him how I feel, but he just doesn't seem to want to know. So now I don't bother – I talk to my friends or my mother instead.'

In the last ten years I have seen an increasing number of men coming to counselling, either because their wives are threatening to leave or because they have already left. Sometimes men don't have any idea of what has gone wrong and are often very confused, saying: 'I don't understand. I thought I had a happy marriage.' Their wives are sitting there in an angry but determined frame of mind, saying exasperatedly: 'It's only now that he is listening to me, but it's too late. Love has died.'

Relationships don't have to go that way if couples try to sort things out before they reach that stage.

The difficulty for men

I believe it is easier for a man to take off his clothes in front of a woman than to lay bare his soul. Most men are terrified of being stripped bare emotionally, just as most women would rather expose their feelings than their bodies unless they happen to look like Michelle Pfeiffer!

Men often fear that if they talk about their feelings they will let women get too close to them. They are afraid that, if they reveal their deeper feelings or areas of themselves that are easily hurt, women might take advantage by thinking less of them or ridiculing this side of them during arguments. If a woman asks a man to open up emotionally he often feels under attack or cornered. Since this feels scary or uncomfortable his way of protecting himself is often to clam up, to go on the attack or to get angry. This response alienates the woman, who feels rejected and confused. So both sides end up angry with each other.

Josh and Penny were in their second marriage. From his first marriage Josh had a ten-year-old son whom he had not seen for four years. Every time Penny asked him about the boy he flew off the handle and refused to discuss the matter. Penny felt totally rejected and cut off from Josh as a result. But after a lot of time and patience and talking together they grew to trust one another. This was difficult as they had both gone through very damaging childhoods and in previous adult relationships had been treated badly, so each was anticipating a recurrence of these emotional injuries. In counselling Josh was able to start talking about the tremendous pain that he felt about losing contact with his son. He had tried everything to maintain the relationship, but his ex-wife had poisoned his son's mind so much that the boy did not want to see him on access visits. Josh could not bring himself to drag a screaming child away from his mother into his own car.

Josh was afraid that Penny would feel he hadn't tried hard enough to see his son, or that she would think he did not love his son, when in fact he loved him deeply. But the situation was so painful that he had buried it away. When he was eventually able to talk to Penny she was wonderfully supportive and understood his feelings immediately. She had a five-year-old daughter and would have been devastated if this had happened to her. So they were able not only to share the pain Josh was feeling, which brought them closer to each other, but also to discuss what they might do to enable Josh to see his son again.

Men often deal with uncomfortable or distressing feelings by reacting aggressively, because they do not know how to handle them. A man confronted with a woman in tears is quite likely to get angry, to tell her to stop being foolish or that she is over-reacting, and he will walk away rather than put his arms around her. But what a woman in tears wants is the comfort of his arms around her and encouragement to tell him what is wrong.

If men and women can only start to understand these differences, they will find it is possible to make changes for the better.

The difficulty for women

If a woman has a problem, what she wants is to talk it through, usually at length. But because men tend to be solution-focused they think they are being asked to make a decision. Yet if they supply one, more often than not the woman becomes irritated.

She feels he hasn't give her enough discussion time. He has cut this process short by offering a single solution – and, what's more, she didn't want to be told what to do in the first place. What she wanted was for him to listen to her views and feelings and to hear about his, so that she could arrive at her own solution or at least a joint one. If the man steps in with an answer she feels it diminishes her own ability to resolve the issue. So the chances are she'll reject his solution. He then feels there is no pleasing her, or that she is just being difficult. If she doesn't want to take good advice, then why did she bother to ask him in the first place? This way both parties end up frustrated and angry with each other. Or, as Professor Higgins continues to complain to Colonel Pickering,

> *Let a woman in your life, and patience hasn't got a chance,*
> *She will beg you for advice, your reply will be concise,*
> *She will listen very nicely, then go out and do precisely what*
> *she wants.*

Perhaps modern man might have a sneaking sympathy for Martial who in AD 98 said to his spouse:

> *Wife, there are some points on which we differ from each*
> *other:*
> *Either change your ways to mine, or go back to your mother.*

Circular arguments achieve nothing

Most people desperately want to sort out problems that are developing, but often they just don't know how to. They get into arguments that lead nowhere because they are convinced that it is their partner's fault for not listening to them or not doing as they say. Or else they score points off each other by being unpleasant without getting to the bottom of what is wrong. But problems in relationships can't be sorted out through veiled attacks, criticisms or sideways digs. They can only be dealt with by talking openly and honestly and by couples really listening to each other.

When Ian and Sarah came for counselling they knew how to argue but not how to sort things out. They were so angry with each other that all they could do to begin with was run each other down, each justifying their own behaviour. Ian said that the marriage was in such a bad way that if it went on like this he saw no future in it. Sarah said that she still wanted the marriage but not in the state it was in.

They had a baby of about nine months, and Sarah's nine-year-old son by her first marriage. Most of the rows started because Sarah felt that Ian expected too much from her son, Daniel, and that he was always bullying him and getting at him. But Ian was jealous of Daniel. He felt Sarah was always putting Daniel's needs first and that she was an over-protective mother. Not having children of his own of that age, Ian didn't realize that Daniel was no naughtier than most nine-year-olds. And what he couldn't see was that, because Daniel had been on his own with his mother since he was a small baby, he too had mixed feelings about Ian arriving on the scene.

Part of the little boy was quite excited at having a new stepfather, but the other part of him resented the time and attention his mother gave Ian. He used to play up because he knew that his mother was more likely to take his side, and doing so reassured him that his mother still loved him.

In many ways both Sarah and Ian needed each other very much. Neither of them had experienced a close or loving relationship with their parents. One of the things that emerged in counselling was very poignantly expressed by Sarah: 'I'm so lonely in this marriage. We never really talk now. We used to – that was one of the things that attracted me to Ian in the first place – but that seemed to go once the new baby arrived.'

Ian was really taken aback by this statement. He said, 'I thought we did talk. It's just that you never listen.'

It soon became obvious that there was plenty of arguing but almost no talking going on, except about day-to-day matters. Each had developed a separate life, and Ian was drinking too much as an escape. He would withdraw into himself and not say how he was feeling. This behaviour had started when he was a little boy: his mother had been in and out of hospital much of his childhood, and when he was complaining or naughty he had always been told: 'Don't say that' or 'Don't do that. You mustn't upset your mother.' So he had learned to suppress his feelings, and later, instead of talking things through, he became withdrawn and silent because he didn't know how to handle problems.

Sarah found this impossible to cope with, because for her it felt like rejection. And this brought back all she had felt when she was rejected by her mother as a little girl. So she screamed and shouted at Ian, which made him withdraw even further into himself. Eventually he would shout and scream back, which of course achieved nothing either.

When they were helped to understand the reasons behind their arguments, and what they were doing to each other, it became possible to make changes in their relationship. Ian agreed not to withdraw and to tell Sarah that he needed time on his own to calm down before they talked things through. Sarah was then able to be less demanding, able not to scream and shout and not to feel she was being rejected.

They agreed not to have the television on all the time, so that there was more time to talk to each other. They also agreed that mealtimes would be taken together – at a time when the television would be switched off. This was a practical but major breakthrough, because both had been accusing the other of being the one who had wanted the television on, which made any real conversation impossible. But with a little honesty they admitted they had both contributed to the problem in their different ways.

Ian also recognized that he was getting at Daniel when it was often not justified. Even though he found it difficult, he did manage to bite his tongue and let Sarah do more of the disciplining. Then, when he and Sarah were alone, Ian was able to tell her what was annoying him and, as he was not tackling Daniel directly, they were able to discuss it without losing their tempers. Sarah no longer felt she had to protect her son at all costs, and so she was able to concentrate on her relationship with Ian and be much more loving. Ian really responded to this – he felt loved and understood, and no longer jealous of Daniel. His relationship with Sarah flourished, and he and Daniel also became much closer. By learning to listen to each other, and to understand each other's point of view, and not just impose their own view as the only correct one, Ian and Sarah had started to learn how to argue constructively and so sort out differences.

The battles between the sexes

'Make love, not war' was the slogan in the sixties, yet behind so many front doors up and down the land many couples are engaged in warfare. The late American rhythm and blues singer Esther Philips sang a very moving and poignant song about marriage and relationships that go wrong. Part of the lyric goes:

Home is where the hatred is,
Home is filled with pain,
So it might not be such a bad idea,
If I never went home again.

This, sadly, reflects the real state of many couples' relationships. When they come home from work and shut the door on the outside world, instead of finding a relationship of love, renewal and support they just tear each other apart.

Some couples, of course, continue the warfare in public. I call it 'the exposure game'. Of course it is not a game at all, but a deadly duel to see who can hurt each other the most.

Couples who argue with each other frequently often find they are arguing about the same old things – like who does what around the house, how impossible her mother is, or why when he says he'll just have a quick drink with his friends down at the pub he rolls in two hours later. If these arguments remain unresolved they cause deep and increasing resentment. Each person ends up feeling that their partner is not listening to them and doesn't appreciate their needs. Each feels frustrated and misunderstood. As they haven't learnt how to discuss problems openly, how to negotiate and reach an agreement, and because they feel ignored and trampled on in private, they often use a public occasion to make their complaints and score points by exposing to those around them how impossible their partner is.

A favourite place for couples at war to play this exposure game is when they go out to a dinner party, or are mixing with a group of friends. Not only is there a safety net in that your partner will probably not retaliate as much as he or she would if you were at home (though retaliation will undoubtedly occur when you are eventually on your own again), you also have an audience who, you hope, will be on your side. The problem is that you often end up exposing yourself rather than your partner and, even to the not very discerning, you certainly end up exposing the state of your marriage. You also end up the loser because your partner inevitably gets the sympathy vote.

Helen bared her bitterness towards her husband Mark in a 'jokey' comment during a drinks party the couple were hosting. A guest who had just arrived latched onto a small group engaged in conversation and enquired about a glass of wine. 'Mark will give you one,' replied one of the number, and the ambiguity of the response prompted laughter. Making capital of this double-entendre, Helen quickly sniped, 'Don't worry, Sally, you won't notice it. I never do.'

John really resented the fact that his wife had put on weight. He knew she was embarrassed but felt she was not trying hard enough to lose it. To a group of friends who were discussing the new health club that had just opened up in their area he remarked, 'Oh, Jo has joined. I think it's only because she fancies the instructor, but with the extra weight she's carrying around he's more likely to be calculating the extra pounds than whether he can take her out on a date.'

Not only is that type of exchange very cruel, it's also damaging to the relationship. The outcome is much more likely to be a deeply hurt wife than what John hopes to achieve – which is to shame her into slimming. John needed to encourage Jo into slimming, not criticize her. She had made a start by joining a health club, but what she needed was reassurance and praise, not a public put-down.

Couples who are separating or divorcing often let spiteful remarks slip out. When Prince Charles was on a walkabout, he reportedly met a woman who told him that she had also met his wife. He was reported as replying, 'And you lived to tell the tale?', implying that contact with Diana was fairly lethal.

Unkind messages are often wrapped up in jokes by couples: they deliver their poisoned dart by exposing their partner to ridicule. But if their partner challenges this, expresses hurt feelings or is even reduced to tears, the attacker frequently denies the hidden message and claims, 'I was only joking, darling.' Heads I win, tails you lose – except that in this kind of scenario there are really no winners in the long run, only losers.

Power battles

Couples struggle daily over the issue of power in relationships. Is it evenly balanced, or does one partner have too much and the other too little? Is one partner bigger, stronger, cleverer, and using those advantages to achieve what he or she wants at the expense of the other? If so, it might bring short-term gratification; but in the long run the partner will start to feel resentful, angry and bullied, and the relationship will either fall apart or stagger on miserably. In any relationship, if one partner continually tries to dominate the other it leads to problems. Relationships flourish best if the power balance is fairly evenly distributed – ideally it should ebb and flow between you, with neither of you feeling you always have to have the upper hand.

When men do try to exercise power over women in marriage, it is sadly often through the use of physical violence or emotional bullying. To outsiders such men can appear very charming and not particularly threatening. But in the home they behave very differently, through an over-developed need to control which often stems from deeply buried feelings of inadequacy and low self-esteem. Men may also behave like this through a fear that, if their wives are well-functioning, confident people they might up and leave them. The irony is, of course, that it's their response to this hypothesis that tends to drive their wives away. Either that or they become desperately unhappy women, too scared to get out.

Power is also frequently exercised by put-downs. A man may undermine a woman's opinion, wanting or insisting on things being done his way, or consistently ignoring her needs, so that she ends up constantly getting at him. Then he blames her for nagging, and so shifts the blame for his behaviour on to her. One man who was constantly trying to control his very intelligent and beautiful wife said to her once, with obvious irritation but deadly seriousness, when they were arguing about politics, 'What you don't seem to realize is that what I say is fact. What *you* are saying is merely opinion.'

If one partner feels unable to make concessions to the other partner's needs because they see their requests as an attack on their independence, it makes for an unhappy relationship. It means that one person is treating the other in a very autocratic way, which creates distance between them and often leaves the couple feeling very lonely in their relationship.

Susan experienced this in her relationship with Gerald. His father had been in the services and had brought his children up in a very overbearing and controlling way. Though Gerald had hated it and been a rather unhappy, lonely little boy, he didn't realize that he was continuing the same pattern with his own family.

Gerald was a slightly pompous, rigid type of man in his mid-forties, with a rather limited sense of humour. He was very dedicated to his work, and so his wife and four children often had to take second place. His wife had been a nurse and was a rather jolly, organized and unflappable woman.

Gerald was constantly late home from work and his wife rarely saw him before eight or nine at night. On this particular evening there was a special function at their son's school which Gerald had agreed to go to, but first he was holding a meeting at home.

Susan, knowing how he tended to let meetings run on, put her head round the door at about 6.30 and said, 'You have remembered that it's the boys' school concert tonight, and that we have to leave no later than seven or we'll be late?'

'Yes,' said Gerald, hardly looking up from the meeting, 'I have remembered.'

'Well, *I* shall be leaving on time,' retorted Susan.

As seven o'clock approached the people around the table were expecting Gerald to draw the meeting to a close. But he just went on, apparently oblivious to the time.

At precisely seven the front door banged and a minute later there was the sound of a car engine starting up. After a slight pause there was a crunch of tyres on gravel and the car accelerated away from the house. Gerald was speaking at the time. There was no pause, no flicker of emotion as he went on speaking.

Gerald's need to control his wife, to hold the power in his hands and to remain independent was so strong that when she made a simple request for him to finish the meeting on time he interpreted this as her taking charge and telling him what to do. This made him angry, so that he couldn't respond to her simple and reasonable request to finish the meeting on time – which after all had already been agreed between them.

Gerald is a fairly extreme example of one person needing to control another, but it is none the less a familiar battle in many relationships between men and women. If one partner hangs on to their need to be independent or controlling at all cost, it causes resentment and anger and erodes relationships. That was what was happening to Gerald and Susan.

In counselling I see more marriages where the man is the

over-dominant partner than the other way round, but that is not exclusively so. Charles, a successful businessman running his own company, is married to Amy, a managing and bossy woman in her late fifties. She has never worked and achieved success in her own right, despite being capable and highly intelligent. So to compensate for this, and against her husband's will, she does her best to run his company. She constantly rings him at work about the day-to-day running of the company, or turns up in the office and talks to his financial director about the company's accounts, or insists on seeing the books to make sure that he is not over-extending. She tries to alter his decisions if she does not agree with them, and if things go wrong she is the first to criticize him. On the rare occasions when he stands up to her they have major rows. Charles, who is laid back, witty and charming, has throughout his married life escaped from his wife's dominance by having affairs with other women. This is one area where she fails to control him, and it is his way of getting back at her.

John Mortimer's invention Rumpole of the Bailey refers to his wife as 'She who must be obeyed', after an autocratic character in a novel by the nineteenth-century writer Rider Haggard. Although Hilda Rumpole is portrayed as being very bossy and in command, her husband does a pretty good job of achieving the upper hand in his work until he goes home at night. But once inside the house she has more say in what goes on. Another example is Arthur Daley's well-known phrase, ''er indoors' – who, it implies, rules the roost. And we are all familiar with the seaside postcard image of the huge, dominant wife with her scrawny little husband.

One of the things that men fear is women taking charge and giving them orders. If a man feels that a woman is trying to rule him he understandably feels that his independence is being threatened, so he will often react by putting her down so as to regain control.

Male power – female manipulation

Even nowadays many women only get their emotional needs met by gently manipulating their partners. In other words, a woman makes a man feel that the idea she was trying to get across was really his, so that he will be more willing to act on it. Previous experience has taught her that direct acknowledgement is difficult to obtain, so she learns to be more devious. This is particularly necessary in relationships where the man is very traditional or rather stubborn.

If a woman is not accepted as an equal decision-maker by her partner she will be tempted to fall back on this more indirect approach. So if being devious is the only way to gain power, women are still going to manipulate men – whether it's by humouring them at work or twisting them around their little fingers in the home. It works something like this.

Confronted with a really obstinate man, a woman will give him a series of options, asking which he would like to pursue. If the husband goes for the one the wife doesn't want she expresses interest, but lets him run with it for a day or so. After that she drops in a few examples of the difficulties associated with that idea. And then, after some thought, he comes up with another of her options which by now he is really beginning to think is his own idea. Eventually he will get round to what she wanted in the first place. This way of negotiating takes a little longer but is quite effective. But it is really only preferable if up-front negotiations are rarely or never successful.

One intelligent and sprightly seventy-year-old said to me about her very good-natured but extremely stubborn husband: 'Not only do I have to make him think it's his idea, I also have to put the words into his mouth.' And she added: 'A really intelligent woman is one who doesn't let her husband know how clever she is!'

We all use a little mild manipulation at times. How many women, when they buy a fairly expensive garment, admit the true price to their partners? Don't most women knock off a few pounds? And how many men, when returning from the pub and asked by their wives, 'How much did you have to drink, darling?' reply, 'Oh! Just a couple'?

'You just don't understand me'

Both sexes would probably agree that it is often easier for men to understand men and for women to understand women. Men and women often have to struggle much harder to understand each other.

When men have close friendships with other men, that friendship tends to be like an alliance, a comradeship, perhaps most intensely experienced in times of war or when all the chips are down. Men don't necessarily talk about how they feel, and are more likely to be at ease talking about what is happening. They don't necessarily deal with emotions, but are just there for each other – and that experience makes them feel close to each other. For me it is an extremely important way of relating and of being friends. As one man in his late fifties said to me, with immense feeling and passion: 'The friends I made in the army were real mates. If we'd been at war I'd have been prepared to die for them.'

When women have close friendships, however, they tend to want to talk about how they feel first and what they think second. They want to be open and emotionally honest, accepted and understood. They like to debate things at length. And among true friends they, like men, are there for each other in times of trouble.

Neither way of handling relationships is necessarily better than the other. They are just different.

In this first chapter I have tried to draw out some of the different ways men and women think and act: how women need to talk about problems thoroughly, which can seem endless and never-ending to men, who are more focused on finding solutions; how in relationships women set more store on intimacy and men on independence; how women are struggling for equality in relationships, where the traditional roles are changing; and how the power balance between the sexes is an endless subject of debate. All of these differences can put pressure on a relationship. In the next chapters I shall be looking more closely at how men and women relate to each other in different areas of their lives: how they cope, and how to improve matters, in the home, with children, over work and money, and in relation to sex and infidelity – in fact, in all areas of their lives together.

2

GROWING UP WELL

THE EFFECTS OF CHILDHOOD
ON OUR ADULT LIFE

*We are moulded and remoulded by those who have loved us;
and though the love may pass, we are nevertheless their work,
for good or ill.*
                François Mauriac, French writer and philosopher

Over the last twenty to thirty years we have been encouraged
by the feminist movement, as well as through books, newspaper
articles, television and radio, to believe that there is only a physical
difference between men and women. This is perhaps because after
thousands of years of inequality, women's justifiable need to be
treated as equal to men in all aspects of their lives has led them
to be over-enthusiastic in minimizing the differences between the
sexes. Declaring their similarities has been seen as a way of reaching
their goals.

When the feminist movement took off in Britain in the late
fifties and early sixties, women seemed to think that to succeed in
a man's world it would be better if they became more like them.
Many believed that assuming what they saw as male characteristics
was the way to equality and success. The Greek writer Arianna
Stassinopoulos recognized this when she wrote in *The Female
Woman* in 1973: 'It would be futile to attempt to fit women into a
masculine pattern of attitudes, skills and abilities and disastrous to
force them to suppress their specifically female characteristics and
abilities by keeping up the pretence that there are no differences
between the sexes.'

But women were so far behind men in the equality stakes that this may have seemed the only way forward. And whether it was in the workplace, at home or in relationships with men, drastic action was needed if they were to catch up. Reflecting on their plight, women may have shared the sentiments of George Orwell when he wrote in *Animal Farm*: 'All animals are equal but some animals are more equal than others.' Burning their bras was perhaps not so much about sexual liberation or a cry for freedom but more about the need to be seen to be like a man.

Few people would now dispute that men and women are equal to each other, though they may not as yet have achieved complete equality. Charlotte Whitton, the Canadian writer and politician, reflected on women's desire for equality when she said in 1963: 'Whatever women do they must do twice as well as men to be thought half as good.' I think we are now at the stage where most people recognize that men and women differ quite considerably from each other in how they think, feel and behave – whether it's in marriage, in relationships, with their children or in the workplace. If men and women stopped seeing these differences as threatening and realized how complementary they could be, there would surely be more harmony between the sexes. In this chapter I want to start by looking at how these differences originated, starting in early childhood and moving through adolescence, and to discuss how these early influences condition men and women in the way they relate to each other in their adult lives.

Nature or nurture

The nature versus nurture debate has been around a long time. But I think most people would now agree that the characteristics we are born with combined with the way we are brought up do influence how we are as adults. Research and observation show that we treat even newborn babies slightly differently, handling boys a little more roughly than girls. We may dress baby girls in blue, but we do not put boys in pink. We also apparently talk to girl babies more than to boys. So right from the cradle we treat them differently and have different expectations.

When a baby is born it has no awareness of self, of being an individual. It is also completely dependent on its mother for survival. The basic necessities of food, warmth and comfort that the womb provided now have to be provided by another human being. So the newborn baby's first attachment is to the breast or bottle. It wishes to suck it and to possess it orally. It is only after many weeks that the baby begins to understand that attached to the breast is the mother. At that point it starts to relate to her, and then to those round about such as the father, brothers and sisters and then family and friends.

As the baby gets older and begins to realize that it has a separate identity from its mother a sense of self starts to develop. The baby learns, for example, that people around it respond to its needs and actions. The first smile, which brings such excitement and joy to the parents, enables the baby to start learning how to relate to others. As the baby becomes secure in its relationship with its mother it can then begin to explore the world around it and its sense of self continues to grow.

How we see ourselves

First and foremost we see ourselves as a man or a woman. Our gender is fundamental to our very being: it conditions how we relate to ourselves and to those around us, and how we treat our male and female children.

In Western society, in the early days of a child's life the mother is the prime carer and therefore has most contact with it. Mothers identify with girl babies because they are the same sex; they do not do so with boy babies. This does not mean that a mother does not love and care for boys just as much or even more, but is just the natural process of gender identification. She experiences girl babies as the same sex and boys as different from her. This early influence means that a baby girl experiences herself in relationships as merged. A baby boy, on the other hand, experiences himself in relationships as separate. As the boy gets older he will start to move towards and identify more with his father, and so become separate from his mother. In this way he will establish himself as the same gender as his father.

These differences – merging and separateness – have a fundamental influence on how men and women learn to expect and
experience relationships in their adult lives. As a result of their
upbringing and gender differences men and women seek a different
intimacy in relationships, particularly in the areas of sexuality,
emotions and feelings. This does not mean that every man and
woman will encounter gender differences in the same way, or that
this situation will automatically lead to problems between the sexes.
If the reasons for these differences are understood the couple can
work out the differences.

Connectedness and separateness

In her book *In a Different Voice* the American writer and researcher
Carol Gilligan describes women's search for intimacy in relationships as wanting to merge with their partner, while men favour
separateness. Women are more likely than men to depend on
intimate connections for their sense of identity because this is
how they define themselves and how they are defined; men, on
the other hand, gain their sense of identity more from the jobs they
do, the money they earn and the status that this brings.

Much of what happens in our upbringing explains why women
tend to look for a close empathic relationship in which they are
fully understood by a partner whom they can trust with their
deepest feelings. For women talking about feelings is the road
to intimacy. Few men feel the same way; most want their woman
to be there for them, but not all men are necessarily looking for
the close, intimate relationship that they often feel women are
demanding.

As one man explained to me: 'Sometimes women are so
emotional in relationships that they just batter your brains as well as
your feelings. Men don't want to engage with emotions all the time
– it's just over the top. Men want to look after a woman. They want
to be close to women, but they don't want an emotional bloodbath.'
Another man said: 'I have such a rotten time at work these days
that by the time I get home I feel completely disorientated. So
what I need at home is stability and security. I don't want to be
put through the mill by an overdose of emotions.' Because men

and women often don't understand or recognize these differences they go into relationships thinking they want the same thing. And because they don't achieve their expectations they frequently end up confusing and misunderstanding each other.

As with love, there is no single definition of intimacy. Different people will explain it in different ways. Over the years researchers have talked about intimacy as an enduring relationship, and a close, confiding one. In *The Fund of Sociability* Robert Weiss suggests that 'intimacy or attachment is provided by ties from which people gain a sense of security and place and where individuals can express their feelings freely and without self-consciousness.' The researchers Brown and Harris investigated whether an intimate relationship protects women from becoming depressed, and published their findings in *Social Origins of Depression*. They claim that 'for a relationship to provide intimacy there must be trust, effective understanding and ready access'. I would add that, although most couples want true intimacy, they also want a loving and mutually satisfying sexual relationship. Though not all women would regard a sexual element as a necessary part of an intimate relationship between couples, nearly all men would. So let's look further at why these early influences affect adult relationships.

What the nursery rhymes tell us

As children we are influenced by our parents, families and those around us, by early experiences such as going to play group or school, and by fairy tales and nursery rhymes. The messages we receive affect how we will be as adults, just as parents' different expectations of their children play a part in the way they bring them up. The different roles of men and women are spelt out for children in stories and rhymes:

What are little boys made of?
Frogs and snails, and puppy-dogs' tails.
What are little girls made of?
Sugar and spice, and all that's nice.

It doesn't say much for little boys, and is hardly going to make little girls think much of them. But it does begin to highlight the fact that as girls and boys grow up they are frequently admired for different things: girls because they are pretty or have lovely curly hair, boys not for looks but for what they achieve. This again reinforces the message that the sexes are valued for different attributes. Parents are often not aware of how sexist they are in their attitudes, yet old ideas and habits linger on. If negative attitudes to the opposite sex are planted in children's minds even unintentionally, they are often carried into adult life.

We see the stereotyping of the sexes all too frequently. Women often knock men, saying: 'Oh! All men are bastards,' or 'Men, hopeless creatures. They can never do more than one thing at a time,' or 'Men – they are only after one thing.' And equally men say about women: 'Scratch the surface of a woman and there's a hysterical one waiting to get out,' or 'Women will always make a mountain out of a molehill,' or 'Don't you worry your pretty little head about that.'

There are many more nursery rhymes which draw attention to the different expectations of the sexes:

> *The King was in his counting-house*
> *Counting out his money,*
> *The Queen was in the parlour*
> *Eating bread and honey.*

The King is depicted as the one in charge, with the money and the power, while the poor Queen has little to do except over-eat and get fat. And sometimes girls are depicted as weak or silly, as in 'Little Miss Muffet':

> *Little Miss Muffet*
> *Sat on her tuffet,*
> *Eating her curds and whey*
> *When along came a spider,*
> *And sat down beside her,*
> *And frightened Miss Muffet away.*

All fairy tales and nursery rhymes abound with these subtle and not so subtle messages. I am not suggesting that children should be deprived of these poems and stories, but merely pointing out how easy it is for them to be influenced in the way they see their future adult roles.

When my own children were very young my son and his friends wanted to play the prince or pirate king in their fantasy games. They would have died rather than play the princess or the fairy queen! On the other hand my daughter and her friends were usually happy to be the princess or a fairy but were equally keen to be pirates, highwaymen or even the prince. After a while the girls realized that the female roles were passive while the male roles were much more fun. But for the boys it would have seemed cissy to play a traditionally female part – even at that tender age maleness was an important commodity. For my daughter and her friends, however, wanting to be a tomboy was totally acceptable. I think, to be fair, there was one other reason why my daughter opted out of being a princess. She used to get very fed up with being tied to a tree without knowing for certain whether the prince would remember to rescue her – he had been known to lose interest and wander off to play some other game.

So for a girl to show her aggressive, assertive, masculine streak is much more acceptable than for a boy to show his softer, feminine side. And that is often true in male and female adult relationships, which is tough on the men.

Different ways of communication

Let's follow boys and girls through childhood and see what happens. When a little boy of seven or eight falls over and cuts his knee, the message very often still given by parents or teachers is that he must be brave about it. Little boys don't cry. A small girl of a similar age is more likely to get a cuddle, and there will be no messages about not crying. The little boy is being told to suppress his feelings, while the little girl is led to understand that her feelings are quite acceptable.

Take the same boy a couple of years later in the school playground. He is being bullied. When he tells his father he is told, 'You must stand up for yourself and don't let them see

you are scared.' Some fathers may even add: 'If necessary get
out there and use your fists – show them who is boss.' When the
ten-year-old girl is being bullied, she tells her mother and they talk
about it at length. The mother suggests that she gets away from the
bullying group. She encourages her to talk to a friend about it, and
to ask her friends to stick around so that the bullies give up trying
to bait her.

These two children have been taught to react differently to the
same situation – the boy modelling himself on his father and the
girl on her mother. The message is: this is how girls and boys
behave, and it's different from each other. What it also shows is
the different expectations that parents often have, depending on the
child's sex.

If his daughter was being bullied, a father would be unlikely to
encourage her to fight it out. And although if her son was being
bullied, a mother would talk it through with him, any suggestions
she made would be influenced by her not wanting him to appear
a cissy. Society, too, encourages these different expectations. Men
resorting to fists in an argument with each other is perhaps
regrettable, but not nearly as unacceptable as if women start to
fight each other.

But most important of all is how the two small children are
learning to relate to each other. So let's take the same boy and
girl fifteen years later, now both in their mid-twenties and just
married to each other. They hit a problem in their marriage. What
she has learnt all along is that if you have a problem you talk things
through, and it is all right to show your vulnerability – to admit you
are upset and need help. What he has learnt all along is that you act
without doing too much talking, you don't show you are running
scared or feeling vulnerable in any way, and most importantly of
all, you aim for the dominant position. With these messages learnt
at their mother's knee, or from their father's fighting talk or in the
playground, is it really so surprising that when men and women are
put together they find it so hard to understand each other?

At a play centre in America in the 1970s, some educational
psychologists studying the way boys and girls develop undertook
some fascinating research with children aged seven or eight. To
start with, two little boys were put in a room with a lot of building
toys such as Lego. The researchers then watched the children at
play through a two-way mirror. The little boys liked the toys

and immediately started to play with them together, skilfully constructing something out of the building pieces and discussing and sharing how it should be done.

Afterwards, two little girls of a similar age were put in the same room and again watched through a two-way mirror. The girls, too, were interested in the building bricks and started to play with them together. Like the boys they talked about what they should build, but very quickly they also started talking to each other. They asked each other their names, where they lived, what schools they went to, whether their Mummy and Daddy had come with them to the play centre, what was the name of their best friend at school, and what was he or she like. The boys' conversation, other than asking each other's name, had been almost entirely concentrated on the task in hand. They had established almost nothing about each other and, like the girls, were quite happy with the situation.

You will not be surprised to know that what they had constructed was larger than and of superior quality to what the girls had managed. No doubt some men might like to interpret this as confirming what they have always 'known' about women – given the chance, they prefer to gossip while the men get on with the important tasks of life. But what is more illuminating about this research is its demonstration that, even at that early age, the female of the species is more interested in getting to know the person she is with, of finding out about her and establishing friendship and even some intimacy through talking. She is developing her verbal skills. The little boys, on the other hand, have concentrated more on the activity of play and the fun of constructing something in which they were both interested. To them this was more interesting than finding out about each other, but it was also their way of forming a friendship. In their way they too were bonding. In adult life men's friendships are often made and developed through a shared activity such as playing squash or golf. Where women are concerned, closeness or friendship is more likely to be achieved through conversation than through activity or sport. Again, I am not suggesting that one is better than the other – only different.

I would be interested to know what would have happened if they had put a boy and a girl together in the room. Would the little boy have wanted to get on with the task of building his model, only to be irritated by the little girl's constant questions? Would she have felt rejected and ignored and gone off to find something else or preferably someone else to play with? Or would they have reached a compromise with the little boy responding to her questions and starting to want to know more about her; and, because that felt good to her, would she then have become more interested in building things together? That would, after all, be a sound basis for the start of a good relationship.

When Terry and Ann came to me for counselling they were like two small children who had not taken time to get to know each other. They were both twenty-two when they got married and both had experienced unhappy childhoods although in quite different ways. Communication between them was deteriorating fast. They had been married for about two years and had a daughter of fifteen months called Lindy. Terry was good-looking, with a very fit, athletic appearance. Ann was pretty, with long blonde hair, and slightly overweight.

When Terry sat down he said that, if only Ann could make some changes, learn how to discuss things and make compromises, there would be no problem. Ann's reaction was to turn away, cross her arms in front of her body and look furious. At this point Terry said: 'You see, I told you she can never discuss anything.'

Trying to pull the counsellor on to your side is very typical behaviour when people first come for help, particularly if they are very angry with each other. Understandably, most people arrive feeling that their partner is more unreasonable than they are; and because they are feeling so awful themselves they long for the counsellor to be on their side and to agree with them, which would feel supportive. But if the counsellor took sides it would immediately alienate the other person, making counselling impossible. In an argument, going into the attack as Terry did only draws forth from your partner anger and counter-attack or withdrawal and suppressed fury – Ann's reaction. So you both end up the losers.

The main area of argument seemed to centre on the amount of time Terry devoted to sport. Ann resented it and felt that, as she didn't work but stayed at home looking after Lindy, he ought to be there at weekends instead of playing squash and rugger. Terry felt that he worked hard all week and was therefore entitled to time away playing sport. Ann's reaction was she didn't have time out from being a full-time mother, so why should he have all this time away from her and Lindy?

Anyway, she wanted to be with him – that's why she had married him.

As in so many arguments like this between couples, it's only when you start looking underneath that you find out what is really going on. Terry came from a family whose father was frequently absent, and when his father was there his parents were always arguing a lot. He remembers as a small boy sometimes trying to pull them apart physically when the rows got really heated. Ann thought her parents had a really close marriage. They were always together, and as a child she thought they were very content with each other. It was only when she looked at her parents' marriage through adult eyes that she saw a bored and lonely couple with few friends. She was an only child, also with few friends, who had frequently felt excluded by her parents.

Both she and Terry had gone into marriage with completely different expectations. They had not talked things through but just made assumptions, both thinking that what they wanted from marriage was what the other wanted. Ann wanted to have a slice of the togetherness she had thought her parents had enjoyed. Terry's only experience of marriage was arguments and if you didn't like it you made yourself absent, as his father had done. Here he was repeating his father's pattern by playing sport all the time. He wanted a wife who was there for him when it suited him, but who did not tie him down.

When Ann was able to stop idealizing her parents' marriage and see it in a more realistic light, she saw that it had been claustrophobic and had excluded the world around them. She was then able to appreciate that being close did not mean you had to live in each other's pockets. She no longer insisted that Terry was there all the time, and because of this he was able to see that continuing to live the bachelor life, playing sport all weekend, was unfair to Ann and Lindy. He began to recognize that he was missing out on time with both of them.

So after some time in counselling and a lot of honest talking together, they were able to reach a solution that they could both live with. Terry played sport on only one day at the weekend. Often Ann and Lindy would go and join him after the game, and they would go and have a picnic together. Ann had also learnt to understand that you can have a good, fulfilling marriage without being glued to each other. When she stopped pressurizing Terry always to be there, he in turn played less sport. They also learnt not to make assumptions, but to test out how they both felt by asking each other what they thought or wanted to do.

What are the male and female characteristics?

Men and women have traditionally been seen as having certain gender-specific characteristics. This does not have to mean that a particular characteristic is solely the preserve of one sex, but rather that it predominates in one sex. There are plenty of aggressive, ambitious (male characteristics) women, and sensitive, caring (female characteristics) men. I think we are now seeing a loosening of these bonds. There is far less stereotyping today, so men and women are able to acknowledge the male and female side of their characters without either feeling threatened by displaying a characteristic which has usually been seen as belonging to the opposite sex.

Among the characteristics usually attributed to men are aggression, logic and ambition. Those associated with women are more likely to be sensitivity, caring and intuition. Ask men to describe how they see women and they might add to the list over-emotional, hysterical, unreasonable and changeable. Women might add to their list on men: domineering, inflexible and critical. Both would at times describe the opposite sex as 'quite impossible'.

Traditional male characteristics such as aggression, ambition and the need to succeed are highly prized in the male world, both by the man himself and by those around him. Yet if a woman displays these qualities she can make others feel uncomfortable or criticize her for being too masculine. Mrs Thatcher was joked about as being the only real man in the Cabinet, just because she had these traits in great abundance.

If men show the caring, sensitive side of themselves this too can be criticized. I remember sitting next to a woman journalist from one of the national dailies as we listened to a talk, given by a man, recommending men to get in touch with the sensitive side of their personalities. 'Oh, what a complete wimp,' she said, sighing heavily and stubbing her pen aggressively into her notebook. Sensitivity in a man can also be frowned upon by other men as well as by women, since it can be interpreted as lacking in backbone – a flaw in their character. A man in his fifties said to me: 'My son-in-law stays at home to look after the children and it seems to work well.' He sighed. 'But it's not natural,' he added with mounting irritation. Obviously his son-in-law did not agree with him, as he was happy with the choice he had made.

One of the many good things that feminism has achieved is that men and women are much more relaxed about the male and female sides of their personality. As a result the traditional characteristics of both sexes are far more integrated in one person, and men don't feel they always have to be the strong ones in a relationship. Men can now be more relaxed about showing tenderness, softness, even tears without fear that this exposure undermines their masculinity. Similarly women can now express their need to take the lead at times, to have control, to be ambitious or aggressive without feeling it a threat to their femininity in any way.

Childhood experiences influence our adult behaviour

In trying to gain more insight into understanding how men and women relate to each other I cannot stress enough how important it is to take into account upbringing, gender differences and particularly childhood family experiences. All these influence people's personalities and the way they behave in relationships with others. In my work as a counsellor I look at the issues that cause so much unhappiness, such as constant rows, infidelity and sexual problems, but I usually also go back with the couple to see where the problems started. It is nearly always true that what people have experienced as children affects how they are in their present lives and relationships. This, of course, is nothing new: Freud, Jung, Melanie Klein and many other psychiatrists and analysts have developed their theory and practice along these lines. The English poet Philip Larkin put it simply, if cynically, in 1974:

They fuck you up, your Mum and Dad.
They may not mean to, but they do.
They fill you up with faults they had
And add some extra, just for you.

The Myers Briggs Type Indicator: feeling and intuition

Understanding different personality types is very helpful to psychologists, psychotherapists, counsellors, individuals and couples. Isobel Briggs Myers achieved fame in the field of personality measurement for her creation of the most widely used personality inventory known as the Myers Briggs Type Indicator. Her research and writings were based on Jung's theory of psychological types, first translated into English in 1923.

In the early days of her work, in the 1940s, the measurement of personality was very controversial. But now, after extensive research, it is widely accepted by psychologists, educationalists and counsellors who are concerned with the realization of human potential in the home and workplace.

In her book *Gifts Differing*, published in 1980, Briggs Myers says that humankind is equipped with two distinct and sharply contrasting ways of perceiving. One means of perception is the familiar process of *sensing*, by which we become aware of things directly through our senses. The other is the process of *intuition*, which is indirect perception by way of the unconscious. There are, she says, also two distinct and contrasting ways of judging, of coming to a conclusion. One is by *thinking*, in other words the logical process aimed at an impersonal finding. The other is by *feeling*, that is by appreciation, bestowing on things a personal, subjective value. I want to explore these concepts a little, because I think understanding these differences can help to avoid unnecessary friction in relationships, or at least help to resolve it more satisfactorily.

'Sensing' personality types perceive mostly by directly relating to the five senses: touching, smelling, seeing, hearing and tasting. Because 'sensing' people also gain their understanding of the world and those around them first and foremost through this process, they tend to be more influenced by actualities than by ideas, which are less concrete. 'Intuitive' personalities too are influenced by their senses, but their intuition is a more strongly developed part of them. They perceive things more by way of the unconscious and not so much by what they see around them. These intangible experiences are then added to the more tangible senses.

In other words, anyone biased towards 'sensing' rather than 'intuition' is interested primarily in the actualities, whereas anyone biased towards 'intuition' rather than 'sensing' is mainly interested in possibilities. Put these two differences together in a couple's relationship, and, though it may be challenging, it is not difficult to see how it could lead to frustration. When the 'sensing' type is trying to approach a problem or understand a situation he or she is not in such close communication with their unconscious, but needs to be prudent, to take all the facts into consideration and not take any leaps into the unknown. Facts really are of prime importance. The 'intuitive' type, on the other hand, often appears to arrive at assessments or conclusions with the intervening steps left out. In fact that is not so – it is just that their thoughts are undertaken at a more unconscious level and with greater speed. The net result is that the 'intuitive' type can appear to the 'sensing' type as not having really thought things through thoroughly, while the 'sensing' person can infuriate the 'intuitive' person by appearing slow or ponderous or over-cautious. Intuitives tend to describe intelligence as a quickness of understanding, whereas sensing types are more likely to see intelligence as a soundness of understanding. This is an important point to remember in relationships at home and work.

In describing the 'sensing type' Briggs Myers shows how they want to look at all the facts when reaching a conclusion – they want to make sure of its soundness, like an engineer examining a bridge before deciding how much weight it can safely bear. They will not skim when reading, and they hate people to skim in conversation, believing that matters inferred are not as reliable as matters explicitly stated. They are annoyed when you leave things to their imaginations. Intuitives, on the other hand, are often annoyed – if not actually bored – when you do not.

During counselling, when a couple are explaining to me or each other something that has happened between them, one partner frequently goes into tremendous detail while the other twists about

.in their chair with frustration or stares out of the window looking bored. When it's their turn to talk, they say how it was for them more succinctly and with less detail. It might satisfy them, but their partner may well pull them up short about what they think has been left out.

Another way in which Briggs Myers categorizes personality type, and one that I think is particularly relevant to the way men and women behave and interact, is to contrast the thinking with the feeling type of person. Again the thinking person approaches a problem, a task or their partner by using the intellect, the mind, the logic of the situation. Feelings are right at the bottom of the list. But the feeling person's approach is quite the reverse. Their first reaction would be governed by how they feel about the situation, problem or partner. How they think about the situation would be the last thing on their mind. Clearly these two ways of reaching conclusions or solving problems can lead to much potential friction between partners.

If couples don't understand these fundamental differences between them, when they find their partner reacting so differently it can be infuriating and confusing and seem quite unreasonable. The feeling person is likely to accuse the thinking one of being cold, unfeeling and bloody insensitive, while the thinking person will consider that their feeling partner is over the top and emotionally out of control.

Laura, a friend of mine, told me that her son had had surgery to rectify his broken nose, and when the plaster was taken off it was clear that the operation had not turned out as he had expected. In fact he was terribly upset by the results. Laura felt awful because of the way her son was feeling. What made it worse was that she felt it was all her fault – perhaps she should have searched more thoroughly for another surgeon, or he should have had a slightly different operation. Her husband, on the other hand, was saying that she was getting things out of proportion, that in a week the bruising would have gone down and the nose would look fine. If not, he said, they would see what could be done. The more upset she got, the calmer and more logical he became. It was only after some time and only when he stopped telling her that she was over-reacting, and that he understood how she felt, that she was able to calm down and take some comfort from what he was saying.

When Larry and Jean came for counselling they highlighted the differences between the thinking and feeling personality types. Larry was a tall, thin man in his mid-thirties. His wife was short and pretty and two years younger than him. They came to see me because they had had endless rows, mostly about how to bring up their three children, who at the time were all under five.

They sat down glaring at each other. Jean started to talk straightaway. 'I feel awful,' she said. 'I'm struggling to bring up the children – and it's not easy with three under five – but Larry says I'm making a bad job of it and that's why they're all so naughty. He says I must discipline them more, but I feel it's much better to be more relaxed with them.' At this point Larry said, 'I don't think this is the right way to approach the problem. Going over the past will not help. What we need to do is agree on the correct way to bring up the children.' He then picked up his briefcase, took out a writing pad and pen and put them down in front of him. 'Now point one is . . . ?' he said, writing the figure one on his notepad and staring at me.

Throughout this exchange I had noticed that whenever Larry spoke it was prefaced with 'I think', whereas Jean immediately referred to how she *felt*. They were both operating in quite different worlds, neither understanding the other. But I realized that if I approached Larry too soon about how he *felt* about a situation rather than what he *thought* about it, the whole process would be a waste of time. So what we agreed was that if he wanted to make some notes that would be fine, but I would not give him ten golden rules for bringing up children. This was something that would have to be worked out together during counselling. As things were, if even at that young age the children felt pulled in different directions by their parents they would almost certainly continue to be naughty and start to play their parents off against each other as they grew older.

When someone operates at such a thinking level as Larry, and as a counsellor you ask him how he thinks his wife feels about being criticized, his answer is likely to be along the lines of: 'I think she should realize that I am making a valid point.' Whereas if you play him at his own game and take the more cause-and-effect approach, you stand a better chance of beginning to break down the barrier between them. By asking Larry: 'What effect does criticizing your wife have on her?' he is able to respond in the way he understands, so his reply is likely to be: 'She gets very angry.'

Larry had said he never got angry – it was his wife, he declared, who did all the shouting and screaming. Jean had said in one of the counselling sessions that sometimes Larry would not talk to her for hours on end. Again, asking Larry how his wife felt about this would not be very successful in enabling him to get in touch with his feelings. The more effective approach would be to ask: 'If you sit in silence for hours on end, how do you think she is likely to interpret this silence?' Since he has now been asked to explain how he thinks rather than how he feels, he is more likely to be able to answer the question by replying: 'I think she realizes I'm angry.' If he does not reply or says: 'I don't know' it is time to try a more direct question: 'Do you think she is likely to interpret your behaviour as one of anger?' This would give him a chance to get in touch with what he might be feeling, but has been ignoring. Then the counsellor could bring Jean in by asking her how she felt about Larry's long silences. In this way the counsellor will have started to approach the couple in ways to which they can respond, and will have started to give them the tools to do this with each other.

As a couple, try discussing which type you think you are and which type you think your partner is. Remember, if you are a sensing type you will already be amassing facts, and if you are an intuitive type you may already have reached a conclusion; so try to allow for these differences as you approach the task. Of course, you might think that the two of you are the same personality types. If, however, you discover you are different personality types, it does not matter at all. What is important is the insight this knowledge can give you concerning the way you relate to the world around you and to each other.

My experience is that more men than women fall into the sensing category, and more women than men into the intuitive category. Most people would agree that it is women who are famous for their intuition rather than the other way round.

I was not at all surprised when reading about some research carried out in America on nearly two thousand college students that a male/female difference had been noted in this context. More women than men were feeling-dominated and more men than women were thinking-dominated; the findings of the researchers' survey were that 68 per cent of those who were feeling-dominated were female.

Problems can arise when one type is married to the other type, but it does not have to be so. Understanding the differences is the first important step. Recognizing that these differences will influence your behaviour means that you can learn to adjust to each other more easily. By appreciating how the other thinks or feels, a good outcome can be achieved – as Laura and Ben were eventually able to discover.

When defining personality types there can of course be combinations of the two different sorts of perception and judgement. The TF preference (thinking or feeling) is entirely independent of the SN preference (sensing or intuition): in other words either kind of judgement can team up with either kind of perception. Thus four combinations occur:

ST   Sensing plus thinking
SF   Sensing plus feeling
NF   Intuition plus feeling
NT   Intuition plus thinking

Each of these combinations produces a different kind of personality, characterized by the interests, values, needs, habits of mind and surface traits that naturally result from the combination.

Male logic – female emotion

Peter was walking back from the station with my husband. He had recently moved from central London to Surrey, as he was taking early retirement. He loved the new house, the space, the garden and the countryside around him, but his wife Clare and three teenage daughters were hating it.

Clare missed having London on her doorstep. She missed being able to drop in on her friends for a cup of coffee or a chat, and her journey to work was now much longer. The house was chaotic, with builders everywhere. The neighbours were complaining about the colour they were painting the house, and how the newcomers' trees were overhanging their garden and the roots damaging their drains. Peter's daughters were in uproar and made no secret of it. They felt they'd been buried alive. They were bored out of their minds, missing all their friends and missing out on parties because they could not easily get home at night.

Peter had been explaining all this to my husband. As they reached our garden gate he sighed deeply, bowed his head and walked off to his household of disgruntled women. Turning round, he said over his shoulder: 'The trouble with women is that they are a seething cauldron of emotions.'

His wife told me recently, as she stared gloomily into her coffee cup: 'The trouble with Peter is he just doesn't understand us.'

Peter and his wife have a good marriage and love each other but are experiencing changes in their circumstances quite differently, and therefore each feels the other just does not understand them. Peter wonders why she can't see how lovely it all is, and he thinks it's unreasonable of her not to like it. Because of this Clare feels trapped, resentful, misunderstood and angry. So they are both stuck – Peter with thinking his wife is behaving unreasonably and Clare with her feeling of being misunderstood. If this goes on Clare could become very depressed as she suppresses her anger, or they could even become strangers in their own home, unable to communicate.

Given a difficult situation, men tend to apply logic. He would say: 'We discussed it, you wanted to move here, so why are you being so difficult?' She can see the logic of what he is saying, but what she is feeling is miles away from logic. She needs time to talk about it, to be unreasonable, to look at options about what they can do if her unhappiness goes on for so long that they need to consider moving again. Maybe Clare will grow to like the place in time, but it's going to take longer than either of them expected.

If the man does not understand this process and fails to give her time, or will not talk about it, she may not adjust to the situation she is in. For her part she needs to try to like it by making friends in the area and joining things so that she starts to feel part of the community. If they both refuse to try they could reach an impasse, with both of them ending up unhappy.

Moving can be a very different experience for men and women, especially if the woman has moved as the result of the man's job. The man has the excitement of a new job. He leaves for work in the morning with enthusiasm, wanting to make a success of it. He has a lot to learn as well as to contribute. There are many people to meet and things to do – it's all very absorbing and sometimes a little scary. All this understandably takes energy and time – often, lots of time!

The woman, on the other hand, may find the empty house lonely and unfriendly. She may have given up a job in order to move, and she may be having difficulty finding a suitable new one. Perhaps the children are having trouble adjusting to new schools. They will certainly be missing their friends.

As a result of all this the woman feels that one member of the family is happy at the expense of the rest of them, while the man feels he is doing his best to look after and support his wife and children and could do with a little support in return. Resentment and anger, or even depression, creep into the relationship. 'He doesn't understand me,' she screams. 'You're not a lot of fun to come home to,' he retaliates.

Peter is like many other men. They tend to think they are uncomplicated, reasonable guys, who, unlike women, are not ruled by their emotions.

What men really think about women

In January 1995 *GQ*, the magazine for men, published a survey conducted for them by Gallup: 635 men aged between twenty and forty-five were asked what they really thought about women. The results showed that they thought women were loving, supportive and adaptable – all endearing features and important qualities in relationships. But some of the other emotions or qualities they attributed to women were also interesting:

	agreed	disagreed
demanding	82%	7%
irrational	68%	17%
jealous	72%	11%
neurotic	52%	24%
nagging	76%	13%
over-emotional	72%	16%

This list corroborates very closely what I hear men complaining about when talking about the women in their life, whether it's their wife, their partner, their mistress or their daughter.

What I hope I have shown in the various case histories in

this chapter is that, if men and women can only understand and acknowledge and enjoy their differences, they can be complementary, exciting and challenging. By exploring and understanding ourselves and each other better, men and women can learn to live in greater harmony with each other. And a good place to start to do this is in the home.

3

THE HOME FRONT

YOU NEVER DO ANYTHING!

Since her children had gone away to school she had wished that she could do her own housework, but that meant getting rid of Edith who came in three times a week and relied on her wages for the money to go on holiday to Malta or Ostend with her mother and her husband and the twins. Claudia was glad that Charles was so untidy, because if it hadn't been for his wandering socks, overflowing ashtrays and muddled papers she would have had almost nothing to do. She was bored, and irritated by her own predictability.

Alice Thomas Ellis, novelist,
The Other Side of the Fire, 1983

Hazel married Rupert in the mid-sixties. Her new mother-in-law told her that when she had married Rupert's father she used not only to wash and iron all his clothes, but each morning she would get his socks, underpants, tie, shirt and suit out of the cupboards and drawers and lay them out on the bed ready for him to put on. Hazel, rather startled, said laughingly that she hoped Rupert was not going to expect that from her, because if so he was going to be very disappointed.

A generation later Hazel and Rupert's son William and his wife came to stay with them while waiting to move into their new home. Hazel was showing her daughter-in-law how to use the washing machine and where the iron was kept. 'Oh, you'd better show William where the iron is kept,' said her daughter-in-law. 'I certainly don't iron his shirts – that's up to him.'

It made Hazel recall her response to her own mother-in-law's 'daily duty' regarding her husband's clothes – yet here she was all these years later doing just the same thing. Just to make sure, she asked her daughter if she ironed her live-in boyfriend's shirts. 'Oh, come on, Mum, don't be silly,' came the reply. 'Why should I iron his shirts? He's quite capable of doing his own.'

'Does he mind?' asked Hazel.

'Oh, yes, he minds,' replied her daughter, 'but that's just too bad.'

Hazel's experience shows clearly how, over three generations, attitudes had changed. And if Hazel's daughter's boyfriend is anything to go by, it also shows that men are not quite as keen on these changes as their women are.

Learning to live together in the ordinariness of everyday life is far from the romantic ideal of marriage, and in the early days particularly it is not always easy to adjust to. This is why so many couples spend hours locked in combat over who does what around the house; why he never puts his clothes in the laundry basket but leaves them lying around the room; why she is such a slut and the house always looks like a tip; why he has taken three months to get around to painting the hall; and why she always leaves her tights dripping over the bath just when he wants to have one.

This chapter looks at the typical arguments that couples have, which often start with who does what around the house but can also go much deeper. It looks at why couples have disagreements, what causes them and how many can be avoided. It also looks beneath the surface of these everyday rows to check whether there is something more seriously wrong with the relationship that is not being resolved but is being masked by bickering and arguments.

Arguments, of course, happen in every sphere of life, and couples argue about a great range of issues, but since many arguments start or occur within the home that is why I have chosen to discuss them in this chapter. The way to handle disagreement and conflict and to resolve arguments is equally relevant to all the chapters in this book.

I also investigate whether the new man really exists, or whether he is just a gleam in the advertiser's eye. And what do women mean by a 'new man'? Are they sending out clear messages about what they want from him, or are they ambivalent and confused? Let's start with the traditional man.

Traditional man

This is a story about the traditional man. When the alarm goes off in the morning he turns over in bed and groans. His wife gets out of bed, showers and dresses and calls to him to get up as she goes downstairs to make a cup of coffee. She wakes the children, telling them it's time to get up and urging them not to be late for school. She goes into the kitchen and starts to make breakfast.

There's still not much sign of life from anyone, so she goes back upstairs to get the children out of bed and shouts to her husband that if he doesn't get up he will be late for work. The children put in a sleepy appearance in the kitchen and begin to eat their breakfasts. When they have nearly finished traditional man appears. He is now running late, so he grabs something to eat from the kitchen table, wolfs down his coffee and urges the children not to be late for school!

His wife, in the meantime, has made him some sandwiches for lunch. She puts the sandwiches, his briefcase and his coat on the back seat of the car. The man of the house kisses wife and children goodbye and dashes outside swearing as he trips over the dog and frightens the cat.

He jumps into the car and sets off for work. The traffic is bad because he is running so late, in fact it's barely crawling. So he takes advantage of the hold-up and turns round quickly to pick up his belongings from the back seat, so as to save time when he arrives at work. But his foot slips from the brake pedal as he is stretching over and the car moves forward slightly. It slides slowly into a bus stop, startling the queue.

Our traditional man jumps out in a real state at what has happened. People gather round to watch and soon the police arrive on the scene. There is quite a crowd by now. The police start to question him, and, really agitated by now, he says, 'It's my wife's fault. She put my sandwiches and briefcase on the back seat and my foot slipped when I turned round to pick them up. And anyway it's a jolly stupid place to put a bus stop!' he adds in exasperation.

This may be a slightly exaggerated story and a little unfair to men. But I didn't invent it – in fact I heard it from a man!

I am not suggesting that it is always men who blame women

when things go wrong – I know from my experience of counselling men and women that it happens the other way round as well. People of either sex often blame each other because they are unwilling to accept responsibility for what has gone wrong themselves, so they shift the responsibility and blame their partner. But what this story and its source show is that, in the small things of daily life, men more than women tend to blame their partners.

This is particularly true if a man loses something. After talking to a large number of women I feel quite justified in offering this typical scenario – it happens in thousands of homes. A man can't find something small but essential like his car keys, so he turns to his wife and utters those immortal words:

'Darling, I know I left the car keys on the hall table. You must have moved them because I can't find them.'

'No, I didn't,' she replies.

'Well,' he says in exasperation, 'they aren't there now, so you must have moved them.'

His wife is now feeling under attack and tension and frustration are mounting, with each now accusing the other of having moved the keys. He rushes round opening drawers and moving things to look underneath them; his wife feels obliged to stop what she is doing and join in the search.

She calls to him: 'Have you checked in your jacket pocket?'

'No,' he shouts, 'because I left them on the hall table.'

So she goes to check just in case, and there in his jacket pocket of the suit he was wearing yesterday lie the keys. She picks them up and plonks them down in front of him.

'Oh!' he says in surprise. 'Where did you find them?'

'In your jacket pocket,' she snarls, now feeling really cross if not a little triumphant.

If they want to resolve the argument, what he should do now is apologise and thank her for helping him find them. Now that the panic is over and he has got what he wants, he is probably quite willing to do so.

It is not easy for either sex to admit they are in the wrong, but if you know you are, and you want to resolve an argument, you must acknowledge the fact. Say you are sorry, and mean it. You must also appreciate that your partner may still be feeling cross, and is not instantly going to be all smiles again.

But those who are on the receiving end of an apology must work at it, too. Try to defeat any feelings of anger that you still have, and accept the apology rather than reject it. And try to avoid escalating the argument by telling him that it was all his fault really – he has already admitted that. If you do continue to blame him, what started as a small incident can flare up again and turn into a major and unnecessary row over something that started as a minor issue. In my experience, when a couple have a row like this and they have a good relationship, it is normally easily resolved. If not it is because underneath that exchange lies a whole series of unresolved resentments, or constant put-downs and criticisms. Just one more item can be the straw that breaks the camel's back, producing anger and outrage which appear quite out of proportion to the situation.

Who does what around the house?

One of the biggest areas of conflict in the home is who does what around the house. When you first fall madly in love with someone they may seem, as Mary Poppins put it, 'practically perfect'. Look at any number of love stories in the cinema or on television. When a couple meet and fall in love they are more often than not shown at the beginning of an affair, having a marvellous time. They may be whirling round Paris, Rome or some other exotic location, with eyes only for each other. When they are not making love – which is most of the time – they are seen strolling through pretty streets, sitting at enchanting cafés, sharing a meal, visiting art galleries or running through the summer rain. What they are definitely *not* seen doing together is cleaning, dusting, washing and ironing. That is because these tasks are neither romantic nor fun – something that neither men nor women would opt to do if they did not present themselves as a daily necessity.

Traditionally the home has been seen as women's work, just as the world of work outside the home has been seen as men's. Most men know that it is not really fair to leave most of the chores to women, especially if the woman is doing a full-time job or has children or both. But the reality is that the new caring, sharing man is a little light on the ground in this area. He is doing more than previous generations, but not all that much more.

All research and surveys into this area of who does what around the home show that, in general, what men actually do is a lot less than their partners would like them to. There are, of course, exceptions – there are men out there doing their fair share and more – but the stark reality is that the vast majority of men are not lining up demanding equal rights to women where the household chores are concerned.

Government surveys into how people live undertaken by the OPCS (Office of Population Censuses and Surveys) and Social Trends surveys show that the new man is a bit of a myth.

80 per cent of women prepare every meal compared with only 22 per cent of men (OPCS Jan 1995).

Social Trends 1995	Mainly Men	Mainly Women	Shared Equally
Household shopping	8%	45%	47%
Evening dishes	28%	33%	37%
Household cleaning	4%	68%	27%
Washing and ironing	3%	84%	12%
Repairs household equipment	82%	6%	10%

The survey found that men had greater involvement in certain tasks like shopping and cooking than in 1983 but not much change in the cleaning and ironing department, and they are still doing a lot less than women. When men and women were asked how household tasks should be shared 76 per cent said that it should be equally. So it seems a case of the spirit is willing but the flesh is weak where the majority of men are concerned.

Men do take more responsibility for the maintenance jobs around the house, though, but these of course do not need to be done every day. So there may not be many new men around who really do share everything fifty fifty with their wives. But perhaps we can see the newish man emerging.

New man or newish man?

The new man, as research shows, is in short supply – but perhaps the newish man is emerging in a snail-like way, especially if you compare him and his behaviour with his father and his grandfather before him. The new man who shares the household tasks equally with his female partner is thin on the ground, according to market researchers Mintel in their lifestyle survey *Women 2000*, published in January 1994. They set out to find the nineties' man who shared the household tasks of cooking, shopping and laundry equally with his partner, but had to abandon the search as the numbers were so small – just 1 per cent of the sample, so small that Mintel were unable to analyse the findings! The couples who were most likely to split tasks equally tended to be under thirty-four and childless. Mintel researcher Angela Hughes said: 'Men seem to set out with good intentions to share the domestic chores but the catalyst appears to be the arrival of children, which we found seems to trigger a major shift in the workload. At this stage the man appears to abdicate responsibility for his share regardless of whether his partner is working or not.'

If you have just had a baby, at this time perhaps more than any other you need extra help. And if you have babies or small children and have also returned to work, full-time or part-time, you really are going to need more help than ever before. So if the arrival of a new baby coincides with the man doing less than he was, or not reorganizing the woman's increased workload, it is not really so surprising that the result is endless friction and arguments, not to say exhaustion on the part of the woman.

The Mintel research also showed that more than eight out of ten married women take on most or all of the responsibility for cooking the main meals, and for planning the household grocery shopping. With the laundry it is worse. Nine out of ten women are doing the lion's share of washing and ironing. This confirms my own mini-survey, which I have conducted while giving talks around the country on marriage and relationships. I often ask in a light-hearted way if there are any men in the audience whose wife or partner has ever said to them: 'Darling, where did you put that blouse you ironed for me last night?' A ripple of laughter usually runs around the audience – from men as well as women. Only once has a man put his hand up in response to my question.

The outlook is brighter

A recent survey of 1700 working women revealed that, while 85 per cent of men claimed to help at home, only 57 per cent of their wives thought they did! But that does leave 57 per cent of men who do help around the house, which is certainly an improvement on previous generations.

Edward, approaching his seventieth birthday, has a very traditional marriage. When his wife went away on her own for a week's holiday, he found that as usual the milkman had delivered six eggs. Normally he always had an egg for breakfast, but such was his dependence on his wife that he rang her on her holiday island in the Mediterranean to ask her what he should do with them. Should he give them away, he asked, as they would probably go bad if he kept them for her return in two weeks' time.

His wife expressed surprise that he was not having his usual boiled egg for breakfast.

'Oh, no,' he said, 'that's too much trouble. I'll wait until you get back.' When he asked his wife again what he should do with them, she suggested that he stuck them back up the chicken and put the phone down.

The old brigade of traditional man who proudly proclaimed he didn't know how to boil an egg is happily becoming a dying breed. Many men are now very proud of their cooking ability, though most do not have to do it every day.

A Social Trends survey shows that, even when both members of a couple are working full-time, 61 per cent of women prepare the evening meal; and if the woman is not working outside the home, or only working part-time, she takes on a much higher proportion of the household tasks. The same survey shows that men have on average ten hours more leisure time each week than women.

So household tasks may not be evenly shared, but all the research shows that the situation is improving. If only men could learn to understand that, apart from being fairer to their wives or partners if they shared tasks more, there are also hidden benefits, a sort of 'household benefits' scheme or a 'bonus system'. Then they might feel encouraged to change more quickly than they are at the moment.

It is the carrot-and-stick approach, and the scheme would work like this. The man arrives home earlier than his wife and, instead of reading the paper or watching television, he starts to prepare the evening meal. When his wife comes in she finds him successfully engaged in this task. As a result she is really pleased and in a much better frame of mind than if she had arrived home to find him slumped in a chair with his feet up in front of the television and the dirty breakfast dishes still in the sink.

So the evening will get off to a much better start. She will feel more relaxed, more loving towards him, less tired and more fun. What is also very important is that she will feel more cared for, and someone who feels cared for usually responds in a caring way. The whole atmosphere will feel good, and the couple will also have more time to do things together and enjoy the evening.

The reason I've highlighted the early evening is because the time when you arrive home from work is one of the biggest flashpoints in a relationship. It's when arguments are most likely to start, and many evenings in households up and down the land are ruined that way. If you have had a hard day at work, the boss has been getting at you, you had to sit endlessly in a traffic jam, your train was late again, or the children have been screaming all day, it is very easy to take it out on each other and set the tone for the whole evening. So if a man helps his partner by being prepared to share and to help out at this time of day and to put her needs before his own, it will lead to more togetherness and fewer rows. It is short-sighted of a man to try to get away with doing as little as possible, because the long-term effect is likely to be a nagging, resentful, distant and worn-out wife. Other common flashpoints or triggers for an argument occur late at night, during the morning rush, or when one or both of you have been drinking or are feeling very tired. Yet others are when you are driving together in the car, when the children are playing up, or when you have money problems.

Women also have to be careful, however, that they are not excluding their husbands from sharing household tasks by giving themselves 'should' or 'ought to' messages. They go like this: 'As a woman I should be responsible for the running of the house, and I want to show I can do a good job,' or 'I am failing to live up to my expectations of myself if I don't do everything for my husband that my mother and grandmother did for my father and grandfather.' Another mistake that women commonly make when the man does undertake tasks around the house is to criticize him or suggest that he does it another way – which usually means her way. He will soon decide that it's not worth the effort, and give up.

Bernard, sixty-five and recently retired, thought Pat, his wife, was being very unreasonable. He felt he had reached a time when he could put his feet up and relax. Pat had a part-time job which they had agreed she should keep on since they could do with the extra money.

After she had finished work Pat would shop for the evening meal before returning home. Bernard was usually watching television when she got in, and soon he started complaining that the evening meal always seemed to be late. To start with Pat did not say anything. After all, Bernard had worked hard all his life. But then she began to feel irritated and resentful that she was doing everything while Bernard just watched TV. So she started to snap at him, or to sulk and refuse to talk to him. As far as she could see, Bernard's retirement might be nice for him but it meant a lot more work and hassle for her.

But underneath the bickering lay a deeper problem. Though Bernard had been looking forward to retirement, it was not turning out quite as he had expected. Part of him resented the fact that Pat still had a job, and he was now feeling rather lost and lacking in status. But he had not been able to tell Pat. Also, he had always regarded shopping and cooking as women's work, as many men of his generation still do. So having to help out in the house while Pat was at work, when he was suffering loss of status and worry about no longer being the main breadwinner, felt too difficult for him.

Pat, too, was doing things wrong. She felt she should do it all, because the cooking and shopping had always been her responsibility. But while this had seemed sensible when Bernard was working full-time, after things changed and he was at home it no longer seemed fair to her, especially once he started nagging her. During counselling they were able to express their thoughts and feelings to each other, and the understanding they achieved enabled each of them to see how their behaviour was affecting their partner. Now, instead of resenting each other, they were able to make changes in their relationship.

So Bernard started to have a go at preparing the evening meal. Not only did he begin to enjoy it, but he became rather good at it – and much more adventurous than Pat. After a while he was to be found scanning the shelves of the local supermarkets for exotic ingredients mentioned in his newly acquired cookery book, a present from Pat. Meanwhile Pat discovered that she could let go of her 'ought to' messages about women doing the shopping and cooking. She enjoyed the results of Bernard's labours without feeling the slightest bit guilty. The fact that Bernard and Pat were able to adjust to each other's needs made a crucial difference to their relationship.

No one can make you change – the will to do so has to come from you. But if you continually take no notice of things that drive your partner up the wall it only leads to arguments, periods of withdrawing from each other or sulking. It also makes your partner feel that you do not care enough to want to please them and to enjoy life together.

Women nag – men do it in their own time

Why do women have such a reputation for nagging? The easy answer is: 'Because men never listen.' But it is a little more complex than that. When a man asks a woman to do something, most women respond to the request. But when a woman asks a man to do something, many men interpret the request as an order. So, to assert his independence, he either does not comply or thinks he will do it in his own time. The woman then asks again, thinking that maybe she has not made herself clear, or that he has forgotten – but perhaps there is a slight sharpness to her request now. By now the man who thinks he is being told what to do will ignore the request even more, because he feels pushed around. With bad grace she asks again, and of course the man then feels that his wife is nagging. A little less resistance and a little more co-operation in the early stages of this cycle could improve a lot of relationships. One man said to me in exasperation, 'If I treat myself to a day off work, to do the things I want to do, my wife thinks that's the time to present me with all the little jobs that need doing around the house. She cannot seem to understand it's my day, not hers.'

The following are the most common complaints that I hear from women about men and from men abut the women in their lives.

Eight things about men that drive women wild

1. Leaves his clothes all over the bedroom floor, or aims them at the clothes basket and misses rather than putting them in.
2. Telephones to say he is just having a drink with his mates and will be back in twenty minutes, only to turn up three hours later, tipsy or worse, after the meal has either burnt to a cinder or she has fed it to the dog.
3. Sits around like a couch potato, undressed, unshaven and uncommunicative.
4. Watches endless sport on television.
5. Plays endless sport when she wants him at home with herself and the children.
6. She comes home to find his dirty dishes in the sink because he can't be bothered to wash them up.
7. Offers to cook the supper, then leaves the kitchen looking like the aftermath of a number nine earthquake on the Richter scale.
8. When she says a meal is ready, he always has one more thing that he wants to do. Telling a man a meal is ready can be the quickest way of clearing the kitchen! One woman told me that she had once cooked Christmas dinner and just as it was ready her husband said he was going off to have a bath. After all that hard work she was furious and threatened him with fish and chips the following year!

Eight things about women that drive men wild

1. Leaves all the drawers and cupboards open with her clothes hanging out.
2. Says she has nothing to wear when she has a wardrobe full of clothes, then tries on one more outfit and makes them late for the party.
3. Her driving, particularly if she is driving his car or him.
4. Complains about how much space his collection of football posters, fishing rods, African art, matchboxes etc. take up.
5. Leaves the iron, cooker or lights on, burning up electricity that he has to pay for.
6. Throws away or gives to Oxfam his most loved and treasured

sweater, trousers, hat etc. that he has been attached to since his college days.

7. Leaves her make-up and dripping tights all over the bathroom.

8. Talks to her friends about what he is like in bed (a source of objection unless it's very favourable!).

What do you as a couple argue about most?

Draw a line down the centre of a piece of paper and make two lists. Head one list: 'The three things about me that I think irritate my partner most' and head the second list: 'The three things that irritate me most about my partner'. List them in order, worst first. Make your lists separately, with no conferring.

Then discuss the lists together, taking each item separately. Start with the list of what you think it is about yourself that irritates your partner. You may be surprised at how wrong you have got it, but at least you will know for future reference. Then see which things irritate you most about your partner and which irritate him most about you. Talk about why it is particularly irritating to you, and find out if your partner realizes how irritating you find it. If so, are you both prepared to make changes so that you will irritate each other less? If you can't agree to make changes to the most difficult one, settle for another from the list – but they must both be at the same level. For example, it would not be fair if one of you agreed to change bad habit number one on your partner's list while the other settled for number three. That would make the task unfairly balanced.

If you find great difficulty in restricting your list to three, and feel that it could easily be a lot longer, maybe you have slipped into taking each other for granted. Or perhaps you don't care enough about each other's feelings. A very long list could indicate that you are so disaffected with your partner that you have ceased to care how your behaviour is affecting them. Unless you take note of this situation and talk about why you have allowed it to happen, and unless you are both prepared to make changes, this could be the slippery slope that eventually drives you apart.

When Garry and Lyn came to counselling there was nothing

either of them could do that pleased the other – they were at each other's throats all the time. Garry complained that Lyn was a dreadful cook, lazy, spent the evening talking on the telephone to her mother or her four sisters, yet never had time to talk to him. Lyn countered by saying that Garry always came in late, expected her to do everything around the house, constantly criticized her about the state of the place, her cooking, even the way she held her knife and fork, and ending up declaring that she was sick of him. There was so much aggravation that the whole counselling session could just have consisted of them hurling abuse at each other.

What began to emerge from beneath all the arguments was the real pain, hurt and resentment that each felt about the other. They had been married for three years, and the year before they married Lyn had become pregnant. Garry had not wanted a baby. At twenty-five he felt too young to take on marriage and a baby and, though they had talked about it, there were no plans to marry at that time.

Lyn had wanted both marriage and to have the baby. She had loved Garry very much, but very reluctantly she had agreed to have an abortion. She did not think she could manage as a single parent, and was afraid of losing Garry if she went ahead with the pregnancy. As the months after the abortion went by, she felt more and more that Garry had forced her into the decision and given her no choice. She bitterly regretted it, and resented Garry for what he had done. She had become very weepy and depressed. Deep down Garry had been very distressed to see how devastated Lyn had been by the abortion. He felt, looking back, that he had married Lyn a year later more out of pity than love.

This was an awful confession for Lyn to hear, but it was also the start of their realization that much more was wrong with the marriage than who did what around the house. Over the months of counselling they painfully acknowledged to each other that a marriage based on so little love, on Garry's part especially, had no future, and so they separated. Garry and Lyn's arguments in fact had little to do with the disagreements around the house – though there were plenty of those. It was only when they were able to draw aside the surface of their marriage and look at the faulty foundations that they were able to see what the real problems were.

Simon and Victoria, a young couple in their early thirties, have lived happily together for five years. When they first started living together, they said, they had had lots of rows about who did what around the house. They both worked hard, long hours, but all that changed when they agreed to employ a motherly cleaning lady. 'Our arguments were reduced by 90 per cent,' said Simon. 'She is worth every penny,' they agree.

Of course, not everyone can afford that solution. But what this illustrates is that Simon and Victoria have a basically good and loving relationship. Their arguments had no hidden depths. Garry and Lyn's relationship, sadly, was so bad that all the cleaning ladies in the world would not have helped reduce the arguments.

Why arguments happen and how to sort them out

As the song goes:

> *You say either and I say eether,*
> *You say neither and I say neether.*
> *Neither, neether, either, eether, let's sort the whole thing out.*

Understanding why you argue, how you argue, and how to turn a negative situation into a positive one can make all the difference to a relationship. How you were brought up, and how your family handled arguments, usually influences the way you argue with your partner. In the couples I see, so many arguments start for what appear to be very insignificant reasons. People can frequently remember the course of the arguments, but often completely forget what started them. Though arguments seem to start over mundane issues, the real cause is often much deeper.

What is important is to understand *how* you argue. Do you find, for example, that by arguing you are able to resolve conflict? Or do you find you just go on and on, round and round, getting nowhere? In the circular argument syndrome you just chase your own tail and end up withdrawing from battle feeling wrung out, totally hurt and ready to telephone the solicitor to start divorce proceedings. A lot of the work I do with couples helps them to argue constructively rather than setting out to be the winner through either insisting on your own way or decimating your partner.

We never argue

If you have a normal, healthy relationship you will also have arguments. It would be fairly unnatural for two people sharing their lives together, living with one another day and night, never to disagree. If a couple say they have such a close relationship that they never argue I am usually a little suspicious. People sometimes say this because they are afraid that if they acknowledge a row, either to themselves or to someone else, it will disrupt the rosy view they have of their marriage. Though they say and feel that their marriage is solid and stable, they fear it might be more fragile underneath than they are admitting to, and they don't want to put this doubt to the test by arguing.

Other couples may say that never a cross word is spoken. But the truth can be that very few words are spoken, cross or otherwise, because they are either sulking or embarking on hours or even days of silence. In other words, they are denying to themselves and/or to their partner that they are angry. Yet this passive aggressive behaviour is more often than not hiding deep anger which they are afraid of admitting or of bringing out into the open. It is very controlling to those around them, because if you continually deny angry feelings they cannot be resolved. So when their partner tackles them about being angry they deny it and say, 'Leave me alone, I just want some peace. You are imagining it.' They may be afraid of anger, or so out of touch with their feelings that they believe what they are saying is true. Or they may be punishing their partner for causing situations or indulging in behaviour which they find unacceptable.

Ruth, a lovely, hard-working woman in her seventies, was brought up in the north-east and went into service as a maid when she was fourteen. She said that her father and mother married in 1916. One day when her mother was in her late forties, her father filled a hot water bottle to take to bed for his usual Sunday afternoon rest. Only after he had woken up did he discover that he had not put the top on tightly enough so that it had leaked and soaked the bottom of the bed. His wife did not speak to him again for twenty years. It was only when Ruth's mother became ill and she had to rely on her husband to look after her that she started talking to him again.

Ruth told me, 'He loved her all his life. After she died he insisted that the coffin should be kept in the house until the hearse arrived. When it did, he did not want the coffin to be closed.' She remembers her father sitting in a chair in the front room with his bowler hat on, waiting to go to the funeral. When the time came he broke down and said very quietly, 'I cannot go.' His fifteen-year-old grandson stayed with him while the rest of the family attended the funeral. Ruth said to me with deep emotion, 'My father was a lovely man. He loved her right to the end, but it is so sad to think of all those wasted years.'

Couples who never or rarely argue often behave like this because of hidden fears. They may well have a reasonable relationship, but deep down they are afraid that rows will lead to its disintegration or break-up. In other words, it does not feel safe to row, to air their differences. This can stem from childhood experiences. The chances are that one or both of the couple come from families in which all emotions were sternly battened down, and differences were not allowed to be expressed nor authority challenged. If that was unacceptable behaviour in their childhood, their internal world will tell them that to argue as adults is wrong.

At the other end of the scale, such people may come from families in which there was so much rowing, even violence, that it led to great disruption and perhaps even to the breakdown of the family unit. Their experience was that arguments were never resolved, that their parents never or hardly ever made things up. As children they watched in fear from the sidelines as their parents' marriage destroyed itself. They were in a situation that they did not really understand and were powerless to prevent. So all they had learnt, and what their internal world told them, was that conflict, rows and arguments were dangerous: families who rowed ended disastrously. As children they had not observed how to argue and reach a satisfactory conclusion; they had never learnt to deal with conflict. These fears still lie deeply hidden, inhibiting their adult relationships. They assume that if they allow conflict to emerge in their marriage it will lead to the same painful events they had experienced as children which are still lying unresolved within them. So they avoid arguments at all costs.

Trying to bury differences between you does not mean they go away – it just means they never stand a chance of being resolved. Someone who has learnt to suppress all their anger, day in and day out, year in and year out, denies themselves the normal outlets for resolving conflict. Such people internalize their anger and end up quietly attacking themselves rather than the cause of the anger. They do not understand that the other side of the coin to suppressed anger is often depression, and so they become depressed without knowing why.

Couples who are always at each other's throats

While some people never row, others are into arguments and rows in a matter of seconds. This too can be the result of childhood experiences if this sort of behaviour is what they lived with and witnessed as a child.

If as a child you constantly watched your parents going at each other hammer and tongs, verbally and possibly even physically, you were deprived of the chance to learn how to negotiate, how to give and take, how to listen to the other person and not just be waiting for them to draw breath so that you can put your own point of view across. As a result, when you grow up and form close relationships you either withdraw from arguments altogether, as I have described, or you try to resolve conflict in the same unsatisfactory way that your parents used.

Try discussing with each other your different family experiences. How did your mother and father handle angry and aggressive feelings? Are you doing the same, and was it similar to or different from the approach adopted by your partner's parents? Are you repeating learnt patterns? Are you happy with that, or do you want to make changes? Does your partner want you to make changes in the way you both argue, and could that help you to resolve problems?

Remember, arguments can be a natural, healthy part of a relationship. They are a way of expressing the differences between you. They show that you exist and function as an individual, as well as being part of a couple. They are a way of enabling you to grow and develop within the relationship, and they can help the relationship to grow and mature as well. They are an important way of expressing your thoughts and feelings rather than brushing them under the carpet or burying them deep down, which gives neither of you a chance to resolve the differences between you.

If resentment and bitterness build up and fester away beneath the surface, it can often result in violent or over-charged outbursts of anger that seem quite out of proportion to the situation. This is because the real cause of the argument lies elsewhere, or has been slowly building up and then comes out in what appears to be a sudden explosion. An extreme example of this was the so-called Pepper Pot Murder. The wife, continually abused, criticized and put down by her husband, had suppressed her angry feelings for years and years. Then he did it just once too often. While they were having a meal together he was ridiculing her as usual. Then, suddenly, all that pent-up anger finally exploded and she killed him by hitting him over the head with the pepper pot.

But in a good relationship arguments can actually be positive things. You can learn to recognize that, while your partner may not agree with you, he or she is entitled to his or her own opinions. And by really learning to listen to each other you can gain greater understanding.

Why are we always arguing?

If arguments consistently go unresolved, or one of you insists on winning every argument, frustrations and resentments build up. This in turn leads to more arguments. If you find the same old rows keep occurring, or you have different ones with a different theme but they fall into the same old pattern of arguing, maybe you are stuck in a negative pattern of rowing without really understanding what you are doing to each other. Knowing how to argue constructively can make all the difference.

Someone once suggested that couples who row a lot should tape their rows. Then, when they feel one coming on, particularly if it's late at night when both are tired, instead of continuing to argue they could just play the tape while getting a good night's sleep.

Of course it was not a serious suggestion, but if your arguments never lead anywhere it could have a point. A tape of how you argue might prove very illuminating, because when you are in the thick of it, it is very hard to stand back and be objective about the part you may be playing in escalating the situation. Most of us, if we are honest, think it is more our partner's fault than our own. So if you are doing some or all of the following negative things that may be why your arguments just go round and round.

The eight most common things people do when arguing

1. *Bringing up old sins*

One way of making sure that nothing gets resolved is to deflect from the point instead of focusing on the issue you are arguing about, to bring up everything about your partner from the past that you feel angry about, and to throw it at them. This not only confuses the issue but also makes your partner feel very much under attack. He or she will therefore be much more likely to attack you in return. A slanging match is bound to ensue.

2. *Having to win*

If you approach an argument thinking that at all costs you have to win this round, that you are definitely right and it is just a matter of making your partner see sense, you are heading for an unsatisfactory outcome. With that approach your partner may in the short term end up agreeing with you, but deep down a bundle of resentment is being stored up at being bullied into submission. So you are both the losers. It will only be a matter of time before the one who has been bullied will want to have his or her point of view heard, and battle will resume.

3. *Ridiculing your partner*

Trying to win the argument by laughing or sneering at your partner makes them feel that you don't respect either them or their ideas. It is like being back in the classroom or playground, being unkindly teased and feeling powerless, and it produces primitive feelings of rage. So your partner is likely either to respond very angrily or to withdraw hurt and unresponsive.

4. *Criticizing your partner*

Putting your partner down, so you can take the superior position, also enlists feelings of hurt, rage or of feeling destroyed. The partner either counter-attacks or crumbles. For example, saying something like 'Oh, you're bloody hopeless! If you'd bothered to read the map properly we wouldn't have got lost. Can't you ever get anything right?' is hardly going to elicit a reasonable response from your partner – only a defensive or attacking one. If you in return criticize them for being angry, you will have a full-scale war on your hands.

5. *Making a personal attack*

Telling your partner that they are stupid, no good, neurotic, hysterical just like their mother, a drunkard like their father and so on, is another ploy that people use when they get really angry with each other. This way of arguing is very destructive, because instead of focusing on the behaviour that you don't like in your partner at that moment you are actually attacking the person for what he or she is. This makes them think or feel that they are rotten, no good, unlovable or unacceptable, and is extremely harmful to their feelings of self-esteem and self-respect. Since people can change their behaviour but not who they are, personal attacks are very undermining and humiliating.

You sometimes see parents doing this to their children, usually out of ignorance rather than because they want to hurt the child deliberately. Nevertheless it does have a detrimental effect.

The child who is labelled naughty, unlovable or stupid, rather than told off for their behaviour, often goes on to act out these negative labels and really does become a naughty, unruly or difficult-to-love child. These negative feelings about themselves are then carried into adult life. And the resultant low self-esteem will cause them great difficulty in forming loving relationships as adults. So it's important always to separate the behaviour of the child from the child as a person.

6. *Finding the Achilles heel*

With this ploy, no matter what the argument is about you home in on your partner's vulnerable areas as a way of gaining the upper ground. You go for the jugular and, having found it, put the knife in. For example, if you know that they are embarrassed by their lack of education or social background, to win a point you might say, 'Well I wouldn't expect you to understand what I'm saying – after all, you were always in the B stream at school,' or 'People from your sort of background always walk around with a chip on their shoulder.'

7. *Dissolving into tears*

Tears are often absolutely genuine – something you cannot help because you are so distressed or because they enable you to release the tension you are feeling. But sometimes they are used to gain control: 'If I cry, he/she will feel a heel and be sorry for me. Then I have more chance of getting my own way.' Tears can also be used as a defence mechanism. You say to yourself: 'My partner finds tears so hard to cope with that if I cry he will back off and leave me alone, so we can avoid having this argument altogether.' This method is used more often by women than by men. It is a way of opting out of responsibility for what has gone wrong and also a means of avoiding having to look at ways to put it right.

8. *It's all your fault*

Blaming your partner for what has gone wrong and never taking responsibility for your own part in events is a gambit frequently used in arguments. 'It's all your fault!' shouts the man. 'If you hadn't asked your mother round for Sunday lunch you wouldn't need to moan about all the shopping and cooking you have to do,' or 'If you'd been stricter with the children when they were younger, they wouldn't be so rebellious now and staying out at all-night parties,' the woman says accusingly to her husband. But someone who is blamed, particularly if it is done angrily, is most unlikely to do anything except retaliate with an angry or accusing response.

All these approaches to arguments between couples only serve to wind each other up. At the end of the day you both end up further apart than before, each thinking the worst of the other and hurting the one you love very much.

How to resolve arguments

There are three golden rules to resolving arguments, and if you both learn how to apply them you will greatly improve your chances of reaching a mutually agreeable solution. This method, of course, is relevant in close personal relationships but also in the wider world of work and leisure.

- Send 'I' messages rather than 'you' messages
- Set a goal
- Use the skills of negotiation

'I' messages rather than 'you' messages

By using 'you' messages in arguments you immediately come across as blaming the other person. And if a person thinks you are blaming them, you are likely to get a defensive or attacking response. Then you in turn are likely to come back on the attack. Let's look at an example of how 'you' messages and 'I' messages work.

Your partner says he will get off early from work and pick up the children from school, then rings half an hour before he is due to collect them and says he is very sorry but a totally unexpected problem has come up at work and he just cannot get away. He is really sorry to spring this on you at the last moment, but can you go and collect them? Because you are understandably cross at this last-minute request, you may respond along these lines: 'Oh, for goodness sake! You're quite impossible – totally unreliable. You never ever think about anyone except yourself.' Your partner will immediately feel under attack and because of this will probably respond angrily. However, if you had said: 'I wish you'd let me know earlier. I do feel cross, because it's very inconvenient and I'm worried that I'll be late collecting them,' your partner would have realized that you were cross not only because it has inconvenienced you but also because you were worried about the children. The first approach would probably mean an all-out slanging match, making you both even later for your respective appointments and raising the tension level considerably. The second way does not mean you won't feel irritated with each other, but it will be at a vastly reduced level. So when you meet up in the evening, the one who mucked up the arrangements is more likely to be conciliatory and apologetic. You will then be better able to share with them your concerns about the children waiting at the school gates, and make them aware that on any future occasion they will not be able to make such last-minute changes to plans.

An 'I' message gives you both a chance to understand each other. There will therefore be much less chance of your message being received badly, which should elicit a non-aggressive response and, with luck, a change of behaviour in the future.

Beth and Rod had been coming to counselling for two weeks. At the third session Beth sat down in the chair, crossed her arms and stared angrily out of the window. When the counsellor asked them what was wrong Rod shrugged his shoulders and looked at Beth. She turned to him and said, 'It's our wedding anniversary today and you haven't even sent me a card. You are a selfish bastard. You never think of me – you only care about yourself.'

Rod replied: 'You might have reminded me. I think you wanted me to forget so you had yet another thing to accuse me of not getting right. You're quite impossible.'

At this point Beth burst into tears of anger and frustration. However, with the counsellor's help and as the session progressed, Beth was finally able to tell Rod what she was really feeling by using an 'I' message.

'I feel so unloved and rejected,' she said. 'Forgetting our anniversary makes me feel "What's the point of being here?" I feel you don't care enough to remember to send me a card.' This response gave Rod the chance to see how much he had hurt Beth by forgetting their anniversary. He was able to say he was sorry, that it had not been his intention to hurt her, and that he had not appreciated how important it was to her.

The next week when they came for counselling Beth said, smiling at Rod, that the previous night he had taken her out to dinner. It was the first time they had been out together for over a year, and it had been very good. They were then able to talk freely together, and agreed how much they both missed doing fun things. They said they would do more in the future, which made for a good beginning.

What Beth and Rod had learnt to do was look at cause and effect. Rather than launching straight into blaming your partner for what in your opinion they have done wrong, start by explaining how your partner's behaviour has made you feel. Look at what has caused the problem and what the effect has been on you. In that way you can give your partner the chance to explore with you what has gone wrong, to understand why you feel the way you do, and then you can work together to see if you can do things differently in the future. It is not possible to achieve this aim every time, but in general 'I' messages prove to be a far more effective way to resolve arguments than 'you' messages.

Goal-setting

What starts as a discussion can sometimes turn into an argument. Your partner says or does something that makes you feel angry, and you respond in this vein. It is very important at this stage, before you get too heated and your judgement becomes clouded, to try to be honest with yourself: are you angry about what has just happened or been said, or is the situation in fact a trigger point for unexpressed anger whose focus lies elsewhere? Beth, for example, flew off the handle about a forgotten anniversary card. What *really* upset her was the fact that she felt her husband did not love her enough to remember to buy her a card. The unsent card was merely a symptom of a deeper issue.

Identifying the real cause of your anger and sharing it with your partner is fundamental to solving a problem. If you don't do so, you can often appear to be over-reacting to some minor event. This confuses your partner and makes them less understanding about why you are feeling angry.

Avoid what I call 'a shopping list of grievances'. In other words, having identified what you are angry about, stick to that and try to resolve it. Don't bring in a whole load of other grievances that you may have against your partner, because if you do you will get side-tracked away from what you are trying to sort out. You may also end up overwhelming your partner, and probably yourself too, with all the things that are wrong. In addition, because you are angry you might introduce issues that are not really important or particularly valid. The result is that nothing gets sorted out and you have just one more grievance to add to your list, which you can attack your partner for next time around.

Think of it as similar to making a very long Christmas shopping list. You know you won't be able to get everything on the list in one go – time is too short, the crowds too dense, and you probably don't have enough money. So you go for fewer things at any one time, and put the priorities at the top of the list. Having an attainable goal, whatever you are doing, gives you much more chance of success.

Another related issue is sticking to the point and being relevant. If you are angry about something else or someone else that has nothing to do with your partner, then say so. For example, if you have had a rotten day at work and your boss has been quite unreasonable, don't come home and pick a fight with your partner. Say instead, 'I've had an awful day at work and I'm feeling so cross. It's nothing to do with you, but can you just give me half an hour to unwind?' Then, when you are feeling calmer, you can talk about it together and you will probably get a sympathetic response.

The art of negotiation

A publican and his wife arrived for counselling one day. He sat down in his chair, leaned forward and looked at me, and said, 'We have come here because we want a negotiator. We're constantly rowing, and we want someone to help us sort the arguments out.' Counsellors sometimes do fulfil that role. But though we may start off playing the part of negotiator, what we are really aiming for is to enable the couple to do this for themselves.

Negotiating is an essential tool in resolving arguments in the home, on the factory floor, and indeed anywhere. Remember that you cannot *make* someone accept your point of view. You can only achieve a satisfactory outcome by expressing how you think and feel and explaining why this is so, and by listening to the other side's point of view. You should not try to make up someone else's mind for them – that is something they have to do for themselves.

You both need to listen carefully to each other. People often claim to be listening when what they are really doing is waiting for the chance to get their word in; they may have avoided interrupting, but they have not really listened at all. They are just working out what they are going to say when their partner has finished speaking.

At one point Jim, the publican, responded angrily to his wife Betty, who had been trying to explain how something he had said had hurt her very much. He burst out: 'That's six times you've cut across what I've been saying in the last ten minutes!' That may or may not have been true. But if he was busy timing her and counting up her interruptions, then not only were his frustrations mounting but he was unlikely to have been really listening to what she was trying to say in the first place. This in turn was making her angry, and in that state of mind she became much more volatile and less able to listen to him, which is what Jim was complaining about in the marriage. What Jim had to learn was not to deliver a monologue when saying what he felt. In turn Betty had to learn that she must let Jim finish what he was saying, because being constantly interrupted does make for angry reactions and, of course, unresolved issues.

One way of showing you have listened to your partner is what is known as the 'reflection process'. When your partner has finished speaking, you say, 'What I understand you to have said is . . . ' Then you repeat what you think you have heard them say. In that way they not only feel listened to, but if you have misinterpreted their words they can try to explain again, giving you both a chance to clarify the issues. Really listening to each other is vital to achieving a positive outcome to an argument.

What is also important is to remember that the situation should be one of give-and-take, and of being able to arrive at a compromise. If you are unable to agree with the other person about what they think, or what they want to do, you both need to concede certain points and to recognize that some of your needs can be met, but not all of them. Without such concessions one partner is bound to end up short-changed; the gains to the apparent winner will only be short-term, since long-term frustration and resentment will build up in the other. Whether or not the worm turns you will probably have a very unsatisfactory situation and the situation may even end in the breakdown of the marriage or relationship.

Sometimes arguments get so heated that you find you are getting nowhere – you are going round and round covering the same old ground, or else each of you is just trying to inflict the maximum pain on the other. Although not easy, it is much better to end the argument, to call a truce, until you have both calmed down enough to be more reasonable and kinder to each other. I do not mean that the arguments should fall off the agenda for good, merely that you should try to sort matters out another time and in another place.

Different approaches to arguments

There are no huge differences in the way that men and women approach arguments. It is perhaps fair to say that there are a few, but they do not apply to all men or all women. In general:

- Women tend to want to pursue an argument longer than men do. They may follow the man from room to room trying to get to a resolution, far beyond the time when it would have been sensible to let things calm down.
- Men tend to opt for the quiet life, often trying to avoid arguments in the hope that they will go away. Alternatively they withdraw from them by finding something urgent to do, or by engrossing themselves in reading the newspaper or watching television.
- In arguments women tend to cry more easily than men. They become more emotionally upset and at times even hysterical.
- Men are more likely to escape to the pub or to drink too much if the going gets rough.
- Women are more likely to telephone their mother, sister or friends, as a way of escape or of eliciting sympathy.
- Men often attribute unreasonableness (as they see it) in their partners to pre-menstrual tension, and though this may be true men can overdo this accusation.

Domestic violence and emotional abuse

A survey by the Association of London Authorities (local councils), called *Zero Tolerance*, found that almost half of all murders of women are committed by current or former partners. Here are some more disturbing statistics and findings. Domestic violence accounts for a quarter of all reported violent crime. A survey in Islington, north London, of one thousand men and women reported that one in three women had been victims of violence. The most common form of attack is grabbing, pushing, shaking, punching, kicking, head-butting, attempted strangulation or assault with a weapon. Sandra Horley, of Chiswick Women's Rescue, says domestic violence is a national epidemic of staggering proportions and claims that one woman in four is abused by her partner.

In a very unhealthy bullying relationship a man can go on for hour after hour, abusing and shouting at a woman in a way that amounts to nothing short of emotional abuse. There are no bruises to show on the surface, but enormous damage can be done to the woman in terms of loss of self-esteem and loss of will to stand up for herself. She can indeed be reduced to an emotional wreck. Fortunately, however, that is not the stuff of the average argument. Nevertheless men are more likely to become violent in an argument than women. They may lash out, hit, punch, push or use a weapon. In the main they are the more aggressive sex. Also, because they are stronger, when men are violent they are usually more dangerous than women.

But to be fair, women too can be violent in arguments. They can resort to kicking, hitting, scratching or biting. At times they can be the ones to start the violence. It is not uncommon for a woman to throw something such as a plate or a glass of wine at a man. In more serious cases women can attack men unexpectedly with a weapon such as a bottle or a knife, but this is more likely to happen after many years of physical or mental abuse by the man. If arguments end in violence it is important to seek outside help before it is too late, either by going for counselling or by contacting the police domestic violence units.

We have seen how home can be where the hatred is, how it can be filled with pain – and that it is possible to reverse or avoid this. In Chapter 4 I will show that home can also be the scene of another kind of battleground – in the sexual arena. Sex can be deeply wounding or wonderfully satisfying. It can bring intense pleasure and total delight – a thread that runs wonderfully and passionately through the whole relationship. But if it goes badly wrong – or never even begins – it can ruin the relationship.

4

IN THE BEDROOM

IT DOESN'T HAVE TO BE A YAWN 'TIL DAWN

What is it men in women do require?
The lineaments of Gratified Desire.
What is it women do in men require?
The lineaments of Gratified Desire.
William Blake, poet, artist and social reformer

As a rule Victorian mothers told their daughters little or nothing about sex. If they did it was frequently left to the eve of the daughter's wedding, when a rather muddled picture would be relayed. This talk would invariably be given with very negative overtones, implying that if she was lucky the prospective husband would be a kind and considerate man and would not trouble her too much. As Oscar Wilde said in the 1890s: 'Marriage is the price men pay for sex and sex is the price women pay for marriage.' But men's and women's attitudes have changed considerably over the last hundred years.

Victorian attitudes linger

In the nineteenth century and well into the twentieth marriage was very much based on double standards. A man, particularly in middle-class and upper-class circles, was expected and encouraged to have sexual encounters with other women before marriage. But this was regarded as neither desirable nor acceptable for unmarried women. Virginity was a pre-requisite to social acceptance. Any suggestion of a sexual entanglement would have resulted in a tarnished reputation and greatly reduced chances of making a good marriage. To safeguard the possibility of anything happening, a young man and woman were not left alone together but usually chaperoned.

So while one class of women was protected, working-class girls were exploited. Because a girl from his own class was not available, the middle- and upper-class man would most likely gain his sexual experience through prostitutes or a mistress. Alternatively he might take advantage of a servant, a village girl, a barmaid or factory hand. If the girls got pregnant, they would be sacked from the household or place of employment, or sent away in disgrace by their own families. She would be the one at fault, and the man would usually get away with his behaviour. He was not perceived as having any responsibility to the woman or to his child.

Working-class girls, already at risk from predatory men, were frequently just as ignorant as their 'socially superior' sisters. Contraception was in any case at best regarded as criminal, at worst non-existent. As a result the illegitimacy rate among working-class girls was very high, which also affected the way society viewed them and their chances of marriage. Unmarried mothers were 'fallen women', but there was no such thing as the fallen man. According to the National Council for One-parent families, even in the early part of this century the state gave no financial support to unmarried mothers, and thousands lived in the workhouse under appalling conditions. They were not allowed to leave until they could support themselves and their children outside; meanwhile many of the children died from lack of proper nutrition and care. Other babies died at the hands of their own mothers, because of the impossibility of their situations and the need to conceal the birth. So for women sexual activity outside marriage was not only socially unacceptable behaviour, but also riddled with danger and laden with guilt.

The reason I have gone back in time like this is because I believe that, even in the late twentieth century, we are still living in the shadow of these sexual attitudes. Some of the double standards and guilt remain, and render many people unable to be sexually at ease with themselves or each other.

Talking about sex

I was in a Relate counselling centre when the receptionist took a long call from a woman in her mid-forties. She desperately wanted help with a sexual problem, but was having tremendous difficulty in asking. This kind of thing is difficult for most people, but the woman in question had the additional problem that under no circumstances must her husband know that she was seeking help. She wanted to sort out the problem without him ever knowing that she had come to counselling.

Even in the 1990s it is still incredibly difficult for many people to talk to their partners about sexual problems. Yet our partner is the one person with whom most of us really need to share our problem. But sometimes talking things through first with a skilled and trained therapist can give you the confidence to go on and talk to your partner. I hope it was possible for this woman.

One thing is certain – she was not alone in finding it difficult to talk to her husband about sex. This is particularly true if things are going wrong. The woman says, 'I want to tell him, but I think he will see it as criticism', so she goes on faking orgasm. The longer she does so, the more difficult it becomes to admit the truth. Nor does it give the man a chance to learn how to satisfy her.

The man often has the same difficulty in talking to his wife or partner. He may say, 'Sometimes I just don't feel like making love, but if I tell her that she'll think I'm rejecting her.' For fear of hurting his partner he is not being sexually honest, so he picks an argument just before bedtime as a way of avoiding sex. Yet most women would much rather he told them the truth and they made love another time.

In this chapter I want to look at how men and women can have equally loving, fun and deeply satisfying sexual relationships. I shall also explore men's and women's most common sexual fantasies and whether men are more able than women to have sex without emotional commitment.

Sexual difficulties can cause havoc in relationships, so I shall also be looking at various problems such as impotence, premature ejaculation, lack of orgasm and vaginismus, as well as mismatch, loss of sexual desire and the differences in arousal patterns between the sexes. I shall explore the sexual differences between men and women and expose some of the myths – for example that men are always ready for sex, with any woman, at any time, or that women are naturally monogamous and men are polygamous. Dorothy Parker put it delightfully in this poem written in 1937:

> *Woman wants monogamy,*
> *Man delights in novelty.*
> *Love is women's moon and sun,*
> *Man has other forms of fun.*
> *Woman lives but in her Lord,*
> *Count to ten, and the man is bored.*
> *With this the gist and sum of it,*
> *What earthly good can come of it?*

Miss Parker is of course well known for her sense of humour. Or this one by William James, psychologist, and philosopher, and a man of course.

> *Hogamous, higamous, Man is polygamous*
> *Higamous, hogamous, Women monogamous.*

Then J.R. Tolkien the author and creator of the delightful books about hobbits, the little creatures of the underworld, writes about his views of men and women and monogamy in a letter to his son Michael in 1941. He reflexes what many men and women thought about women's sexuality. He suggests that only women who are flighty, or wanton, are tempted into unfaithfulness. He says of women: 'even though false teaching, bad upbringing and corrupt fashions may encourage them – but they are instinctively, when uncorrupt, monogamous. Men are not, no good pretending, men just ain't, not by their animal nature', and he points out to his son that however much a man loves his wife it is only natural for men to have a roving eye, to desire women other than their wives and it was only self-denial that prevents men from acts of unfaithfulness.

Whereas apparently for women only the corrupted and the depraved had these thoughts or behave in such a way. I could perhaps add how lucky for men that there are so many depraved and corruptible women around. But that is slightly tongue in cheek, I am not criticising Tolkien far from it, he was after all only reflecting commonly held views of the time. Many women because of their upbringing had learnt to suppress their sexual feelings, and thought that well brought up women should not feel sexual and they frequently had no real knowledge of their sexual potential.

The currency of power and the currency of intimacy

I believe passionately that men and women have an equal capacity for sexual enjoyment and fulfilment. But I also believe that men and women frequently have very different attitudes and expectations of sex and of loving, intimate relationships. By recognizing and understanding the differences between the sexes, rather than ignoring them or pretending that they do not exist, men and women can achieve much deeper and more fulfilling relationships. Gaining more insight into and understanding of how each other thinks and feels sexually can create an important bond between a couple.

To understand how men and women behave in sexual relationships, let's first look at how they behave in the world at large. As we saw earlier, men tend to view the world, and particularly the world of work and that of relationships, in terms of power and status. Women are more likely to relate to the world, and to the world of relationships, through a desire for closeness, intimacy, a wish to communicate and a search for equality. Intimacy is the currency that women use in relationships, whereas men go for power. This is particularly so in the workplace but is also true in sexual relationships.

Most men, for instance, enjoy chasing a pretty woman whom they find sexually attractive. Pursuing and conquering is exciting. It is not just the possibility of a new sexual experience that is a turn-on, it is also the power that the chase and conquest hold for them. The thought or anticipation of the woman surrendering to them is a great aphrodisiac for most men. And if a woman is honest with her feelings, most would rather be persuaded and wooed by a man whom they find desirable than have to give chase! The American politician Henry Kissinger, writing in the *New York Times* in 1971, said, 'Power is a great aphrodisiac', and many women are attracted to powerful, successful men.

Men sometimes equate money or the spending of it with acquiring power over other people – 'buying' them if you like. An example is the recent case of a solicitor who, having taken a girl out for the evening and in his opinion spent a lot of money on her, was reputed to have felt that, because she had been fairly flirtatious, he was entitled to have sex with her. She thought otherwise, took him to court on a rape charge and won.

Nowadays when young women accept dinner or lunch invitations from men they will often insist on going Dutch, not only because they may well be earning as much as him or more, but also because they feel this ploy gives them more control about what happens afterwards – *they* decide whether they want to go to bed with him or not. A very pretty woman of about thirty, who had just returned from three days' work in Paris, told me, 'I had a wonderful time. I went out with a different man each night but I insisted on paying my way – I didn't want to be compromised by letting them pay for me.'

Men are frequently brought up to believe in what the American author Jay Mann calls the three As of manhood: Achieve, Achieve, Achieve. In the world of work men are socialized to strive for power and believe it's better to be the boss than the subordinate. But if men try to extend this attitude to their intimate personal relationships with women they frequently run into resistance if not actual trouble. Because of this need to achieve, men invest a tremendous amount of themselves in their job. It is one of their most important ways of evaluating themselves and those around them. They get much of their personal identity from the work they do, how much they earn and how successful they are perceived to be by themselves and those around them.

Women's jobs are, of course, also important to them, but the majority of women are not so status-driven as men are. They are more likely to gain their belief in themselves from a wider base. Women acquire much of their sense of identity from what they invest in relationships as wife or partner, good mother, caring sister or loving daughter. A good brain, looking great or achievements outside work may also enter the equation. In other words, their sense of identity will probably be based on a combination of many things.

So whether in the board room or bedroom, men and women are constantly engaged in the task of establishing the finely balanced needs of both sexes for power and intimacy in their relationships with each other. (Power, of course, is not always in the hands of the man. In the classical legend of Lysistrata the women, fed up with their warmongering menfolk, got together and agreed among themselves to withdraw their sexual favours. It was their way of getting the men to stop fighting.)

Different paths to sexual intimacy

Sometimes men and women's interpretations of love, intimacy and sex are very different from each other. Understanding these differences can make relationships between men and women much more satisfying, and can give each sex a chance to understand their partner better.

For example, if you have had a row, which although it has abated has left you both bruised, a man may want to re-create intimacy and closeness by making love. That makes him feel loved and loving and close again. Although this also works for some women, the majority can only really feel close to their partner again by talking to him, by the man touching her affectionately, possibly without sex on the agenda, by perhaps sharing a meal together. Most importantly of all, women usually need time in this situation before being ready to make love.

A man's path to intimacy with the woman he loves or desires is frequently established for him through making love to her. Most women's path to intimacy in a relationship with a man is established by communication – by talking, by feeling listened to, by feeling desired, which then culminates in the intimacy of making love.

Another way in which men express intimacy towards a woman is by caring for her. A man's need to look after and protect a woman is multi-layered and can be shown in quite practical ways. In counselling I have often heard a man say: 'I love her, I look after her, I provide for her and we have a good lifestyle – what more does she want.'

The woman will more than likely reply: 'I love you too, but what I want is more time with you. I want you to be more interested in me and the children. The lifestyle you are providing comes at a high cost to the relationship. I feel you are more committed to your work than you are to me.'

Protecting and looking after a woman is a very deep male instinct. Being able to provide for her and the children, to take her out for a meal and to give her presents are his displays of love and intimacy. It is important for women to understand and recognize this need.

On the other hand, men also need to recognize that, if striving to provide a good lifestyle is really about a need to succeed at work, and if showering her with gifts is really an attempt to buy peace so that he can continue to spend time away from her, he should not be surprised if the woman rejects these things. Men need to see that what women really want is more of their time and attention. If a man does not recognize that he will feel frustrated and at a loss, claiming he just does not understand women. One woman complained bitterly to me that her husband was never there for her and the children. 'Maybe he was physically in the room, but if we wanted to talk to him we were constantly interrupted by his work calls, and he cancelled more holidays than he ever took.' It's an obvious way for both partners to end up feeling angry and confused until they learn to talk the issues out. This situation is described poignantly in the following poem by Ella Wheeler Wilcox:

The Husband
Of course I love you, and the children too.
Be sensible, my dear, it is for you
I work so hard to make my business pay.
There, now, run home, enjoy your holiday.

The Wife
He does not mean to wound me,
I know his heart is kind.
Alas! that man can love us
And be so blind, so blind.
A little time for pleasure
A little time for play;
A word to prove the love of life
And frighten care away.
Tho' poor my lot in some small cot
That were a holiday.

The Husband
She has not meant to wound me, nor to vex.
Zounds! but 'tis difficult to please the sex.
I've housed and gowned her like a very queen
Yet there she goes, with discontented mien.
I gave her diamonds only yesterday.
Some women are like that, do what you may.

Enter arguments, exit sex

In marriage and committed relationships it is rare for the sexual element to be working wonderfully if the rest of the time you are at war with each other. Though some couples do get a sexual charge by moving from rowing to sex, for most couples constant arguments and resentments have a damaging effect on their sex life. Making love happens less frequently, or else it is over very quickly and either one partner or both derive little enjoyment or satisfaction from it. This was true for Sarah and Roger.

Sarah walked into the room looking sullen and cross, with Roger following her smiling anxiously. They were both tall, slim and good-looking. They had been married for ten years, and had two children. Roger started to say how much he loved Sarah and he wanted the marriage to stay intact. Sarah looked impatient and sighed deeply, then turned to Roger and said:

'You say that now, but it's only because you're frightened I am going to leave you. When we were first married you were everything to me, but you've just trampled on everything I had to give. Now I don't think there's anything left. It's all too late.'

Roger looked devastated. 'But I'll change, I'll change,' he pleaded. Over the next few months of counselling he tried, and did indeed make many changes. He became much more reliable – if he said he would do something such as coming home from work or the pub at a certain time he did; and he started to do more with the children. He talked much more to Sarah instead of reading the paper and watching television. He encouraged and supported her in her attempts to return to work. The rows stopped, and the two of them were getting on better than they had done for years.

But there was still an underlying sexual problem. Sarah had lost all interest in sex with Roger, and that had not changed. They made love very infrequently, and it was always Roger who initiated it. Although Sarah went along with making love, there was little in it for her. Looking back over the marriage, it became clear that she had cut off emotionally from Roger shortly after the birth of their second child, who was now five. There was only eighteen months between the children and it had been a very difficult birth. Sarah had left hospital feeling worn out, collected by her mother because Roger, as usual, could not get away from work. When they got home, they found the place in an awful mess, with dirty dishes piled up in the sink. Roger said: 'I had no time because of work and visiting Sarah in hospital.' Things went from bad to worse. Sarah was trying to cope with both a toddler and a new baby, and Roger was hardly ever there. When he was there, he did little to help out. They had row after row.

Sarah became depressed and Roger could not cope. His response was to throw himself even more into his work. Sarah said: 'That was when I just started to feel frozen inside in my mind and body. I resented the fact that the only time Roger seemed interested in me was when he wanted sex.'

At the time of the counselling sessions she turned to Roger with tears streaming down her face. 'You just used me! You were never there for me or the children,' she shouted.

'But I didn't realize,' Roger said desperately.

Sarah replied: 'You didn't want to know. That's the truth and now it's too late.'

'No, it's not,' Roger said. 'I'll change that – I'll make it up to you.'

Often what is happening in the sexual relationship between a couple is a reflection of what is happening in the rest of their marriage, as it was in Sarah and Roger's case. There had been no closeness for many years. Roger had been cold and unavailable to Sarah, and in response she had withdrawn from him emotionally and sexually. Sex between them had, like the relationship, been fairly unloving. Sarah never kissed Roger when they were making love and touched him as little as possible. Though she had the occasional orgasm, afterwards she always felt intensely lonely and let down – just as she did in the relationship. So Sarah's resentment had grown and grown. Roger had failed to recognize that sex was as unsatisfying as the relationship itself. He had to a large degree been ignoring what was going on in the marriage, and had been using work and the pub as escape routes. Yet, sadly, neither of them had been able to tackle the underlying problems.

As far as Sarah was concerned, too much damage had been done. She no longer loved Roger and felt nothing for him sexually. For her the relationship was dead. So despite the changes that Roger had made, and the fact that the relationship had improved, Sarah was unable to recommit herself to the relationship. She had also met someone else and, though this was not an affair, it opened up the possibilities of the sort of relationship she wanted. So even though the future was uncertain, Sarah filed for divorce.

This marriage might not have ended like this if only Roger and Sarah had been able to talk their problems through before they became so deeply entrenched, or if Sarah had not been determined to hang on to the wrongs of the past which were getting in the way of rebuilding the future. If you continue to blame your partner for what has gone wrong, rather than accept responsibility for your own behaviour as well, if you cannot let go the hurts of the past, you can get bogged down. The relationship is unable to move forward, and eventually it can break down altogether. It is vital to try to tackle problems, sexual or otherwise, before they become too firmly entrenched.

Common sexual problems

It is easy to think that nowadays, with so much talk and knowledge about sex, sexual problems are a thing of the past. Unfortunately it's far from true. Research shows that couples have sexual problems both early in marriage as well as when they have been together for some time. Here are some of the most common problems that men and women have in their sexual relationships.

Men	Women
Impotence	Non-orgasmic, or lack of orgasm
Premature ejaculation	Loss of sexual desire
Retarded ejaculation	Vaginismus (contracting of the vaginal muscles, which makes intercourse impossible)
Loss of sexual desire	Dyspareunia (pain on intercourse)

There is one more problem experienced by both men and women, and that is mismatch of sexual desire.

Impotence and ejaculation problems in men, and lack of orgasm, vaginismus and dyspareunia in women respond well to treatment in sex therapy. They can also be helped through counselling. When a couple seek help with sexual problems, even though only one of them may declare a problem (such as vaginismus), their partner often has a sexual problem (like premature ejaculation) too. One problem is masking the other.

Most therapists and marriage counsellors would probably agree that perhaps the most elusive of all sexual problems, and sometimes the most difficult to understand and treat, is loss of sexual desire, sometimes described as 'impaired sexual interest'. Consultant psychiatrist Dr Keith Hawton says in his book, *Sex Therapy. A practical guide*, that in his clinic, out of 257 women who came to him with a sexual problem 52 per cent had impaired sexual interest, while of 258 men who presented with a sexual problem 6 per cent had impaired sexual interest but 60 per cent also had erectile problems. Many difficulties in getting and maintaining an erection are related to impaired sexual interest, making the balance between the sexes here rather more equal than it would at first sight appear.

Loss of sexual desire increasingly seems to be top of the list in most clinics and counselling centres for people with sexual problems. I know from my own clinical experience that, though it is much more common to see women presenting with this problem, over the last few years an increasing number of men have been in this situation.

If you are having sexual problems, it can cause you to avoid making love because it has become a disappointing or totally unsatisfactory area of your life. If you anticipate that sex is going to give little pleasure, then it is not surprising that you stop wanting to put yourself through that experience. So desire for your partner fades away.

Common causes for loss of sexual desire

First of all, what's happening to you in the rest of your life can and does affect the level of sexual desire in both men and women.

External pressures

Think of possible external pressures that might be causing the change in you or your partner. See if it coincided with or started shortly after some significant event in your life, such as the arrival of a new baby or being made redundant.

Overwork, or work in general, is why an increasing number of men are experiencing loss of sexual desire. Work can be very stressful and the British really are the workaholics of Europe, especially in terms of working hours. Many companies have a ten hours a day or more work culture, and if you are not prepared to go along with that there are plenty of people out there waiting to fill your shoes. Add to that the commuting time on busy roads and overcrowded trains, and by the time many men get home at the end of the day they are worn out. All they want is peace and quiet, a meal that someone else (preferably) has prepared and no demands made on their mind or their body. When women are worn out by their job, children or a combination of both, instead of looking forward to making love it can just seem like one more chore at the end of the day.

So if you have put every last ounce of yourself into your job, when you return home you just want to switch off and not even talk very much to your partner, particularly if you are a man. But most women do want to talk – and there's the rub. I shall be looking at this further in Chapter 8, which is about men and women and work. But if, as a woman, you want to spend time together and talk and your man doesn't, and if he at the end of a fairly silent evening wants to make love, the chances are that you won't want to because there will have been too little communication between you. So you both end up feeling rejected and resenting each other. These feelings grow causing ever-increasing emotional and sexual distance.

Here's a list of external life stresses that can cause loss of sexual desire. See if any of them apply to you.

- Overwork and stress can also, it is said, alter the chemical processes in your body, which can be a real depressant to sexual desire.
- Unemployment or redundancy can have a devastating effect on your sexual appetite. It can lead to loss of self-esteem, loss of

identity and a sense of pointlessness, which in turn can cause depression. All these factors can suppress sexual desire.

- Treatment for diabetes, high blood pressure and depression (ironically!) can suppress sexual desire. So if your sexual desire has changed or seems to be dwindling, and you are taking some form of medication, check with your GP about any side-effects which are known to suppress the libido.
- Debts, money worries and drinking too much can have the same effect.
- The death of a close family member or a close friend.
- Having an elderly relative come to live with you.
- The arrival of a new baby.
- A teenager who is worrying you like hell.
- A sick or disabled child.
- Major or disfiguring surgery.
- Mid-life crisis.
- A negative reaction to the menopause.

This is not a comprehensive list, and maybe you can add other things specific to you. See if your partner is prepared to do the same, and then discuss the list with each other. It really is important to check whether some external cause might be causing the problem before moving on to look at other reasons. And remember you are not looking to blame your partner, but to gain understanding of what might be causing the problem.

If it is an external reason that is causing the difficulties, the first stage is identifying it so that you can then tackle it. See if you can make any changes to the circumstances giving rise to the distress. If you can, in time your sexual desire will return naturally. Identifying the problem helps immediately, in any case. It can stop the one suffering from loss of libido feeling there is something dreadfully wrong with them, and can stop their partner feeling either that it is all their fault or that they are being rejected by their partner. So the problem can be tackled together rather than letting it drive you apart.

Differences between male and female external reasons

Men more than women appear to be affected by work and work stresses, drinking too much and money problems. Women, on the other hand, are usually more affected by problems within the family, particularly by what is happening to their children. Nothing has greater potential for totally reducing sexual desire in women than worries about children – whether it's because they are ill, awaiting an operation, being bullied at school, involved with unsuitable friends, experimenting with drugs, having just failed their exams or arriving home hours after they said they would.

That does not mean to say that men do not worry about these things as well – they do – but somehow they are able to distance themselves a little more than women are. I think this difference is partly because women, even in the relatively enlightened 1990s, still think that children and family are their main areas of responsibility, and partly because women do more day-to-day looking after of their children and therefore still feel very responsible and involved with them. The physical and emotional welfare and happiness of their children, their husband and the family comes, they feel, under their jurisdiction.

The state of the relationship

The state of your relationship is a very good barometer for assessing why you may be experiencing little or no sexual desire. This seems a simple statement, but behind it lie some very complex issues. When you first meet someone and fall in love, sexual excitement is very high and it's hard to imagine that it won't go on for ever. But why is it at such dizzy heights?

The novelty factor plays an incredibly large part, of course. But what is also important is that you are spending time together, really talking about things that matter to both of you, listening to what the other person has to say, making the other person feel good about themselves, making them feel special, desirable and the one person you want to be with. All these things combine to make a warm, loving, supportive relationship, which, together with the exciting newness of each other, leads to high levels of sexual desire. And if sex is good it's only natural to want to make love frequently.

So if the relationship is good in this way, and if these things continue, the chances are that you will continue to feel sexual desire for each other. But if these positive feelings for each other slip away, the same can happen to sexual desire. If the good feelings are replaced by rows, arguments, constant criticism, boredom, taking each other for granted and never spending time together, all this may well result in loss of desire in one or both of you. If that is what's going on in your relationship, is it really so surprising that you have turned off each other sexually?

Think about whether you are harbouring deep resentment, constantly shouting at each other or having endless arguments that just go round and round and get nowhere. Are there deep, withdrawn silences that feel rejecting and distancing? If this is constantly happening, it really can reduce or even kill sexual desire. If you cannot sort these problems out together, counselling would be a good next step. You will probably find that, as the relationship improves, sexual desire returns too.

When Derrick and Claire came for counselling even the sound-proofing in the counselling room was having difficulty coping with the noise level of the arguments. Neither of them was listening to what the other said and they were constantly blaming each other for the present state of the marriage. Derrick had been married previously and had three children from his first marriage. They were living with his ex-wife, Ann. He and Claire had a three-year-old daughter.

In the early days of their relationship sex had been superb, they both agreed, but during the last year Derrick had hardly ever wanted to make love and Claire felt totally rejected. Over the weeks of counselling they were able to start unravelling what was triggering the rows, which were almost always about Derrick's children. Claire felt they were completely taking him over and that there was nothing left for her and their daughter. Whenever his children telephoned they seemed to have a problem which would send him into the deepest gloom. He spent more and more time arguing with his ex-wife over how often he was going to see them and he would buy them presents all the time, even though money was really tight and there was not really enough to support his new family unless they budgeted very carefully.

It became clear that two things were happening to Derrick. One was that he was absolutely guilt-ridden about having walked out on his first marriage. Ann had found this, his Achilles heel, and was using it as a way of expressing her own unresolved anger over the break-up of the marriage and trying to get more money out of him. Secondly, there was a new man in Ann's life and Derrick was afraid he would displace him in his children's affections. This was making him demand more and more of their time. But as teenagers they wanted to be out with their friends, while Derrick interpreted this as rejection of him. All of this was making Claire feel more and more excluded, and the lack of sex seemed to prove that he no longer loved her.

In counselling Claire was able to see that her response created even more problems. Even though deep down she knew her attitude was unsatisfactory, it was the only way she felt she could gain his attention. She had slipped right back into a childhood pattern – her strict and unloving father had never had time for her, and she had become a naughty child as a way of trying to get his time and interest. When Derrick was able to accept that the break-up of his first marriage was not all his fault, and avoid falling into the trap his first wife had so expertly laid for him, he was able to get the guilt into proportion. Also he was able to see that having another man around did not have to mean that his children would feel any differently about him. They were just growing up as normal teenagers. Derrick could now see that his behaviour was threatening his present marriage, and when he and Claire were able to support each other rather than tear each other apart the return of a good sexual relationship reinforced the love between them, which had been in danger of slipping away.

Sexual desire for someone else

Falling in love with someone else, or having an affair, can result in loss of desire between you and your partner. It is not always so – sometimes an affair can actually heighten desire for the permanent partner, or it may not change things at all. But for most people, being involved with someone else, thinking about them constantly, planning illicit meetings, spending hours making love to them, wishing you were with them rather than with your partner, or finding them a wonderful escape from the demands of everyday life makes their libido take a downward turn where their regular partner is concerned. And if the partner is aware of the situation, they will feel hurt and rejected and probably not feel like making love.

Of course your partner may know nothing of the affair, or may be colluding unconsciously with you in not wanting to know about it, and therefore feel very confused by what is happening. And if, as is usually the case, you don't want to admit to the affair, you will often be in the position of thinking up excuses or lying to your partner. Deceit and guilt can kill sexual desire.

Sexual boredom

When former President Calvin Coolidge of the USA and his wife were on one of their official engagements, they visited a state chicken farm at which they were being shown around separately. Mrs Coolidge arrived at a pen full of hens and cockerels.

'How often does the cockerel mate with a hen in a day?' she enquired.

'Oh, several times a day,' she was told.

'Tell that to the President, will you please?' his wife requested.

The President duly arrived at the same pen and was told what his wife had said. He paused for a moment and then asked: 'Same chick?'

'No, Mr President,' came the reply.

'Tell that to my wife, will you?' requested President Coolidge.

Ever since then loss of sexual desire has been known as the Coolidge effect or the Coolidge factor!

Imagine if your partner prepared the same meal for you every day, which you ate at the same time and in the same place. Both of you would very soon be fed up with it. Yet that is the sexual routine into which all too many couples slip all too quickly.

Variety in lovemaking is very important: if you always know what he or she is going to do next, that is not very exciting, and if you only have two or three different positions in which you make love, that too will soon become boring. Sex does not always have to take place at the end of the day, when you are both tired and it can be over too quickly.

It may not be easy given the demands of children, work and other pressures, but it is important to keep variety and spice in your sexual relationship. So plan occasionally for the children to go to their grandparents, or to a friend's house – you can do the same in return. Spend those few free hours just being with each other and making love. Or go to bed early, starting with a relaxing bath, and take a bottle of wine or champagne with you. You could try making love in front of the fire, or in the open air if you can find somewhere that you will not be disturbed. Try a weekend away together, just the two of you, and so avoid, as Madame Bovary said of her husband, 'My husband's lovemaking has lapsed into routine; his embraces keep fixed hours. It is just one more habit, a sort of dessert he looks forward to after the monotony of dinner.' Well, maybe Monsieur Bovary was still finding pleasure in his sexual relationship, but his wife was undoubtedly not.

There are so many different ways of making love, so don't just limit it to a few over-used positions or think that sexual intercourse is the only way to give each other pleasure or to reach orgasm. Don't forget the delights and the sexual excitement of kissing and caressing all of your partner's body with your tongue and fingers.

Female sexual problems

Lack of orgasm

Very few women have an orgasm every time they make love, but if it never or hardly ever happens it is not unusual for the woman eventually to lose interest in sex with her partner altogether. You may be non-orgasmic possibly because you do not know or understand your own body enough to know what pleases you sexually. Or you know and your partner does not, and you cannot tell him. It may be because the relationship you are in is unloving, or full of argument and rows. If you have never had an orgasm the reason may be a fear of letting go, of being out of control.

The majority of women do not achieve orgasm on penetration alone but need the extra stimulation of their clitoris, either with the man's fingers or their own, but frequently a woman cannot tell or show her partner what it is she wants. Or she feels that he might take it as criticism, and resent it or be hurt. Inability to achieve orgasm through penetration can often be overcome through oral sex, where the woman's partner caresses her clitoris and vagina with his mouth and tongue. Or a woman can learn to become orgasmic through masturbation. What is important is that a woman has enough trust in her partner to be able to share her body and thoughts with him.

Sometimes the problem is more complex and more deeply rooted. If there has been past sexual abuse or rape, or very strong and overbearing religious influences in a woman's childhood or early adult life, this can result in inhibited sexual desire. Women who have grown up in such authoritarian families have often taken on board so much guilt about sex that they are unable to relax, to trust and to take pleasure in their own bodies. Sometimes trusting and talking this through with a loving and understanding partner can overcome the problem. If not, it is advisable to seek outside help through counselling or psychosexual therapy. This problem does respond well to treatment or to what is called a sensate focus programme (see page 102), which can be done at home with each other but is probably best done with the help of a therapist (I recommend a very good book called *Becoming Orgasmic*, by Julia Heiman, Leslie and Joseph Lopiccolo).

Vaginismus

This involuntary contraction of the vaginal muscles is often caused by fear, and makes it impossible for the penis to enter the vagina. If the man tried to force his penis into the woman, he would cause great pain. That should never be attempted, as it would only make the problem worse.

Many couples put up with this condition for years because they are too embarrassed to ask for help. It is often only when they desperately want a baby that they come forward and seek treatment. With the encouragement of a loving partner the problem can usually be helped through psychosexual therapy. The therapist will teach the woman to relax, to get to know her own body, to be able to touch herself and to learn to insert first one and then two fingers into her vagina. Then the man gently starts to do the same, at the woman's own pace. It can be done through a sensate focus programme which I describe briefly a little later in the chapter. A non-consummated marriage does not necessarily mean there has been no sex. Often the couple have made love in every other way, but penetration has not been possible.

Dyspareunia

Possible reasons for pain on intercourse in women include a difficult childbirth; stitching that may still be sensitive, or too tight after an episiotomy; or vaginal dryness at the menopause. The man, too, may experience pain if his foreskin is too tight. It is important to seek medical advice and to check that there are no physical reasons, as it is not possible to enjoy sex if it is painful.

Male sexual problems

Impotence or erectile problems

It is quite common for a man, at some point in his adult life, to suffer from not being able to get or maintain an erection. If it happens more than once or twice, however, men often feel that it is the end of them as sexual beings, rather than just a passing phase.

So as a man you are often straight into performance anxiety. And if you *think* you are going to fail, you can end up with your worst fears coming true. Most women are very understanding and caring if this happens to their partner; that can be the first step in overcoming the problem, and indeed it is often all that is needed. It is very important for a woman not to criticize a man in this situation. The man feels bad enough already, and a critical partner can make the problem a whole lot worse.

As a man it is important to realize that, given time, the problem will frequently right itself naturally. It will also do so a lot more quickly if you don't worry about it. Easier said than done, perhaps. But understanding what the cause may be is an important first step.

Earlier in this chapter I looked at the causes for loss of desire; if you are suffering from impotence when previously there have been no problems, it might be similar to loss of desire – for example because of external pressures, or a difficult and unhappy relationship. Sometimes impotence can happen after a divorce or the death of a partner, or when you enter into new relationships – either because you have been very sexually undermined by the previous relationship, or because if you have lost a partner through death you may feel guilty about having sex with a new one. It is important to try to identify the cause. I suggest you read pages 90–97 and see if you recognize any of that in yourself or your current relationship. Then talk it through with your partner, so that you can share your anxieties and both gain more understanding and support.

So if it's a problem with the relationship and you cannot sort it out, seek counselling. If the relationship is fine but the problem is still there, look at your external pressures and see if you can do anything about changing them. And always consider a medical check-up. It may be something like a lowering in the level of testosterone, the male sex hormone (which can happen as you get older), or possibly the side-effects of some medication that you are taking. There are also ways in which you can help yourself at home or with the help of a psychosexual therapist, using sensate focus (see page 102).

Premature ejaculation

This is a very common sexual problem, especially in young men or those who have not made love for some time. This problem often starts by hurrying over sex – maybe you were once made to feel guilty about masturbation, so you have learnt to get it over with as quickly as possible. Or perhaps your early sexual experiences occurred in circumstances where you were at risk of being interrupted, such as on the sofa at her parents' home or on the back seat of the car, so that you set up a pattern of hurrying sex. And teenage boys find it's easy to come too quickly because of all the hormones coursing through their bodies. So the problem can often stem from a learnt pattern which can equally well be unlearnt. Sensate focus (see page 102) is a good way of dealing with the situation. Start as suggested with non-genital touching in just the same way, and then when you are ready to move on to the next stage incorporate the squeeze technique (see below) into the programme. By learning to use the squeeze technique or the stop-start art of controlling your ejaculation this problem can usually be overcome.

So first read the piece on sensate focus and then, if you want to, incorporate the following suggestions into the second stage of sensate focus, which is called 'genital sensate focus'. The man lies on his back, and the woman very gently caresses his penis. The man agrees to let her know just before he is about to come. She must immediately stop caressing him, and let the erection subside a little. She should do this two or three times before bringing him to orgasm, while the man should be concentrating on recognizing the moment before the point of no return. The aim is to gain more control, and really to identify that crucial moment. This may take a little practice, but is usually very successful.

A variation on this theme is called the squeeze technique. When the man indicates to the woman to stop, she presses firmly with her finger and thumb just below the ridge of the penis. This should not hurt, but should reduce the desire to come. This, like the other exercise, should be done several times, bringing the man near to orgasm and then squeezing with the thumb and forefinger before finally bringing him to orgasm. It is important to learn this technique before moving on to penetration. When you do move on to the next two stages, to begin with just let the penis lie in the vagina without moving. Then withdraw and use the squeeze technique if necessary. The fourth stage is vaginal containment with movement. When the penis is in the vagina and you feel you are about to come, indicate this to your partner. Then both of you should stop moving immediately, or else withdraw and let your partner use the squeeze technique. Continue to do this several times before going on to orgasm.

Retarded ejaculation

Most men can ejaculate through masturbation, but some men occasionally have difficulty ejaculating when making love. With retarded ejaculation the man usually has a very firm erection when he is inside the woman; he feels a high degree of excitement and desire and wants to come. But it is elusive: despite the desire he is unable to come. After some time the desire begins to fade without the man having ejaculated.

The reasons are not always fully understood by those suffering from this condition. Sometimes it is because the man is inhibited about masturbating or coming in front of his partner, or inhibited about letting the woman masturbate him, or coming inside her. Perhaps he had an over-strict or over-authoritarian background, so feelings of guilt take over and he cannot let himself go – he unconsciously denies himself the pleasure of orgasm. Or the problem can be the result of past sexual abuse, either because he is struggling with guilt or because he is subject to flashbacks of disturbing experiences. For some men it is a fear of being out of control. Sometimes, because of a damaging early sexual experience, the man is only able to ejaculate with the assistance of sadistic or masochistic or fetishist practices, which his partner may not want to be involved in but are necessary for him to reach orgasm.

To overcome problems of retarded ejaculation it is first necessary to establish the cause. When that is identified, the problem should be talked through with a loving partner, or possibly a therapist. The way forward then could start with the sensate focus programme, in which the man can let the woman bring him to orgasm with her hand or mouth and then in time move on to sexual intercourse. But understanding the causes, talking things through and seeing what is possible between you as a couple is very important in trying to overcome the problem.

Retarded ejaculation can also be the result of the man's partner having had an affair. The man is thinking of that when he makes love to his wife or partner, and this can prevent him coming. Once the affair is really finished – and given time and a genuine desire on the part of both partners to repair their relationship – this problem will go away.

Sensate focus

Sensate focus can be a helpful and enjoyable way of overcoming a number of sexual problems. You can try this together, but it usually works best with the help of a trained psychosexual therapist. It is a way of getting in touch with your own and your partner's sexual feelings, to encourage you both to talk more openly about sex, to be better able to tell or show each other what you like sexually, and to enjoy sensual touching and caressing.

You may think it surprising, but you must both agree that sexual intercourse will be banned. In the case of impotence or erectile problems, you might smile to yourself and say that intercourse is not happening anyway. But you are probably trying too much to make it happen. So banning of sexual intercourse is particularly relevant because it removes the anxiety of having to perform, which means that the man can relax much more. If you are embarking on a sensate focus programme because you, as a woman, are non-orgasmic, it is equally important, so that trust and the chance to relax and explore your own feelings can be built upon.

You have to agree to set aside two or three hours a week, an hour at a time, where you can be alone together without interruptions. Make sure the room you are using is warm, with comfortable, low lighting. Then take a bath or shower, to help you both relax. There are certain tasks that I will guide you through, but it is very important to make sure that you are happy and relaxed before you move on from one task to the next. If you try to rush things, you may be setting yourself up to fail. So before you move on talk things through and, if you are uncomfortable with anything, always tell your partner.

The first task is to get you to relax, and to enable you to give and receive, to touch and be touched, to enjoy caressing each other very much like you did in the early days of your relationship. You may become aroused, and if so that is fine, but it is not the intention. What you are both aiming to do is to discover what you enjoy, what gives you pleasure as well as what you don't like. You are also discovering or gaining affirmation about what your partner likes and dislikes.

After your shower lie down together naked. Agree which of you will be on the receiving end and which of you will take the active role. After about half an hour you will reverse roles.

If you are taking the passive role, lie on your tummy to start with and then on your back while your partner caresses every area of your body except the obvious sexual parts such as the penis, vagina, clitoris or breasts. The first stage should be 'non-genital touching'. The person doing the caressing should do what gives them pleasure, while the person on the receiving end should just enjoy what is happening and think about what they are feeling. If they dislike what is being done to them they should explain what they would like instead – perhaps a lighter touch, or more slowly, or with the use of some lotion or cream that you like the smell of as well as the feel, so that as many senses as possible are stimulated. This should be done over several sessions and maybe for several weeks. Only move on to the second stage when you both feel really comfortable with each other and can discuss the experience and sensation in a relaxed way. Don't rush to get to this next stage, or feel too disappointed if, to start with, you don't enjoy it very much. As you learn to relax and trust each other your enjoyment will increase.

The second stage involves taking turns as before and doing the same thing, but now include the areas you have been leaving out – the penis, genital area, vagina, clitoris and breasts. This is likely to be arousing, but remember that sexual intercourse is still off the agenda. If one or both of you becomes aroused, stop for a while and then continue. If you are both happy with oral sex, this too may be included. This stage is known as 'genital sensate focus'.

The next stage is to introduce the penis into the vagina, and is called 'vaginal containment without movement'. By now you will have found that your ability to talk sexually will have greatly improved, trust will have been built up and you know what you and your partner enjoy. So you are probably ready to make love fully or to masturbate each other to orgasm, but it is important not to rush things, particularly if the problem is to do with impotence. The penis may well by now have regained its former firm state, so gently put it into the vagina but be careful to move as little as possible. This stage is called vaginal containment. Repeat this process two or three times, but do not go on to orgasm while the penis is in the vagina.

The fourth stage, 'vaginal containment with movement', involves the first three stages, but now when the penis is in the vagina you can start to move. Only do this gently, however, concentrating on your feelings and stopping before reaching the point of no return. Do this several times. Withdraw, and continue to pleasure each other in different ways before moving on to full sexual intercourse.

It is important when making love not to see penetrative sex, or coming together, as the ultimate goal. What I hope you will have learnt from this pleasuring is that there are many ways to make love, and that sexual intercourse is just one of those many ways.

Men's and women's different arousal patterns

In giving pleasure to each other it is also important to understand the differences between men's and women's arousal patterns. In the very early days of a relationship there may not appear to be very much difference. Part of being madly in love is that you are both operating on a sexual high. But there are in fact quite fundamental distinctions. The average man can become aroused and, if stimulated, go on to orgasm within three to five minutes. It can take longer as the man gets older. But generally, although women may start to feel sexually aroused fairly quickly, to follow through to full arousal or to orgasm almost always takes longer than for men. The differences were nicely illustrated in Margi Clark's television series on sex: *The Good Sex Guide* (Carlton television

1993) 'Think of it like a clock. If you start with both hands of the clock at twelve o'clock, most men could be fully aroused and ready for orgasm by five past. For women it would take longer and be some time between fifteen and twenty minutes past and twenty to the hour. That really is quite a substantial difference.'

If both men and women can avoid seeing this as a problem, and if the man takes time and knows how to stimulate his partner, and she him, delaying his orgasm can bring greater pleasure for him as well as her. To be taken to the point of nearly coming, and then delaying it, can be very exciting; and if you take longer over foreplay it gives you both an opportunity to discover a wide variety of ways of making love, including stimulating each other with your fingers and tongue as well as trying different positions. Remember, too, that arousal patterns even in one individual are not always the same. It can depend on the person's mood and how he or she is feeling about their partner. Sometimes a woman can be very quickly aroused by the heightened desire that the man is showing her. She may respond very sexually to this as long as she knows that, if she does not want that approach, he will not take her against her will. Nothing is ever entirely one-sided where sex is concerned, and of course the man too can sometimes take longer to become aroused than the woman he is with. In sex, as in all aspects of relationships, nothing is ever set in tablets of stone.

Mismatch of sexual desire

Mismatch should not be confused with loss of sexual desire. Different people have different needs and different sex drives – high, low or somewhere in the middle. Most research shows that the length of time you have been together and your age also affect this particular aspect of sex.

Though it used to be thought that men had a higher sex drive than women, this is not necessarily so. Sex drive tends to be individual rather than gender-related.

Lovemaking is usually at its most frequent at the beginning of a marriage or long-term relationship, with the majority of couples making love at least three times a week in the first two years. The average then alters to about once or twice a week. According to the Wellcome Foundation's sexual attitudes and lifestyle survey, published in January 1994, people between the ages of forty and forty-five are having sex six times a month, and in the fifty to sixty age group it is about once a week. But life events also affect the frequency of sex. It tends to drop off considerably after the birth of a baby, or if there are teenagers in the household. It often takes an upward trend on holiday or when the children leave home. If you are both happy making love once a month or seven times a week that is no problem – averages are not important. A problem only arises if the person who wants to make love no more than once a month is married to the person who wants to make love every night.

In counselling, it is men more than women who complain about the infrequency of sex, just as more women complain about sex being too hurried and with little or no time for foreplay. Maybe the two are related? After all, if women are complaining that sex is unsatisfactory, that could surely be one of the reasons why women in general do not want to make love as much as men, and why a greater number of women than men report loss of sexual desire.

Mark and Jenny came for counselling because of mismatched sexual desire. They were talking about their different needs when Mark turned to Jenny and said, 'Sex is like spinach – it's good for you to have it every day.'

His wife sat there in silence for a moment, then snapped at her Popeye: 'What you mean is that it's good for you, but I get bored with spinach every day.'

Couples often do not discover a mismatch in sexual desire until they start living together or marry. That is for two reasons. In the early days of a relationship sexual feelings are heightened and you both tend to want to make love all the time, and secondly the opportunities are less frequent than when you are living together full-time. It's only when you are together all the time that you discover each other's natural rhythms.

So what can you do? First, don't resist what I am about to suggest because it seems unreasonable or boring. But the answer to this one really is 'compromise'. 'How can I compromise over sex?' I hear the more sexually active ones cry. If you don't, a destructive pattern can be established with both of you ending up as losers: what happens is that the partner who wants sex more often is always pursuing the other one. 'She was warm towards me. She kissed me affectionately when I came home. Perhaps that's the green light for sex tonight.' But to the partner who does not want sex as frequently, this sort of behaviour feels like constant pressure; and the natural reaction to pressure is to resist. This feels like rejection to the one who is seeking sex, and the result is a sort of obsessive zeal because you are feeling unloved or rejected. You then not only want sex because sex is enjoyable, but also as a way of being reassured that you are loved. The more your partner resists, the more unloved or angry you start to feel – so you switch off, look elsewhere or pursue the reluctant partner with even greater interest. That can understandably lead to such a bad atmosphere between you that all the rest of the relationship is affected.

If you are the one who wants sex less frequently, just imagine for a moment what it must be like to feel constantly rejected. No, it's not good, is it? You start to think there is something wrong with you. You may start to have doubts about your desirability, and maybe you are tempted to look elsewhere to make yourself feel better.

Does all this sound familiar? If it does, first try talking to each other about how it feels to be on the receiving end of your behaviour. Really listen to what they have to say, then talk about how it feels to be the one doing the rejecting or the pursuing. Whatever you do, avoid blaming each other. Just try to understand the differences. Then look to see whether the problem really is a mismatch of desire or whether it is masking other problems.

When John and Paula came for counselling one of the things that struck me about them was how very different they looked. John was very slender, wearing either some sort of training outfit or very beautifully cut and co-ordinated casual clothes. Paula, on the other hand, had a rather delightful but chaotic layered look, with skirts and scarves and cardigans flowing in all directions.

They had been married two years and had no children. When you sense that one partner has dragged the other along for counselling you always check this out, and it certainly turned out to be the case with John. Paula said that what was wrong between them was that, over the last year, John had been less and less interested in making love and more and more keen on being down at the gym working out. In the first year of marriage they both acknowledged that Paula had wanted to make love more than John, but their needs then had not been very different. But Paula added: 'During the last year things have got a whole lot worse.'

John did not say a lot – just that he was sorry, he did not want to hurt her, but that was just how things were.

After a couple of weeks of counselling Paula had to go away for a week's conference, and John asked if he could come on his own. Paula was happy with this.

In his single session John obviously found it hard to talk. Eventually he said that he could not tell Paula, but she had put on so much weight since they were married that he no longer found her attractive. When he asked her to try to lose the extra pounds she always got aggressive, or burst into tears and said that if he really loved her he would not mind how much weight she had put on. John was helped to see that, by not explaining to Paula what was wrong, he was also hurting her. So he agreed that in the joint session the following week he would see if he could tell Paula about the problem.

When he did, there was uproar. Paula shouted and screamed and said he was a selfish bastard. John looked white and withdrawn, full of suppressed anger. He said to Paula: 'There's no point in my telling you anything. You never listen to me. I don't want to feel this way, but I just do.'

What they were able to start to talk about was the fact that John felt Paula never really listened to his needs within the relationship. After a while she turned to him with a watery smile and said: 'I know I've put on over two stone in the last two years, and I hate it. I try to cover it up in the way I dress, but that doesn't really work in bed, does it?'

John was able to admit that he had been a very fat little boy and had been dreadfully teased at school, so he was ultra-sensitive about people being overweight.

'Is that why you're always at the gym?' Paula asked.

John agreed, smiling, that it probably was. Paula admitted that she wanted to lose weight almost as much as John wanted her to, so she would have a go. John agreed to try to talk things through much more openly, rather than withdrawing and cutting off emotionally from Paula when they encountered a problem.

As the counselling continued he was able to start doing this. It emerged that it was something he wanted as much as Paula did – just as Paula wanted to lose weight as much as John wanted her to. What is important in bringing about change in a couple's behaviour is that both members agree to some change. Otherwise they can just end up feeling resentful because only one of them is working at the relationship.

Timetabling for sex

As a couple, you must learn to negotiate over how often to make love. The partner who wants to make love more frequently agrees to settle for, say, once a week. The more reluctant partner agrees to this as well – and that they won't make excuses to get out of it. You must enter into the agreement with enthusiasm, which is much easier if you are not feeling pressured all the time. If that works well, you may be able to increase it to twice a week. What is important is that both of you concentrate on the quality of the lovemaking rather than the quantity. There are plenty of variations on this agreement, so find one that suits you both and remember that compromise is about getting some of your needs met some of the time, not all of them all of the time. And that does not come easily to any of us.

There is a lovely scene in the Woody Allen film *Annie Hall* where you see a split screen. The Woody Allen character and the Annie Hall character are with their psychiatrist – who else – who is asking each the same question:

Psychiatrist to Annie Hall:	'How often do you make love?'
Annie Hall:	'Oh, all the time. About three times a week.'
Psychiatrist to Woody Allen:	'How often do you make love?'
Woody Allen:	'Hardly ever. Only three times a week.'

So it really is a matter of what seems normal to you, and that may be at odds with your partner. Neither of you is right or wrong – just different.

Sexual expectations

How you feel about your body and your sexual attractiveness also affects your attitude to sex. If you think you are reasonably OK – and I don't think there is a man or woman in existence who is totally satisfied with every part of themselves – you are more likely to be able to relax sexually. If you hate your body and how you look, you are more likely to try to prevent your partner seeing you naked. So you insist on making love with the lights out, or underneath the bedclothes. So accepting your own body and not being too critical is important when it comes to sexual enjoyment.

One of the biggest changes that has taken place in this century is women's understanding of their sexuality, their own bodies and their attitude to sexual enjoyment. Because of this, men's attitudes have changed as well, as they have realized that women's pleasure in sex is equal to their own.

In previous generations many women saw sex as a wifely duty, not as something they could enjoy equally with men. Most men accepted this in their wives, because if a woman had no expectations of her own sexual pleasure the man tended to have no expectations either – or if he did, it was of women who were not his wife. This was because he had been conditioned to think that sexual pleasure was not appropriate in wives, because nice girls did not behave like that. Victorian moral attitudes and hypocrisy, as well as religion, have a lot to answer for in the way that people were made to feel guilty about sex.

Even in the early 1960s, during the obscenity trial following the publication in Britain of D. H. Lawrence's novel *Lady Chatterley's Lover*, the prosecution said that it was 'not the sort of book that you would want your wife or servants to read'. So what was apparently all right for men even then was not seen by some to be all right for women.

But expectations have changed now. Women and men have a much better understanding of their own bodies, their capacity for lovemaking and their right to sexual enjoyment. This was greatly helped by the work of Masters and Johnson and others in the late fifties and early sixties. Sex was much more openly talked about and written about, enabling men and women to understand each other better.

Sex may well be for procreation – that, after all, is what makes the world go round – but it is also for recreation. The expectation is no longer that sex is something a woman does for a man, lying there immobile 'thinking of England', as the saying goes; it is something a woman does with a man, with each of the sexes having the same opportunities for giving and taking sexual pleasure.

Sex without strings

Although men and women have equal capacity for sexual enjoyment, there are still sexual differences between men's and women's attitudes to having sex without emotional commitment. Young men and women are often looking for quite different things in their early adult relationships. The adolescent boy of seventeen, eighteen or nineteen is much more likely to be looking for sexual adventure – the more experiences the better. He is, after all, at the highest peak of his sexual potential. Quality may not come into it, but quantity certainly does. The girl of a similar age is much more likely to be wanting sex to be part of a loving, romantic and committed relationship. For her a one-night stand is more likely to be the result of pressure from the man to have sex, peer group pressure, or too much to drink, than because she wants to experiment sexually. Many young women can get very hurt as well as pregnant because of the different needs and expectations of young men of their age.

By their early to mid-twenties things are evening out between the sexes, with young men as well as young women wanting and valuing a committed relationship of which sex is an important part. For some women – although they are very much in the minority – sex can be enjoyed without much commitment, provided that they know what they are doing and that it is their choice. They feel they can take sexual pleasure without commitment, as men have done traditionally. But for most women differences still exist, and I describe these more fully in Chapter 5. It comes down to the fact that men seem more able than women to separate out sex from loving relationships. There are times when men need little or no relationship with a woman to have really good sex with her. But for most women good sex is in the head as well as the body, and is therefore usually part of a relationship. That relationship does not have to be years long – it may be only months or even weeks – but intimacy, trust, liking the person and feeling that they as a person are liked or preferably loved are important to most women. What men also say is that the greatest sex is usually with a woman they can relate to emotionally, physically and mentally – in fact on all levels. But they can also enjoy sex with no strings and no commitment more than most women can.

Sexual myths

Men can't help it

A few years ago I was co-presenting a programme on a local radio station. One of the guests was an anthropologist who quite seriously suggested that, through his study of the animal kingdom as well as the human animal, he was convinced that men were naturally polygamous and women monogamous. I have not studied the animal kingdom, but after twenty years of working with and studying the human animal I certainly do not agree.

The cynical side of me thinks that it would be jolly convenient for men if they could get women to accept this myth. You can hear them now. 'Well, darling, I know I was unfaithful. I'm very sorry, but it's just nature. I couldn't help it. Men are, after all, polygamous, while women are naturally monogamous. I can't really expect you to understand – that's how we chaps are.'

No, I think not. I don't think modern women will buy that one. And anyway, statistics show that women are almost as unfaithful as men.

The way I see it is that for most people monogamy is not a natural state. When you marry or settle into a committed relationship, there is no little switch that operates so that you no longer find others sexually attractive. If that were so, the waiting lists for marital counselling would probably plummet overnight. Everyone contains the potential for unfaithfulness, but you are not forced to go down that road. You can always say no, hard though it may be. If you value the relationship you are in and know how much it would hurt your partner, you will perhaps resist temptation. 'Tis one thing to be tempted, Escalus, another thing to fall,' wrote Shakespeare in *Measure for Measure*.

The James Bond syndrome

One of society's myths is that men are always ready for sex – at any time, anywhere, with any available woman. Because this is such a commonly held view men tend to hold this expectation of themselves as well. And what makes it even more difficult for them is that if they fall below society's and their own expectations they think they are the only man in that position. They convince themselves that every other man out there is 100 per cent successful with women, able to make love at the drop of a hat. That is, of course, far from the truth. But because of the myth men frequently cannot share their fears and thoughts with other men, because it would feel like exposing themselves to the competitor. They fear criticism, that the other man would secretly laugh at them and tell his friends – or, even worse, pity them.

But women know – and, after all, they have more experience of men than men do of each other – that men are not always ready for sex. They are affected by what is going on in the world around them, just as a woman is. Work, stress, money problems, drink, worries about a sick child, death of a family member or problems in the relationship can all lower a man's sexual drive. But men and society often fail to recognize this, whereas women have more realistic expectations of themselves – so that if on occasions the female libido takes a downward spiral it is not such a traumatic event. In this respect it is far easier being a woman than being a man.

Men are not machines, zipper-happy and ever-ready. Nor are they like James Bond, able to make love even in the jaws of death or when the world around them is collapsing. That really is the stuff of fantasies.

The nymphomaniac syndrome

If a man has a strong sexual drive and sleeps around, this is condoned as he is only doing what is regarded as coming naturally. But a woman who takes her sexual pleasures as freely is soon negatively labelled – as a slag, an easy lay or a nymphomaniac. The reality may well be that she just enjoys sex without too much commitment, so why should she be judged more harshly than men? I would suggest that nymphomania does not really exist, but is just a moralistic word for women with a high sex drive.

When women who have had many sexual partners settle down to a committed relationship, they are often economical with the truth about how many partners they have had. This is because many men really mind about a woman's sexual past. In contrast, a man will see his own sexual conquests as something to be proud of.

There is a lovely story about a Fleet Street journalist who was very pleased with himself because he had heard that in the women's washroom there was a notice over the mirror saying he was the best lay in the office. He was slightly less pleased when one of the women journalists who heard him boasting about this took him aside and said, 'No, it doesn't say you are the best lay, just the easiest.' I feel a woman would not want either comment made about her in the men's room.

Penis envy or another sexual myth?

I think Freud was wrong when he said this was something that only women suffered from. Maybe they do, but they are not the only ones. Behind the male exterior his sexual ego is a tender and fragile plant. Nearly all men, from their mid-teens upwards, worry at some time about the size of their penis. Therapists are trained to assure the man that his penis is not shorter than that of the man next to him in the shower – it's just that he is getting a sideways view, whereas he sees his own penis from above and it is therefore a foreshortened view, a matter of perspective. Or when he was a little boy he compared his penis to his father's, which was then naturally much bigger, and so the man grows up not really recognizing that his is now just the same. And naturally the caring, loving woman, when she realizes what is worrying her man, is usually the first to reassure him that 'it's not the size that counts, it's what you do with it that matters'.

One man's penis does vary quite a lot from another when they are not erect, but when erect they are much the same size – approximately five to seven inches long. In the many years I have been counselling, one thing I have never heard a woman complaining about is the size of her partner's penis. So stop worrying.

Sexual honesty

Do men have more difficulty telling the truth about sex than women do? Surveys say they do. This story sums it up rather nicely. At a man's annual medical check-up his doctor asked him, 'How often do you drink?'

'About three times a week,' replied the man.

'And how often do you have sex?' enquired the doctor.

'Around seven times a week,' replied the man.

'Right,' said the doctor. 'If we reverse those figures we will probably be nearer the truth.'

The three most common complaints that men make about women

- They don't initiate sex enough.
- They would like more variety in the way they make love.
- Their partners are inhibited about giving and/or receiving oral sex.

The three most common complaints that women make about men

- Lovemaking is over too quickly.
- Men rarely or never touch them affectionately without it in some way being sexual. 'He confines his affection to times of erection,' some say.
- Their partners are not romantic enough or forget to say, 'I love you.'

Sexual fantasies

Sexual pleasure involves both your mind and your body. Sexual fantasy gives you the opportunity to think about having sex in a variety of ways. Imagining yourself in different sexual circumstances can be fun and exciting. It can be used as a way of sexual arousal either individually or with your partner.

For some people sexual fantasy can be a way of exploring their sexual feelings, of discovering sexual pleasure and excitement, but with the safety of knowing that is where it stops. It is in your imagination, it heightens your sexual pleasure and desire, but you do not want to put it into practice.

It has also frequently been said that sexual fantasy is a substitute for actually carrying out that fantasy. But according to some surveys this is not necessarily so. It has been shown that in some cases people do want to act out their sexual fantasies. For example, if a person fantasizes about orgies in the daytime they are also more likely to have fantasies about orgies at other times, and to wish to attend orgies and to participate in them, or have done so in the past. But for most people sexual fantasies are just that – something that exists only at the fantasy level.

Many people have also thought that sexual fantasies are a substitute for good sex, but research shows that this is likely to be the reverse. People who are sexually liberated, have a high sex drive and are sexually active are more likely to be relaxed about using fantasy, either during masturbation or by sharing it with their partner.

According to psychologist Dr G. D. Wilson in his survey entitled *The Secrets of Sexual Fantasy*, men reported more fantasies than women. But what I think is particularly interesting is that his survey also showed that men and women demonstrated a significant difference in the type of fantasy to which they were attracted.

Though the most popular fantasy for both men and women was making love to a loved partner, there is a significant difference. Men were more into impersonal or exploratory fantasy and having sex with a woman with a good body – the shape of the body, not who the woman was, being the important factor. They also fantasized about having sex with two women, being promiscuous, seducing an unknown woman, attending orgies, whipping or being whipped or spanked, or being tied up. All these fantasies were popular with some men, whereas women's fantasies were more intimate and relationship-orientated.

Women fantasized about having sex with a loved partner, or with someone they knew and fancied at work or among their friends. They thought about making love out of doors, in romantic settings like in a field of flowers or on a beach at night, or in front of a log fire, of being seduced or overpowered sexually (but not raped), receiving or giving oral sex, or having their clothes slowly taken off.

For many couples sharing a fantasy adds to their sexual enjoyment. Telling the other person about your sexual fantasies as part of foreplay can be fun and a turn-on. But it is not something that they want to go any further than that. Other people would rather keep their fantasies to themselves – for them sharing it would spoil the fantasy, or they feel their partner would be disturbed or turned off by it. If you are wondering whether to share a sexual fantasy with your partner, try one that is not your favourite and is fairly low-key.

If your partner responds well, that means it is probably safe to share your fantasies with him or her, but if your partner seems to hesitate or is reluctant, or even shocked, then leave it well alone.

Some people wish to act out some of their fantasies like making love out of doors, dressing up in sexy clothes, being the seducer or the seduced. If this is something you are both happy with, there is no harm. But forcing or coercing someone to share or act out your sexual fantasy is not fair, and should not be done. In time it would certainly become a sexual turn-off for them.

The joy of a good sexual relationship

If sex is not working in a marriage or committed relationship it can overshadow everything else and cause deep and lasting unhappiness that can lead to affairs, unhappy marriages or marriage breakdown. But when sex is working well in a relationship it is loving and binding. It enhances the feelings between you and makes your relationship feel great. It makes you feel loved, desired and fully alive. It filters through into all aspects of your life together, and is an invisible thread that moves between you. In the fulfilling sexual act you are merging with one another to become one. You are aware of your own feelings, but totally open to one other person. The sexual dance between you moves with intricate and delicate steps, encouraging you to give and take pleasure. You are emotionally open to each other and trust your partner enough to know that he or she will not take advantage of you, will not try to manipulate or control you. It is a partnership of equals, in which the feelings you have for each other can be expressed in this ultimate act of love. Making love is a way of expressing deep emotional love – it is an affair of the heart, the mind and the body.

So often sexual excitement is portrayed as existing only in relationships that are newly formed or in affairs (as will be seen in Chapter 5). But married sexual love, or that in a committed cohabiting relationship, where two people really know and trust each other and have shared the ups and downs of their lives together, can be the best of all. For most couples, when that is right between them it is something that is of great joy and sustaining to the relationship. Seven years after their marriage the nineteenth-century author Charles Kingsley wrote to his wife

Fanny: 'Oh that I were with you, or rather you with me here. The beds are so small that we should be forced to lie inside each other, and the weather is so hot that you might walk about naked all day, as well as at night. *Cela va sans dire*. Oh! Those naked nights at Chelsea! When will they come again?'

5

LOVE AND BETRAYAL

HOW AFFAIRS AFFECT
MARRIAGE AND RELATIONSHIPS

may i feel said he
(i'll squeal said she
just once said he)
it's fun said she

(may i touch said he
how much said she
a lot said he)
why not said she

(let's go said he
not too far said she
what's too far said he
where you are said she)

may i stay said he
(which way said she
like this said he
if you kiss said she

may i move said he
is it love said she)
if you're willing said he
(but you're killing said she

but it's life said he
but your wife said she
now said he)
ow said she

(tiptop said he
don't stop said she
oh no said he)
go slow said she

(cccome? said he
ummm said she)
you're divine! said he
(you are Mine said she)
E.E. Cummings, 1935

Michael and Tom had been at university together. Afterwards they had not really kept in touch, except for occasionally hearing about each other through mutual friends. When they were in their late twenties and both married, they met up again at a friend's party. It was very good to see each other and they were delighted that they liked each other's wives and that their wives seemed to get on with each other.

Over the next few years the friendship between the four of them deepened. Michael's wife, Miranda, produced two children – a son and a daughter in fairly rapid succession. And Rosie and Tom had a little girl, Hannah. Miranda and Rosie saw a lot of each other because they were both at home with the children, and the four of them would often meet up at weekends at each other's houses, spending long summer days playing with the children, or winter evenings playing bridge, talking, sharing meals and glasses of wine.

Then one day Miranda was at home on her own, as the children had gone to play school, and Tom called in unexpectedly. He was driving past her house on his way back to work from a meeting. Miranda made some coffee, and they sat in the garden and talked. When Tom stood up to go, he unexpectedly put his arms around her and kissed her. When they met as a couple they always kissed hello and goodbye, but this felt very different. Both were instantly aware of the great rush of sexual excitement that passed between them.

Miranda found that whenever they met as a foursome she just wanted to be alone with Tom, as he did with her. She tried to resist this desire, but found it increasingly difficult, especially as Tom appeared to be making every effort to catch her on her own. She constantly thought about him and, when she did, little darts of excitement would shoot through her entire body.

One day Tom asked her out to lunch and she accepted. A friend agreed to collect the children from play school, and said they could stay for the afternoon and play with her own children.

When the day arrived Miranda knew she should cancel the date, because she recognized how much she wanted to go. Also she felt she was not being fair to Michael and Rosie. She took great care over dressing, knowing she looked good. It was so lovely to feel like a desirable woman again, rather than a mum at the school gates waiting to collect her children. As the weeks and months followed Tom and Miranda stole more secret time together with the occasional shared lunch.

The two couples continued to meet just as usual. They all still got on well together and it was great fun. For Tom and Miranda the highly charged sexual attraction, plus the secrecy of their relationship, heightened every meeting the four of them had. Miranda told herself there was no harm in this – she was not hurting Rosie, since nothing had happened and she would not let it go any further. Then Michael went away on a business trip for three days. Tom telephoned Miranda and she agreed to have lunch with him.

When they met, they did not go out to their usual place – on this occasion Tom had brought a picnic and a bottle of champagne. They drove out into the country, ate their picnic and drank the champagne, and in the afternoon sunlight in a quiet corner of a cornfield they made love. The affair was fully consummated. But as in all affairs, though not necessarily in the same way, it also changed things, as Miranda and Tom were to discover.

The risk factor

When someone embarks on an affair, however much they think they are in control this is rarely true. You may, for example, start off thinking you are quite certain you will never be discovered, because you planned everything so carefully. Then someone you know sees you in a restaurant with someone who isn't your wife. They may mention this to someone else you know, who in turn may mention it to your wife. Or your car breaks down, and you have to explain to your husband why you are in a different place from where you said you were going. The seeds of suspicion are sown, your partner no longer fully trusts you, and questions begin to be asked. This can be the first step on the road to discovery.

Another mistake made by many people who start an affair is thinking they really are in charge of their emotions. But you can never guarantee this either. It may seem like no more than a wonderfully exciting relationship with great sex. Then, as time goes on, the desire to be with that person increases. It is not just the sex that is the turn-on; you are becoming closer to them, and the intimacy between you is suddenly much more than sexual. It's emotional, intellectual – perhaps shared dreams and talk of the future that stretches beyond the next illicit meeting.

You can never guarantee that in an affair, whether it lasts weeks or months or more, one or both of you will not fall in love with the other. The outcome you anticipated when you embarked on the affair may turn out quite differently.

You may think you really know your own feelings, that the affair will be just an affair, that it will not interfere with or upset your marriage. From your point of view maybe it won't, but what you can never be quite sure about is whether the person with whom you are having the affair will feel quite the same way – or what will happen if the affair is discovered.

This was vividly portrayed in the film *Fatal Attraction*, in which Michael Douglas had a very passionate relationship with Glenn Close while his wife was away for a few days. He thought it would end when she returned, for he had no intention of the affair upsetting his marriage. Bu the other woman had very different expectations. When he tried to break off the affair she pursued him to his house, on the telephone, by any means she could. She would not let go. And she took revenge for being used and thrown away. She went to his home and, while the family were out, caused havoc around the house, wrecking everything in sight and killing and cooking his child's pet rabbit. The film was said to have had a great impact on American men, even if it was only short-lived, and that for a while they thought twice before embarking on what they thought might be a fun, but brief and inconsequential, affair.

The outcome is always unpredictable

If you embark on an affair you can never be entirely sure what the outcome will be, whether it's because what you thought you could keep secret is discovered, or because one or both of you fall in love, or even because of the unpredictability of the other person. All these things can have repercussions on a marriage or a committed relationship.

When Tom and Miranda began their affair they had not thought about the future implications at all. If they had done so they might have thought twice about it, and that was not what they wanted to hear at all. For example, was this going to be just a one-off occasion or the beginning of a long affair? Could they keep it secret from Michael and Rosie? Did they both have the same expectation about the future? Was the affair more important to one of them than to the other? Did they feel guilty, and if so, could they handle it? Would one of them want to tell their partner? Would the other keep it secret? Could they really trust each other not to tell anyone else about it? Could the friendship between the four of them still continue? And how did Miranda feel about her friendship with Rosie and Tom about his with Michael? Could they all survive this complex betrayal?

Tom and Miranda thought, as countless couples do, that a fleeting kiss, a secret lunch, snatched time alone together, was something they could handle, that it would not go any further and would not harm anyone. It's often only once the affair has begun that all these issues come flooding in.

Things did change. Miranda started to feel uneasy about her friendship with Rosie because she felt guilty. So she started to see less of her. Rosie was hurt by this and did not understand what had gone wrong. The affair with Tom continued, but they were so afraid of being found out that their meetings became few and far between. Miranda went back to work, and combining that with two small children left her with hardly any time to see Tom alone. He started to resent this and they argued about it.

Then Tom was promoted, which meant that he and Rosie moved to Paris. Miranda was devastated by this, but she did not feel that Tom minded quite as much as she did, which made it worse. The affair really started to fall apart over the next few years. Tom did not seem to have much time when he came to England, and she, understandably, could not go to Paris. So they only saw each other about three times, and though as a couple they continued to send Christmas cards to each other, the affair drifted to an end.

Miranda heard through friends in Paris Tom had been involved with several women. But somehow Rosie never knew, or perhaps chose to turn a blind eye. Tom and Rosie's marriage survived. But not so Miranda and Michael's. Looking back on things, Miranda felt that the affair had been the start of their growing apart. Their dissatisfaction with each other mounted, the arguments increased, and five years after Tom's move to Paris they split up. Like the majority of affairs, it never came out into the open. Neither was it the cause of the marriage breaking down. But in some ways it was the catalyst, and for Miranda it was the start of recognizing the many differences and difficulties that had been rumbling around under the surface of her marriage.

How many people are having affairs?

Researching into affairs is always difficult. Do people respond honestly to questions? Are both sexes equally honest? Men are usually shown to be a little less honest than women, especially when it comes to sexual exploits where they have a tendency to exaggerate.

A friend who has a nice sense of humour and who says she had not had any affairs once answered, unknown to her husband, an advertisement in a newspaper. It was looking for couples who had not had affairs, as well as ones who had, who were prepared to be interviewed. She seemed to be much more certain about her husband's behaviour in that direction than I was. When she told him, he agreed to be a guinea pig and be interviewed on the not-having-had-any-affairs side. But if he had not agreed to go along with her it would have looked suspicious, and he would hardly have been likely to disclose to the interviewer in front of his wife that things might have been otherwise.

The great majority of people go into marriage promising and expecting faithfulness in their partner and themselves. Even after people have been married for some time and answer questionnaires about what they consider to be important qualities in a marriage, faithfulness is always high on the list.

Open marriages, where the couple agree that each of them can look outside the marriage and have sex with other people, are still very uncommon.

But how people behave is very different. Even allowing for some dishonesty from research and survey figures, it is estimated that between 50 and 70 per cent of married people have affairs, despite what they said when they embarked on the marriage. Surveys also show that more men than women have affairs: between 60 and 70 per cent of men have affairs compared with 40–50 per cent of women. But the gap is getting narrower.

Research by Annette Lawson shows that affairs are now happening far earlier in marriage. Men and women who married before 1960 and who were going to have an affair waited on average fourteen years before their first liaison, whereas by the 1970s and 1980s it was a little over five years before men and women embarked on their first affair.

Interestingly, Lawson's research also shows that those people who have a variety of sexual partners before marriage are more likely to have affairs after marriage. She says:

> Premarital sexual experiences lead in significant ways to postmarital behaviour, the faithful more often being inexperienced before marriage and the most adulterous the most experienced. For example, of those who remained faithful, 60 per cent had sex only with their future spouses or had remained virgins until marriage, and the opposite was true of those who had experienced many liaisons. Only 40 per cent of those reporting at least four affairs had been virgins or had had sex with a future spouse at marriage. Furthermore, the greater the variety of lovers before marriage, the more likely it was that people would have affairs following marriage.

This certainly turns on its head the popular notion that if you sow your wild oats before you marry you are more likely to settle for faithfulness afterwards. I would suggest that there are also other reasons why, if there has been no sex or very little before marriage, people are more likely to remain faithful. Often it is those people who remain virgins prior to marriage, or who only have sex with their future spouse, who possess strong religious beliefs that sex outside marriage, whether before or during, is wrong. Because of these strong convictions they are more likely to resist temptation. Or they may have avoided sex before marriage because of deep inhibitions and sexual hang-ups, or because they have a low sex drive. If that is so, these conditions are more than likely to continue into marriage, making sex a not very positive experience and therefore making faithfulness more likely.

That is, of course, not to deny that some people who have reluctantly settled for few sexual partners prior to marriage can change afterwards. Once married, and perhaps experiencing sexual boredom or disillusionment, they may well go out and make up for what they see as lost time.

How do you define an affair?

An affair is always sexual, but quite what that means is open to interpretation. Some people think that unless there has been full sexual intercourse it is not an affair. But secret lunches, touching, kissing and undressing each other can also constitute an affair. A one-night stand while you are away on a conference may be considered by the person involved to be meaningless, but it is nevertheless an act of unfaithfulness. The classic male response when discovered on these occasions is to say, 'But it didn't mean anything, darling.' But in my experience it usually means a great deal to the wife, just as it does if it's the other way round.

Ken and Marjory came for counselling because he discovered she had been involved in an affair. It was now over, but he could not get over his wife's unfaithfulness. At one point in the counselling Marjory turned to Ken in a fury and said: 'You've had affairs, so why are you making such a fuss over my one brief affair?'

'Oh, no,' responded Ken. 'I have had several flings, but no affairs.'

This understandably infuriated Marjory even further. To her, the fact that Ken had had sex with several other women, yet was trying to diminish the importance of what he had done, meant he was refusing to recognize how important his unfaithfulness was to her, how hurt she was by what he had done and how each occasion had been a betrayal. If he had been so ready to betray her, why was he now being quite so unreasonable about her affair, which she said was more a retaliation than anything else.

Ken could not believe that Marjory would have an affair unless it meant more to her than she was admitting. 'She wasn't,' he shouted, 'that sort of woman!' What he meant by this was, that she was not going to be unfaithful just for sex like he was. That was too basic – it had to be for more than that.

So a one-night stand, a brief liaison when one of you is away on holiday or at a conference, a relationship that lasts over several months or even years – all of these constitute an act or acts of unfaithfulness and come under the definition of an affair. I would add one more to that, and that is the relationship between a man and a woman where sexual tension fills the air but there has been no sexual infidelity. Nevertheless there is a deep intimacy, friendship, closeness and delight in each other that transcends mere friendship – the glance, the look, the slight touch on the arm as you guide someone across the road are all kept secret from your partner, because they are too important to share.

Different attitudes to affairs

No one will deny that some men fall passionately in love with the woman they are having an affair with or want to have an affair with. They feel totally overwhelmed by feelings of love. They cannot sleep, they lose their appetite, they are unable to concentrate at work. Whatever they do, the woman they love invades their every thought. But many, many more men than women embark on affairs that are more about lust and sexual excitement than a search for love, commitment or intimacy. In affairs, as in the rest of their lives, most men have much greater ability than women to compartmentalize their affairs.

Just as women seek in marriage the all-loving, compassionate, romantic relationship, they are also more likely to be looking for at least part or some of this relationship in any affair that is more than a one-off occasion. But men tend to have a different approach. Their needs are different – they are less likely to be looking for the emotional involvement or intimacy that women so often want in an affair.

A man, for example, can spend a wonderful afternoon making love to his mistress, which is fantastically exciting and all-absorbing. When the afternoon is over, he can put that part of his life aside, or into a nice, neat, self-contained compartment, and then happily go back to work or home to his wife and children. He can just leave behind or shut out thoughts of his mistress as his everyday life takes over. But most women find this very difficult to do. They spend more time thinking about their lover, wondering what he is doing now, what his wife is like and whether he makes love to her.

The majority of men find it easier to have an affair or a brief fling just for sex because the opportunity presented itself, or for the novelty of the experience, than most women do. The average woman embarking on an affair is usually looking for a little more than just sex. It does not have to be love, but she does at least want to like the man, to feel there is a little commitment and affection between them, and on top of that she is often looking for intimacy as well. The man, on the other hand, is more often than not looking for the sexual excitement of an affair; or he is interested in the pursuit, the chase and the conquest. But the last thing he wants is too much emotional intimacy or commitment.

Men are, for many of the reasons I have already suggested, more able to indulge in no-strings-attached sex. Prostitution still abounds, whether it's in Soho or on the streets of Bangkok. Men go in pursuit of sexual stimulation and are prepared to pay for it. Some want to feel that the prostitute is enjoying it, maybe because that makes them feel better about themselves as potent sexual beings. But they don't usually need to feel that she is the slightest bit interested in them in any way, other than when they are actually having sex.

In the main, women do not seek out male prostitutes. Totally uninvolved sex is not really what turns women on. Quite frankly, if a woman had to pay for sex it would not only seem tacky to her but would do her self-esteem no good at all. Women may go to see shows like the Chippendales, but that is usually a group activity when they laugh at them and with each other, rather than an exciting sexual experience. (Though I did hear an interesting conversation from three women talking on the Underground. They had been to see the Chippendales the night before, and one said to the others, roaring with laughter, 'They have great bodies, especially if you compare them with what I have back at home!')

Vulnerable moments

There are times in the life of all marriages when circumstances make one or both of you more susceptible to the possibility of an affair. In the early years of marriage, before the children arrive, if what you expected from it does not materialize and disappointment and disillusionment set in, you are more likely to look outside the marriage for what you feel is missing. This is especially so if you are in love with the idea of being in love and think you can continually live at that dizzy high, rather than recognizing that it should move to a deeper and more enduring love which copes with the ups and downs of everyday life. That does not mean to say you have fallen out of love, or that there is something wrong. But unless you understand that, you may be tempted to go searching after what you feel you have lost.

One of the most vulnerable times of all is after the arrival of a baby. The woman is so involved with the baby, or chronically tired – or probably both – that she frequently loses interest in sex. Her partner may try to understand, but he often resents the fact that he is getting little of his wife's attention and less sex than he would like. If a woman at work or elsewhere shows that she is interested in him and finds him sexually attractive this is very appealing. For the woman, once the first few months with the new baby are over, if she has lost confidence in her own attractiveness because she is still a little overweight, or her husband is not giving her the reassurance she is looking for – but someone else does – she too is vulnerable.

A marriage can become susceptible to an affair if a couple are having to cope with problems (such as redundancy, constant money worries or the sudden death of a close family member). If these things distance you as a couple rather than draw you together, an affair can be used as an escape from all these struggles or a little light relief from the day-to-day toll.

The mid-life crisis is a commonly recognized stage of marriage in which one or other partner appears all too frequently to stray. Whether it's the man with the younger woman, trying to hold on to what he sees as his lost youth, or the woman who wants to discover herself and move on from feeling that her main role in life is looking after her husband and children, an affair seems like an exciting opportunity.

When children leave home couples are often thrown into turmoil. They look at each other, knowing that they no longer have that mutual interest in the children, and are left wondering if they have anything else in common. They discover they have been so busy with their own individual lives that they have become strangers under their own roof, and the empty years seem to stretch endlessly ahead. So one or both of them often escapes into an affair – perhaps an easier option than recognizing what the problem is and trying to do something about it.

Martin and Deborah had just celebrated their twenty-fifth wedding anniversary. Their three children, the youngest of whom was twenty, had arranged a special party to celebrate the occasion and had invited all the family and friends. They thought it had been a happy day, but four days later Martin walked out on their marriage, saying he no longer loved her and didn't want the marriage to go on. It turned out that he had been having an affair with his secretary for the past four years, had fallen in love with her and was planning to set up home with her.

Deborah and Martin lived in a village where everyone knew everyone, and they were both very much involved in village life. Martin worked in the family firm and was a churchwarden. Deborah too was a very active member of the church, and ran the local Brownie pack. They had been seen as a very happy couple, and the whole village was taken by surprise. Deborah, who had always been seen as a wonderful coper, organizer of village fetes, the Brownies and meals on wheels, felt her whole life had come to an end. She begged Martin to come back, and so did the children – but to no avail.

He said: 'For years I felt I had been forced to take second place, not only to the children but to all Deborah's activities and everyone else in the village. I'm fed up with being organized, I'm bored with it all. Sally – the woman I have fallen in love with – makes me feel alive again. When I'm with her, that's all I want. Sexually my marriage had been dead for years. That didn't worry Deborah, but it's important to me. The children have left home, and I'm entitled to a life of my own. I don't enjoy hurting Deborah, but I just couldn't go on any longer.'

Martin and Deborah are like many couples I see in counselling. They have grown so far apart that one of them is not prepared to see if the marriage can be revived. If one of the couple is quite set on ending the marriage, counselling cannot keep them together. What it can do is offer the partner who is left a chance to talk through what has happened, so as to gain more understanding of why the marriage broke down. And most importantly, it can help them pick up the pieces of their shattered lives and rebuild them.

Why do men and women have affairs?

Problems in the marriage

The reasons why men and women have affairs are complex, but most counsellors and therapists would say that the biggest reason is dissatisfaction in the marriage. There are problems in the relationship that are not being tackled, or are being pushed under the carpet. An affair can be seen as an escape from all this.

If a couple have drifted apart, or are bored with each other, an affair can be a very attractive alternative. If they are spending very little time together, and that time is only spent talking about everyday things like who is collecting the children from football or how are they going to pay the gas bill, life becomes very humdrum. The marriage has lost its sparkle. If someones else comes along who makes you feel alive again, who wants to be with you, is interested in what you have to say and seems to value you, this can seem immensely attractive and very seductive and all too often can lead to an affair.

Sexual boredom

This is another very powerful reason why couples have affairs. If, like the marriage, sex has become boring and humdrum – the same time, same way, same place kind of sex – it's not surprising that couples lose interest in each other sexually.

Sexual problems

If there are sexual problems in the relationship one or other of the partners will often look outside that relationship for another one, hoping that with another partner it will be different, or feeling that the problem is their present partner's fault. This is covered more fully in Chapter 4.

Affairs that signal the end of the marriage

Since an affair can definitely signify that the erring partner wants to end their marriage, so they embark on an affair more as a way out rather than as a supplement to marriage. The affair may be a real love affair with someone with whom they want to spend the rest of their lives.

It may, on the other hand, be with what is known as a transitional person. At the time the affair seems very important and exciting, but the reason for it is the bad state of the marriage rather than the actual person involved. When the unfaithful partner is out of their marriage he or she realizes this and does not want to continue with that relationship for very long. What was really going on was that the marriage was in its terminal stages and the affair was a stepping-stone out of it. If you are the transitional person – for whom it was a serious love affair – you can end up getting badly hurt, especially if you were single or unattached or had left your marriage for your new partner only to find that he or she did not really love you after all and that it was soon all over.

The right to be me

This is a need that I think applies much more to women than it does to men. Women are nowadays seeking self-fulfilment, individual growth, an escape from being the carer, the nurturer and the emotional prop to the demands of family life.

Some women see an affair as an enhancement to their marriage and an enrichment to themselves. If this is how they feel they are less likely to be weighted down by guilt about their own behaviour. They do not see it as, or even want, an alternative. They would say they are not in the category of marriages with major problems, or of ones they want to leave, but are looking to express important hitherto unfulfilled areas of themselves.

Men too sustain marriages that they would describe as happy yet at the same time have affairs. But traditionally men have always been into the having-your-cake-and-eating-it syndrome, so looking outside marriage to an affair is often less about self-fulfilment and growth and more 'penis-driven'. That is not to say that women are not wanting good sex from these relationships – of course they are. But their approach is rather like holistic medicine, an all-over body and mind experience which involves what happens below and above the belt in a more integrated way than the one in which many men regard affairs.

Traditionally, men have never been expected to subordinate their own interests to those of their family in the same way as women. Men are not motivated to find self-fulfilment through affairs as women are. They also have a longer tradition of self-development through work, sport or endurance activities such as mountain-climbing, trekking across the North Pole as a way of personal challenge and growth. Until recently many of these outlets were not so readily available to women, and if they have children are still not so.

Women's reasons for having an affair

If you look at the research and the reasons why men and women have affairs (such as Lawson, *Adultery – Analysis of Love and Betrayal*, 1988) some very striking differences emerge.

1. I felt compelled by my emotions to have an affair.
2. My husband/partner and I had grown apart.
3. I had sexual needs which were not being met at the time.
4. My life felt empty.
5. Life is for living.

Men's reasons for having an affair

1. With care the affair would not harm my marriage.
2. I was curious to know what sex would be like with someone else.
3. Life is for living.
4. I had sexual needs which were not being met in the marriage.
5. I felt compelled by my emotions to have an affair.

Interestingly, emotional reasons are at the top of the women's list and at the bottom of the men's list. The women seem to be searching for some form of emotional attachment, while the men are more motivated by sexual curiosity and variety and declare that they want the affair as well as their marriage – not as an alternative – as indeed many women do. If men and women understood these differences more when they embarked on an affair, it would at least give them more understanding of what to expect of each other.

I was talking to a man, now in his early seventies, who had spent many years as an army officer. Throughout his married life he had been consistently unfaithful to his wife. She had found out about some of these affairs, but there were also many others of which he claimed she knew nothing. He said: 'Once I arrived home in the middle of the morning unexpectedly, and my wife had four or five friends round for coffee, and as I looked round I realized I had slept with them all.' He appeared to have no guilt feelings about this situation – more a sense of pride and achievement. But the women also come out of this story rather tarnished, since each had betrayed the woman who was pouring them coffee and inviting them into her house as friends.

Addicted to affairs

I have counselled many men and women who, like this man, appear to be addicted to affairs. They are often good-looking, self-assured and charming, take a great delight in the opposite sex and are at ease with them. But very often underneath this façade they are constantly looking for reassurance of their own attractiveness, and an affair is a way of achieving this. Or it can be masking the fact that they find emotional closeness quite hard to handle, so they seek to be close to someone else through sexual intimacy – often not being able to distinguish between the two.

Forbidden fruit

To confess or not to confess, that is the question. More affairs are conducted in secrecy than get discovered, I believe. There are some people who want their affair to be discovered because they want to introduce a crisis as a way of signalling to their partner that the marriage is over. Some people want the affair to be discovered because they are finding it incredibly difficult to cope with the guilt. They believe, totally foolishly, that if they tell their partner about the affair – and this is usually at the time when the affair is moving towards a close, or has just ended – that their partner will forgive them. They know their partner will feel hurt, but they also hope and even expect him or her to forgive them, thus making them feel better.

But life's not like that and their partner is not into forgiveness at that stage – it's much too soon. So the person who confessed, far from being forgiven, suddenly finds themselves on the receiving end of all the normal feelings that the discovery of an affair brings. These are outrage, anger, hurt and the desire to destroy or murder their partner or the person with whom their partner was involved. Because their need to be forgiven was so great they failed to anticipate what effect their confession was going to have, so they are often unprepared for their partner's reaction.

The desire to confess can be a very self-centred, selfish act if all you're trying to do is relieve your own guilt. But if your partner really suspects that you are having an affair – perhaps there are tell-tale signs like telephone calls that are always 'the wrong number', or a hotel bill for two is discovered in the suit being taken to the cleaners, or some friend has told your partner that they think they have seen you with someone else – it can be very cruel not to confess. If they really do want to know, then to continue the deception is not only cruel and unkind, it's also not fair.

Richard thought he had a happy marriage, loved his wife and children and worked hard for them. But over the last two or three years Polly, his wife, had become increasingly unhappy. She felt she was always overshadowed by Richard and that, though he said he loved her, she took second place to his job. She felt he continually wanted everything to revolve around him, and that her needs came way down the list of priorities. If she went along with him he was happy, but if she resisted or opposed him there was friction. So she had rather given up trying to tell him what was wrong, because he never seemed to understand.

Resentment and bitterness grew, eventually she fell out of love with him. The marriage might have gone on like this if she had not met someone else and started an affair. It was very important for her, and it also showed her how much she was missing in marriage. She told Richard she wanted a divorce. He was stunned. He said he had not realized she was so unhappy. He then did everything to try and change, because he did not want to lose Polly. But for her it was too late: she secretly loved someone else. Richard went through months of agony trying to win her back, but to no avail, of course. They had many conversations about whether there was someone else, but Polly always denied it.

Richard said: 'I know she is telling me the truth, despite what has happened. She would not lie to me. I love her and don't want the marriage to break up, but neither do I want to keep her in a marriage that she does not want and is unhappy with.'

Polly just continued to say she wanted a divorce, and that the marriage was over – no more. After a few months they separated and put their house on the market, and Polly filed for divorce. Richard still continued to do everything he possibly could in the hope that she would come back. He did not find out about the other man until many months after Polly had left.

Though the other man was not the main reason for Polly leaving the marriage, it would have been kinder and fairer to Richard if she could have been honest about the fact that there was another man. There are times when it is fairer to be honest and other times when it's better not to confess.

If an affair is over, and particularly if it is some time in the past, there is little point in suddenly telling your partner all about it because for them it will not feel over at all. Not only is it likely to hurt them deeply, but they will want to know all about it just as if it had happened yesterday. Equally a one-night stand, or a brief but regrettable encounter because of foolishness or too much to drink, would be deeply upsetting to most partners even if you felt it held little importance for you. And becoming involved sexually with another family member, such as your wife's sister or your father-in-law, usually causes uproar, if it is confessed to – not just because of the act of unfaithfulness and betrayal, but also because it is felt to cross some sort of deep incest taboo.

The secret affair

For many people the secrecy of an affair is part of the attraction. It takes them back to the idea of sexual relationships being slightly illicit. They enjoy planning snatched meetings that are more often than not spent in making love. They are excited by the uncertainty of where and how and when they can meet, which is different from a marriage in which their partner is always available. They like the thrill of a special relationship that the rest of the world does not know about.

I believe that most people want to keep their affair secret because they want both the marriage and the affair. Many people claim that their affairs help to sustain their marriage, or to fulfil parts of their lives, desires and needs that are not being met in the marriage. They are not saying they are unhappily married, or that they want to leave the marriage for the person with whom they are having the affair. They frequently recognize that the person with whom they are having the affair is not offering what they would want if the relationship were on a full-time basis, but they are nevertheless providing something very important.

Isobel, who had been married to Mark for twenty years and had been having an affair with Henry for the last five, said: 'Henry's such fun to be with and has so much get up and go. He always makes me feel great. He'll suddenly suggest that we drop everything and find time in a busy day to meet and make love, to go to an art gallery, to visit an antiques fair or just walk by the river. With Mark it's always me who has to make the suggestions. Then he takes three days to decide whether he wants to do it and how much it will cost, and by that time I've lost interest. Mark is very reliable, but sometimes I'd like to put a bomb under him just to get him to do something that is spontaneous and fun.'

Isobel has not been able to find in one man the necessary combination of stability and a lively, fun, get-up-and-go attitude. So she is married to the stable Mark and has looked outside marriage for spontaneity and fun.

Henry married when he was twenty-three. Now, thirteen years on, he said that, though sex was good within the marriage, it was a little predictable. He had had a number of affairs, in some of which the sex had been great, in others not as good as it was with his wife. But he was always curious about sex with other women. He liked the feeling that he was desirable and attractive, and if it seemed to be on offer he was not going to turn it down.

Neither Isobel nor Henry seemed to think that their affairs affected their marriage. Both were rather of the opinion that it added to it. They did not expect their marriages to provide all their needs, neither did they feel weighted down by the betrayal element in what they were doing. Their life was segmented into fairly neat little pieces. The rewards of the affairs outweighed the fact that the deceptions they were involved in might be stopping true intimacy in the marriage. Or perhaps for them a secret affair sustained their marriages, which might otherwise have broken down.

What happens when an affair is discovered?

When Stella discovered that her husband Dominic was having an affair it was New Year's Eve and the ground was covered in thick snow. But she got into her car and drove round to the other woman's house. There was no one in, so she took her lipstick out of her bag and wrote over all the downstairs windows right around the house: 'My husband's whore lives here.' She then tore down the fairy lights from the tree in the garden and threw them into the dustbin. When she returned home she rushed upstairs and snatched out of the drawer a new jumper that her husband had produced, because she had put two and two together and realized who had knitted it for him. Then she slashed it to ribbons.

One of the most frequent reasons why people come for counselling is the discovery of an affair. It creates turmoil, trauma and intense pain, particularly for the person who has not been unfaithful, but also, though in different ways, for the partner who has had the affair.

It is traumatic, because for most couples it constitutes the ultimate betrayal. Marriage vows, in which you committed yourself to each other to the exclusion of all others, have been broken. Trust has been broken, which is quite devastating, because being able to trust each other is one of the foundation stones of a good marriage.

The faithful partner

Whether it's the man or woman whose partner has been unfaithful, the pain is equally intense and the recovery path is broadly similar. But the reactions of men and women to the discovery of an affair have some fundamental differences as well as similarities.

The first feelings are very intense and primitive. Apart from the initial pain, shock and sense of rejection there is often a sense of extreme anger, or the desire to hurt or even to kill the person who has caused you such intense pain.

With men these thoughts are more likely to be directed towards their wives or partners. With women the very intense violent feelings are directed more at the other woman – as with Stella. This may be because women know that in reality they can do less damage to men than the other way round. Crime figures bear this out: a high proportion of domestic violence is done by men to women after finding out about an affair. But I think there's another reason, too. Because of the caring, nurturing role that women play in marriage, they cannot allow such intense feeling to be directed at their partners. It's too frightening, so they direct these feelings at the other woman. Sometimes they even justify the behaviour of their partner by saying, 'Well, she threw herself at him/lured him away/set out to get him.'

The other reaction that women often have is to focus on what they think are their own inadequacies. They say: 'What's wrong with me? Aren't I pretty enough? Is she prettier or younger than me? Has she got a better figure? Have I been taking him for granted, allowing sex to become infrequent or boring? What have I done wrong?' This usually also runs alongside: 'How could he have done this to me? How could he have broken my trust/my heart/ both?'

Men tend to look less at their own possible contribution to their partner having an affair, more at their partner's behaviour. 'She's been two-timing me,' or, to use an old-fashioned expression, 'I've been cuckolded.' There is no similar description for a woman in that position. The man is very concerned at being exposed to his friends, his neighbours or, if he is well known, to the public, because it is such an attack on his masculinity. The whole thing is tied up with society's and men's expectations of themselves. Real men, they say, satisfy their women in bed. So if the woman strays it is seen as an enormous attack on their sexual potency. That is also one of the reasons why men find it harder to forgive women for having an affair than vice versa. Women's self-esteem is less bound up than men's in their sexuality and sexual performance.

After the initial feelings of hurt, pain and sense of betrayal comes the long haul to see if the marriage can recover. Many more marriages recover than break up, but it's not easy, and it frequently takes much longer than anticipated. It is certainly not days, or even weeks, but many months or even a year or two before the marriage has really recovered. Over time forgiveness is possible, but the memory cannot ever be completely forgotten; and even though the trust can be rebuilt there is usually a little bit that never quite comes back.

To start with, the person who has not had the affair often becomes obsessed with the details. Who was it with? Where did it happen? What did you do together? What was he/she like in bed? Was it better or more exciting than with me? How deep were the feelings? Did you, do you love her/him? Was it just sex, or was it more than that? All these things go round and round in people's heads, driving them mad.

The memory of the lies and the deception is usually just as hard to cope with as the sexual acts of unfaithfulness. When their partner said he or she was working late at the office, or at the gym, or away on a conference, something entirely different was going on. Julie said of her husband's affair: 'What I couldn't bear was that while I was at home collecting the kids from school, giving them their lunch, he was sitting in a wine bar with her, talking to her, listening to her, laughing and having fun, having time together, then spending the afternoon making love. All the things I wanted to do with him he was doing with her.'

The unfaithful partner

The partner whose infidelity has been discovered has a different but far from easy set of feelings to cope with. They probably did not want the affair to be discovered unless they fell into the category I talked about earlier. So now that the affair is out in the open they have to confront a whole lot of unexpected issues.

There are the demands from their partner to know who the other person is, perhaps combined with insistence that the other person's husband or wife, if any, should be told. There are the hurt, betrayed and often outraged feelings of your partner to whom you have caused so much pain. Your partner may be considering a divorce, screaming at you to leave the home, or threatening suicide. And if the affair is not already over, your partner may be demanding that it is ended and that you never see that person again.

Then there are the children. They are so often involved because of the arguments, the tears and the recriminations which they see in the daytime and hear as they lie in bed at night.

The rest of the family can get involved, too, because it's almost impossible for most couples to keep the whole thing contained. So parents and in-laws are soon having their say. A classic example occurred at the time of the politician David Mellor's affair with an actress. His father-in-law was interviewed soon afterwards, saying without mincing his words what he thought of his son-in-law's behaviour. He was responding in the way that any caring father would over a wronged daughter, but because of Mellor's position in public life a show had to be made to the outside world. So shortly afterwards the whole family poised for the press, and so was published an extremely insensitive and demeaning picture of David and Judith Mellor, their children and the in-laws, all smiling grimly over the garden gate.

Most of us do not have to face such public debate, but we do have to face our family, friends, neighbours and colleagues. They all get to hear about it, they talk about it, and many of them take sides: 'Well, I'm not surprised,' they say. 'She's really let herself go.' Or, 'After all you've done for him, I should kick him out – he doesn't deserve you.' But of course it's never as black and white as that. The reasons for affairs are many and complex.

If the affair was an important one, ending it may be very painful. Some people are not sure whether they want to leave the marriage or stay. In counselling I have seen many couples where the man or woman who has been unfaithful vacillates between the two – their partner and their lover. They say the affair is over. Then they decide they cannot bear it and contact the lover or arrange to meet for another final goodbye – only to start the affair up again. Then there is more secrecy, more deceit and more hurt all round. Yet ending it quickly feels brutal and too sudden if the affair has meant a lot to you.

I see couples where the lover has been given up as soon as the affair was discovered; the person who has had the affair then suffers the pain of losing a loved one. They are grieving, unhappy, missing someone they really cared about. They know this is the price they have to pay to keep their marriage. They have made the decision because both they and their partner want to stay married to each other, but the other person cannot always be cast aside easily, quickly or painlessly. There is the added difficulty, for you and them, of your husband or wife watching you missing the other person. Either they feel angry or, worse, it increases the hurt you have already caused them. Yet if you are seriously attempting to rebuild the marriage the affair does have to finish. At times some people hang on to the belief that they can have both the marriage and the affair. But most husbands and wives, unless they have agreed to have an open marriage, will not accept this situation.

Is guilt evenly shared between men and women?

I believe that at the beginning of time when the world began, when different qualities, strengths and weaknesses were being handed out, women were right up there at the head of the queue for guilt. Even if little girls are not born feeling more guilt than boys feel in almost any given situation, they soon acquire it.

Look at the story of the Garden of Eden. Adam was doing fine until he was tempted by Eve to eat the fruit of the Tree of Knowledge. He did so, and then everything changed. They were thrown out of paradise and into the tough old world. If Eve had not been tempted by the snake, and in turn she had not tempted Adam, how different things would have been, the story implies. Poor, guilty Eve – and of course the Bible stories were written by men.

I am not suggesting that men are solely responsible for the guilt that so many women feel about many areas of their lives and relationships. Many things have contributed to the load of guilt that women carry around, and I have written about this in particular in Chapter 6. But when it comes to the impact of affairs on their partner, the women whom I see tend to feel more guilty about the affair than the men do. This is, I think, because women feel that they are the carers, the people who look after the emotional life and practical needs of their husband and children. So for them to put this under threat, possibly to destroy it, makes them feel worse about what they have done, particularly if the affair is discovered and they see the pain it is causing.

Also there are, I would suggest, double standards working here as in so many areas of men's and women's lives. Women – and society – judge women more harshly than men if they step out of line. It goes against the script they have for how women ought to behave. It is being selfish, taking something for yourself, and as children we are taught that that is not the way to behave.

Unfaithfulness is perhaps less of a problem in terms of guilt for men, because they are more used to looking outside their marriage and family for self-fulfilment. So male misbehaviour strikes them with less of a sense of betrayal.

Rebuilding the marriage

If this is something you both want and are both committed to, it is possible to achieve, as I have said before, though it is not easy. It takes time and a lot of talking. The person who has not had the affair usually needs and wants to talk much more than the unfaithful partner, who rarely wants to be questioned about the relationship and the details of the affair. This partner sees a fresh start as a matter of trying to put the affair behind them and getting on with repairing the marriage. But the injured partner has to be given the time and opportunity to express all their negative feelings of hurt, disbelief, anger, grief, rejection, loss of confidence and self-esteem.

Some questions have to be answered honestly: who the affair was with, how long it had been going on, who else knew, where they had met, and what the affair meant to them. This is very painful to hear, but if it remains unsaid it gives their partner no chance to start to deal with what has been going on. This process may have to be gone over time and time again. It is not usually a good idea to talk in detail about intimate sexual details, because they can stay in the mind of your partner and haunt them for years to come. When they ask, as most do, it may be difficult. But it is, I think, kinder not to be too explicit. Also, if you say too much it can get in the way of your sexual relationship with your partner in the future. It is fairly likely that when you and your partner make love again they will imagine that what you are doing together you probably also did with your lover. It takes time for these memories to fade.

Why did the affair happen?

The next stage in the recovery process is moving from recriminations to looking at what went wrong and what led to the affair. This is often particularly difficult for the partner who has not had the affair. For them it is often easier to stick with the thought that it's all their partner's fault and to go on blaming them, rather than look at what they might have contributed themselves. But until this shift can be made it is not possible to move forward to acknowledging, perhaps, some joint responsibility for what happened.

Bob and Libby had been married for twelve years, with two little girls of ten and eight. Bob left for work every morning around 7.30 and was not usually home until eight o'clock at night. He was very ambitious and doing very well in his job. When he came in at the end of the day he was fairly tense. He never seemed to want to spend time with Libby, and was always too tired to talk to her except to say what a terrible day he had had at work.

He also found his two daughters a strain on top of a heavy day, so he would snap at them when they asked him to play a game of cards or if he thought they were making too much noise. Libby resented this as she not only did a part-time job but took on most of the childcare as well, with very little help from Bob. Surely he could do more to be part of the family?

She said: 'Bob never seemed to have time for any of us. I just felt he wanted me there to look after the children and the house, to make sure everything ran smoothly. He was just not interested in me. When we did make love it was very infrequent, and over very quickly. He didn't really seem to care.'

When she met Jack at the local tennis club, even though she knew he had quite a bad reputation with women, she was very attracted to him. He seemed very interested in her and they would relax and talk over a drink after a game. She felt desirable again and interesting, not just a mother and household drudge – so she began an affair with him. But it was a small town and people started to talk. Bob got to hear of it, and when he confronted Libby she confessed.

To start with Bob threatened to end the marriage, which is why they came to counselling, but as he started to understand what had led to the affair, and how much he would be losing, he became deeply upset. He loved Libby and the children, but he was also under tremendous pressure at work and at risk of redundancy – he had not told Libby this as he had not wanted to worry her. But to her this had felt like rejection – he had just seemed preoccupied and cross all the time, as if there was no space in his life for her.

To Bob, Libby had seemed nagging and demanding when he came home at the end of the day – which was the last thing he wanted. It was only by sharing what had been going on before the affair that they were able to understand and realized that they both cared very much for each other, which enabled them painfully and slowly to rebuild their marriage.

Making love again

It is usually better not to rush into lovemaking too quickly after the discovery of an affair. Some couples do so because the person who has not been unfaithful and wants their partner to stay feels it is a way of keeping them, or of repairing the relationship. It's more often a woman who thinks this than a man. She may think it is a way of showing she still loves him; and sometimes it is just an attempt to compete with the other woman.

It usually does not work very well – because the man is still missing his mistress, or feeling guilty, or both. This can result in loss of interest in sex or inability to get an erection, which feels like further rejection to the woman. Or else the woman is too plagued by thoughts of his mistress, this applies the other way round as well. Either way, both of you can end up getting hurt.

Can trust be rebuilt?

I believe trust can be restored, but it's never quite the same as before. If you imagine trust as a circle, once an affair has happened that circle is broken into little pieces. Over the weeks, months and years following an affair those pieces can be put back together, forming an almost complete circle again. But there will probably always be a little gap, a little question mark, and complete trust can never be totally rebuilt. If another affair happens the circle will break again, and the gap will get larger each time. And each time the marriage will be put more at risk.

The person who has had the affair needs to show a lot of patience to their partner by assuring them not only that they still want the marriage, but that they do love them, despite what has happened. But the unfaithful partner will probably find that they need to account for where they are going, who they are with and when they will be coming home. Trying to lay doubts and fears is not easy, but it is necessary. This is particularly important in the early days.

It is difficult for the other person not to spend their time wondering where their partner is or to question where they are going and whom they are seeing. But if constant reassurance is not enough for you, maybe you are becoming obsessional and need help to get things into perspective. It is not easy rebuilding a marriage after an affair, and if you are finding it very difficult, or seem to have got stuck along the way it is a good idea to consider counselling.

In this chapter I have looked at how most people enter marriage expecting faithfulness from each other, yet in reality the majority end up being unfaithful. I have looked at the risks to which people put their marriage or current relationship when they embark on an affair; why there are times in the life of a marriage when you are more vulnerable to an affair than at other times; why some affairs remain secret and others get discovered; what happens when an affair is discovered; and how it is possible to rebuild a marriage after an affair. I have also explored the different reasons why men and women embark on affairs, and their different attitudes to them.

The following piece is from Alison Lurie's book *The War Between the Tates*, which illustrates extremely sensitively how two people can behave towards each other in the aftermath of an affair if their relationship cannot move forward to the stage of forgiveness and rebuilding. What happens then is that both people, the offender and the offended against, unnecessarily hurt each other.

For years they were moral and social allies; together they observed and judged the world. Now she judges him. They judge each other, and each finds the other guilty. 'Yes, perhaps,' Brian thinks, standing among the lettuces, but he had committed no overt act of aggression against Erica, deprived her of nothing.

And even if he is guilty, he is guilty of adultery, a form of love. Erica is guilty of unforgiveness, a form of hate. Besides, his crime is over, hers continues. Three months have passed; but still in every look, every gesture, Erica shows that she has not forgotten, has not pardoned him.

It is as if he has incurred a debt which his wife will never let him repay, yet which she does not wish to forgive. 'She likes to see me in the wrong,' Brian thinks, looking across the dark lawn at Erica. 'She intends to keep me there, possibly for the rest of my life.'

But remember: things do not have to end up like the Tates' marriage. It is possible to do something about it.

6

ROCKING THE CRADLE

THE KEY TO HAPPY FAMILIES

If children live with criticism they learn to condemn.
If children live with hostility they learn to fight.
If children live with ridicule they learn to be shy.
If children live with shame they learn to feel guilty.
If children live with tolerance they learn to be patient.
If children live with encouragement they learn confidence.
If children live with appreciation they learn to appreciate.
If children live with fairness they learn justice.
If children live with security they learn to have trust in others.
If children live with approval they learn to like themselves.
If children live with acceptance and friendship they learn to
find love in the world.

Anon

This chapter concentrates on the fine balancing act involved in combining the important relationship between husband and wife with the delights and demands of being parents. These two very different roles can be complementary. But because men and women have such different needs they can also, if not handled sensitively, cause such mammoth friction that they can drive couples apart. It is easy for a woman to become so submerged in the roles of wife, mother, carer, homemaker and worker to experience a tremendous loss of identity because of the demands of raising a family. She finds she has little time left over for herself and her own needs and interests.

Absent fathers, absent husbands

It is equally easy for men to feel weighed down by the financial responsibilities of providing for a family and the demands of a job, which often militate against being a loving husband and involved parent. He can also feel pushed to the sidelines by the arrival of children, which means less time as a couple and less time and space for himself. When I was talking to a fifty-nine-year-old sales director of a large company about the demands of work and home, he told me, 'Tomorrow will be the first time I will have been home in thirteen days, and that is not unusual. It's par for the course in this sort of job.'

'Is she your first wife?' I asked, wondering how she put up with this situation.

'Yes,' he said, smiling ruefully. 'She doesn't like it, but she's had to learn to adapt to it. It has also meant that in the last few years I have hardly seen my three children, and now the youngest one is just off to university.' It seems that we don't just have absent fathers now but absent husbands as well, virtually turning the traditional family into a one-parent family.

I think the concept of the absent husband highlights one of the main differences in the way men and women relate to their children. Where men are prepared to accept very long working hours or, because of the demands of the job, considerable separation from their children, women are not. They feel guilty enough being away from them from nine to five, or not being able to attend the school sports day, or not staying at home when their children are ill, without adding to their guilt by being away for days and nights on end. I am sure that this is one of the reasons why the Houses of Parliament and the board rooms of this country and elsewhere are so male-dominated, and why women with children are attracted to jobs in which they can combine the two demands more easily.

A very successful feminist woman in an extremely high-powered job, who had worked out her life with her partner on an exactly fifty-fifty basis and had equality down to an art form, said to me, 'Do you know what makes me really mad? When Al goes to work he shuts the front door, walks down the drive and gets into his car, and in those few minutes any worries he has about the children are left behind him for the day. But when I go to work, despite the fact that I know they will be all right, emotionally I take them with me. I just do not have the ability to switch off like he does. We do everything split down the middle, we both have equal involvement with the children – and yet I just can't do what he does and it drives me wild.'

For her book *The Second Shift* Dr Arlie Hochschild interviewed dozens of career couples and found that women:

- feel more responsible than men for home and children
- are more likely than men to think about their children when they are at work
- are usually the ones who keep track of doctor's appointments
- are usually the ones who arrange for playmates to come over
- are usually the ones who make packed lunches and shopping lists

During counselling I often hear women saying, 'I just don't understand him. I know he loves the children just as much as I do, but he can sleep in a chair or read the paper or watch television while the children can be all around him shouting for his attention. And he can just sit there oblivious to them all. How does he do it? I just can't switch off like that.' One man, talking about the first night out he and his wife had managed since their baby was born, said: 'Eventually, when the baby was six months old, we managed to go out to dinner for the first time. And what did she do but spend the first half talking about the baby and the second half worrying if the babysitter was all right? In the end we went home early.'

I also want to look in this chapter at how parents relate to their children; at the importance of bringing children up with love, tolerance, acceptance, encouragement and consistency; at the potential damage to children of criticism, hostility, ridicule and relentless pressure to perform; and at the importance of striking a balance between over-authoritarian parenting and providing few or no boundaries. I also want to show how important it is for couples to work out together how they are going to approach the joint task of parenting.

New life, new emotions

I still remember feeling wonderfully excited when I first discovered I was pregnant. I drove back from the doctor's surgery far too fast through the Wiltshire countryside, with the leaves turning to the beautiful deep red and gold colours of autumn, to the little cottage we were then living in. My husband had just arrived home from work and I ran into the house to greet him.

'What is it?' he said, turning round. 'Are you all right? Has something happened?'

'Well, in a way, yes,' I replied. 'I think this may come as rather a surprise.' Then I told him I was expecting our first child.

He was simply thrilled. Fortunately he had always wanted children, though it was a lot sooner than either of us had planned. We had only been married a few months, and I was very young, so something had gone wrong somewhere, and what's more we were terribly broke. Aware of all these things, I said, 'Don't worry, darling – having a baby won't change a thing.'

How could I have been so utterly foolish? I think it must have been a combination of excitement and youth, and the fact that I was an only child of two only children. So I had never had anything at all to do with babies or small children. As I was soon to discover, the arrival of children does change your life completely. Even if you are rather more sensible than I was about things and you realize that a new baby will indeed make a difference, you never anticipate that the changes will be quite as dramatic, as far-reaching or as long-lasting as they turn out to be.

Making the sudden transition from being a couple, with just yourself and your partner to think about, to being responsible for a totally vulnerable and totally dependent new life is scary. The demands it puts on you both are enormous. New babies do have a habit of taking over your life.

The other thing I was quite unprepared for, as I had never even stooped over a pram or picked up a baby, was the absolute intensity of love I felt immediately for both my son and, eighteen months later, my daughter as they were put into my arms after the birth. For me it really was love at first sight. I realize how very lucky I was to experience this, because it does not happen for all new mothers. It frequently takes longer, or they have to struggle with a mixture of emotions, some of which are very positive while others can be very negative, causing guilt feelings. For a few, the close bonding between mother and baby continues to be elusive. I take no credit for how I felt. I was just very lucky.

Two's company, three's hard work

Child development expert Dr John Bowlby wrote: 'When a couple have their first baby, the honeymoon is over and the work begins. Both parents discover that where two's company, three can make friction. Strong feelings are aroused and old conflicts relighted. A new equilibrium has to be found.'

Most couples imagine that the birth of a new and often much longed for baby will bring them closer together, and for many couples this is so. But at the same time there are losses: loss of freedom, lack of sleep, never being able to go out to dinner or the cinema at the drop of a hat. You can't enjoy long lazy Sunday mornings in bed, just the two of you making love, because babies have a remarkable sense of timing: as soon as you are really starting to enjoy it they wake up, or start to cry, and you just can't go on. You have to work hard to prevent intimacy being eroded when there is always a tiny pair of hands demanding your attention. The fact that you have to meet these demands, sometimes at the expense of your partner's needs, can lead to arguments and emotional distancing if you haven't adjusted to the arrival of a new baby very well.

'You're more interested in the baby than in me,' he shouts.

'I wouldn't be if only you helped me more and understood how tired I feel,' she snaps back with tears streaming down her face.

The fact is that, however much children may complement a marriage, they also make it more difficult for you to maintain the intimacy and closeness you had when there were just the two of you. Research shows that marital satisfaction starts on a downward trend after the birth of children and – this will be no surprise to parents of adolescent children – also takes a dive in their teenage years.

But remember that, even though 73 per cent of mothers report a decline in marital satisfaction by the time their babies are just five months old, things can and do recover. So the more that couples can support each other through this period the better the chances are that the marriage or relationship will not only survive but flourish.

The transition to parenthood

Professor Jay Belsky, a leading expert on child development and family studies at Pennsylvania State University, undertook an eight-year study of couples going through the experience of adjusting to parenthood. He identified six characteristics which he says are vital in facilitating a couple's smooth passage through this transition period.

- *Self*: the ability to resolve individual goals and work together as a team.
- *Gender ideology*: the ability to resolve conflicts about the division of labour and career sacrifices in a mutually acceptable way.
- *Emotionality*: the ability to handle tensions in a way that does not over-stress either partner or the marriage as a whole.
- *Expectations*: the realization that, however good a marriage may be after the birth of the baby, it will not be good in the same way that it was before.
- *Communication*: the continued ability of the partners to communicate in a way that is nurturing to the marriage.
- *Conflict management*: the ability to fight constructively and maintain a pool of common interests despite diverging priorities.

I would add one more item to this list:

- *Sexual deprivation*: the ability to understand that your sexual relationship will probably be at best infrequent, or, for a few months at least, practically non-existent. But this should be combined with the belief (and indeed the reality) that as a woman you will again feel sexual desire and sexually desirable; and for men, given time, the woman in your life will move her focus back from how to have at least one decent night's sleep to wanting to make love again. As one new mother said, 'We used to make love first thing in the morning. But now, after the 2 a.m. feeding shift and the fact that first thing in the morning is now two and a half hours earlier, making love is just a lovely memory.' A father of four young children said to me with a tired smile. 'My horizons seem to be limited to how to manage a good night's sleep. But I do love them all.'

My kingdom for a good night's sleep

No new parents – and the mother particularly – are ever fully prepared for just how exhausting a new baby can be. Charlotte said that when her son was three, her daughter two and the baby just six months, her husband's company held a party at a smart London hotel. She was so tired that she did not really want to go, but knew it was important to her husband. But she was wondering how she was going to get through the evening without falling asleep – sleep having been in short supply over the past three years.

At dinner she was quietly congratulating herself on managing to talk animatedly to the man on her right when she noticed he was staring at her with a look of intense surprise. She looked down and realized, with horror, that she had moved on to auto-pilot and had quietly and efficiently cut up all the meat on his plate, just as she did for her two-year-old daughter when trying to feed the baby at the same time. He looked quite relieved when she explained the situation, and they were both able to laugh about it.

Why becoming a parent is more difficult for some

On the whole women adjust more easily to becoming mothers than men do to becoming fathers. Maybe – feminists forgive me – it's partly inborn. But you cannot ignore the fact that most little girls want to cradle a doll and most little boys prefer to cradle a toy gun. Certainly conditioning and modelling have an important influence as well. But if a man or woman is really having a lot of difficulty making the transition to parenthood, it is often because of their own childhood experiences. Someone who has had a very emotionally deprived childhood, with little or no love, can be quite damaged. Behind the adult exterior there is such a needy child lurking that finding the resources to be a good and loving parent in turn feels either impossible or immensely difficult. Or maybe as a child the arrival of a new baby in the family was not handled very well and you either felt, or really were, pushed out from your mother's or father's affection. This memory is often buried within you – particularly so with men, who tend to talk less about their feelings. So suddenly in adult life, when a new baby arrives all these feelings of loss and rejection are reactivated and you find yourself resenting the baby; or, as a man, you find it particularly hard to share your partner with the new arrival. If this is happening to you, adjusting to becoming a threesome might need some counselling. If you are a woman suffering from post-natal depression it's very important to discuss it with your health visitor and your doctor. Help is available, so do not be too proud to seek it. Research estimates that as many as one in three mothers of children under five suffer from depression.

How you adapt to the change from couple to threesome is, I believe, of crucial importance to the future of your marriage. Frequently in counselling when I start to look at where things began to go wrong in a marriage, it turns out to be after the birth of a baby. Some couples make the transition better than others, and it is not unusual for one partner to make the changes more quickly than the other – most often the woman gets there first. This is perhaps not surprising, since she has been carrying the baby around inside her, then giving birth and breastfeeding, none of which men can ever experience.

No man should ever underestimate how crucial it is to love, support and help his wife or partner through pregnancy, the birth and during those crucial first few months. And every woman should appreciate how easy it is for the man to feel excluded by the arrival of a baby – however much he loves her and his new child. Achieving this understanding of each other is one of the key factors that unites a couple and lays the foundation for successful parenting and a happy marriage.

Fathers and children

One of the biggest changes I have seen in the twenty years I have been counselling is the relationship between men and their children. Men in their twenties and thirties are usually more involved with the children than previous generations of fathers were. This is also true for men who are taking on fatherhood the second time around, in their forties and fifties. Many first wives observe with anger and regret that their ex-husbands can now be seen pushing their second set of offspring around the supermarket with pride, hurrying home for bathtime, or reading them bedtime stories – something they did all too little of twenty years or so earlier when their first brood was young. I suspect there are two reasons. Modern women expect it of course; but also the men, being older and wiser and perhaps more established in their jobs, now realize how much they missed out first time around and don't want to let it happen again. Indeed, one executive now in his fifties and with a new wife and baby said: 'I didn't see my children from my first marriage grow up, and that has really got to me. I'm going to make sure I devote more time to my new wife and child – rather than giving everything to my job.'

I am not suggesting that parenting is as yet shared equally, but the father is frequently more involved. He may not be changing many more nappies, but he plays with his children more and wants to spend more time with them. An important bond is being forged between father and child. This has its downside, though – it is particularly agonizing for the man who acts like this if the marriage breaks down and he loses day-to-day contact with his children. But at least the motivation to continue his relationship with them will be far more developed than if this bond had not been formed. The sad fact is that nearly 50 per cent of fathers lose contact with their children within two years of a divorce, which is usually very sad for the fathers and for the children because they often feel they have been abandoned or are unwanted by their fathers.

Emotional security

It is very easy to become submerged by parenthood. The couples who tend to make the best parents are those who recognize how important it is to pay time and attention to their relationship as a couple and not let it suffer at the expense of parenting. Maintaining and nurturing that loving adult relationship so that you continue to fulfil each other's needs and desires will enable you to extend that love and emotional support more effectively to your children. The more sustaining a marriage is to a couple, the less likely it is that either member will inflict their unfulfilled needs and desires on to their children.

Diana turned to her children for what she was not getting as part of a couple. She had given up trying to have a close relationship with her remote and distant husband, and now her life revolved totally around her two small children. She was so angry with their father that she tried to exclude him more and more from their lives. To start with, the children welcomed the attention their mother was lavishing on them. But then, as they began to enter their teens and wanted a more independent life with their friends and hobbies, they found their mother becoming very possessive. She always found something wrong with their friends, or said that go-karting and soccer were too dangerous. And anyway, she moaned, what was she going to do while they were away doing all these exciting things and she was left at home alone – after all, their father was away working all the time.

Jeremy, a very good-looking man in his forties, was also looking to his daughter for what he didn't find in his wife. In his opinion his wife had gone to seed. He complained that she was overweight and always looked a mess, whereas sixteen-year-old Poppy was slim, tall and very pretty, just as her mother used to be. He would look for any excuse to take his daughter out and about rather than his wife. If there was a party in the village where he lived he encouraged Poppy rather than his wife to come with him. He had always promised his wife they would go to Paris for their twenty-fifth wedding anniversary. But then he announced that he was taking his daughter to Paris for the weekend before the anniversary, as he felt she was the right age to enjoy the experience. This made his wife feel even more pushed out of his life – and resentful of her daughter. Poppy had by now got so used to her father's time and attention that she had begun to share his feelings about her mother and felt that she was an embarrassment. In both these relationships, Diana's and Jeremy's, the children were being used, probably unintentionally, by one parent to make up for what they saw as the inadequacies of the other.

To use your children as an emotional prop or support, a confidant or substitute partner puts tremendously unfair demands and pressures on them. And in the more extreme forms it sometimes robs them of their childhood. Lizzie, the eldest of three, had few good memories of her childhood. She remembers little of her parents except their constant rowing until her father suddenly walked out when she was eleven, leaving her to cope with her mother's final breakdown. Her other memory was of always cleaning the house and washing the dishes from the age of five, because her mother was either too exhausted or did not care and her father was shouting at her mother about the constant mess. Lizzie said, 'I felt if only the house was clean my father and mother would stop rowing and we could all live happily together. But that never happened.' To this day she finds it difficult not to be obsessional about cleaning. Lizzie was being expected to be a parent to her parents and look after them – rather than the other way round. This was totally unrealistic and not something that should happen to a child.

In my experience, couples in a happy marriage or relationship which is emotionally and sexually alive make a better job of parenting because they provide their children with the chance to experience a loving couple relationship and are more able to be receptive to the needs of their children. They have more natural energy and resources to do so, because their own relationship is a sustaining one and they are not spending their time draining their partner emotionally.

Making parenting work

As parents we tend to have fairly set ideas about how we are going to bring up children, based on a highly charged emotional factor. It's either going to be like the way our parents brought us up, we feel, or, because they made a right old mess of it, completely different. For example, the woman who was very strictly reared as a little girl may try to bring her children up the same way, or she may feel it was all much too authoritarian and throw everything to the winds, providing no discipline and few boundaries with her own children. What she should be striving for, of course, is a balance somewhere in between. What is also important and vital to good parenting is not doing it his or her way – but as parents doing it their way. How you are going to approach the parenting task is something that you have to negotiate and work out together. The issues in question range from attitudes to breastfeeding, where the baby sleeps, potty training and the importance or not of homework to discipline, dealing with truculent adolescents, developing teenage sexuality, drugs, green hair, deafening music and unspeakable bedrooms. Remember that children flourish best where they have consistent, loving, kind parents whom they can't play off against each other, who let them rant and rage at times, who give them enough flexibility to develop as individuals and also learn self-discipline, and who give kind but firm boundaries.

Four golden rules for bringing up children

- *Separate out the children from their behaviour*. Always make it clear that you love them and that, whatever they do, you will never withdraw that love. You may condemn their behaviour sometimes, but you should never condemn the child. You should never say, for example, 'If you do that I will no longer love you,' or 'you are a bad child.' You have to make it clear that it's not they who are unlovable or bad, but what they are doing or saying that is unacceptable and needs to be changed. Children need to feel secure in their parents' love.
- *Give them a belief in themselves*. Give them a feeling of acceptability, self-worth and self-respect. Children need a tremendous amount of approval and encouragement in their formative years if they are going to make a successful transition from child to adult. We are not all Einstein, Michelangelo or winners of the Nobel Peace Prize, but we

all need to feel we are good at something, that we are lovable and acceptable human beings. Unless we can learn to love ourselves as children we will find difficulty forming loving relationships in adult life.

* *Give them tolerance and not criticism.* Criticism severely undermines a child. If a child is brought up by critical parents, their self-confidence is eroded. This often makes them very self-critical, which is destructive. They can also in turn become very critical adults themselves, carrying this attitude into their own adult relationships and so on to the next generation.

* *Give them encouragement, but do not pressure them.* Never make your children feel pressured to perform, or set them unrealistic targets. This only leaves them with the feeling they are never good enough, or that they always have to achieve that little bit more. In my counselling I am constantly aware of the lovely, talented, bright, intelligent people – often high achievers – who sit before me, weighed down with needing to do better. They are not really able to appreciate what they have achieved. They endlessly and often unconsciously try to prove to their mother or father that they are as good as they think their parents wanted them to be.

Emily, a highly intelligent and articulate woman in her late thirties who was a director in a large corporate company, said to me, 'As a child I remember my mother always pushing me to get into the best schools and obtain the best exam results. Yet when I did just that there was never a word of praise or encouragement – only another goal set for me to achieve. When I was in my late twenties I was the youngest person ever to get a really top job in a particular company. I wrote to my mother to tell her about it, but I heard nothing. Not a letter, not a word, not a telephone call – absolutely nothing. I realized then it was pointless looking for some recognition, yet I am still driven to do it.'

I once saw a sadly humorous cartoon depicting a huge statue of a man – it could equally well be a woman – captioned: 'The President of the United States, Commandant of all Russia, Prime Minister of Great Britain, Chairman of Warner Brothers, the World Bank and ICI and Nobel Peace Prize winner – yet still a disappointment to his mother.' This lack of praise and encouragement from parents to their children is, I believe, perpetuated not only in many people's personal lives but also in the workplace. All too few managers and people in authority seem to praise and encourage people when they have done something well. Surely that is one of the main tools of management, yet it is often sadly missing. A lot of counselling work is concerned with trying to restore people who have been badly undermined or even traumatized by unkind criticism or lack of encouragement received, as a child, from a parent, grandparent, teacher or other significant adult figure.

Jennifer was the outstandingly intelligent child of a relatively old couple. Both parents were very bright but had not achieved what they wanted in their careers, so all their frustrated hopes and dreams were focused on their daughter. At eleven she won a scholarship to a very academic school where all the children were intellectually gifted. Jennifer would constantly get high marks, often ten out of ten and sometimes nine out of ten. If she got ten out of ten she was praised, but if it was nine out of ten her parents would look disappointed and ask why she had not managed ten. In exams she usually came within the top three, but if she did not come at the very top she would get the same reaction. She did not rebel, as many children would have done, but tried harder and harder. She got consistently good marks and was the envy of other ambitious parents around her, but approached exams in a state of total nervous tension, working day and night. After each exam she was quite convinced she had done badly and went through weeks of unmitigated pain waiting for the results.

She got into Oxford without any problem. But then came pressure from her parents to get a first-class degree. Was she really working hard enough? they wanted to know. They didn't want her to have any boyfriends because that might get in the way of her work. She could have sailed through a first, but the trauma and tension had reached such a pitch that her lack of confidence caught up with her. She got a good second, which anyone else would have been delighted with, but to her it signified failure. It was only many years on, and after several unsatisfactory and abusive relationships which fed into her feeling of total lack of worth and self-love, that she finally met someone who loved her for the kind, loving person she was. His belief in her helped her to restore some of her belief in herself, but he was not good enough for her parents and they never came to her wedding.

Sometimes parents criticize their children by making jokes at their expense. Deep down it really hurts and can damage a child's self-image. Matt's grandfather always used to refer to him as Billy Bunter. Even when he became quite a slim young man he had recurring dreams that one morning he would wake up fat. And Wendy, whose mother spent her life mocking her appearance, particularly her legs, once said to her, 'With your short legs, if you walked in the gutter you wouldn't reach the pavement.' For years Wendy was embarrassed by her legs, despite the fact that they were of fairly average length. It was not until she was able to rebuild her shattered confidence as an adult that she was able to recognize this fact.

Love, acceptance, encouragement and tolerance are the best gifts we can give our children.

The 'good enough' parent

Most parents want to do the best for their children and to give them as much as they themselves had or even more. This is only natural. But it's important to accept our limitations, to realize that we are after all only human and that 'good enough' parenting is what most of us end up achieving. It is said of the child-parent relationship that although children often forget they rarely forgive. That may be so, but in any case by the time our own children reach their adolescence they too are having to come to terms with their parents' limitations, so we might as well do the same.

What we can do as parents is to lean to recognize that everyone has different strengths and weaknesses which enable one person to cope with a particular situation better than another. That applies to parenting as well. If we encourage these strengths and differences in our partners, our children can benefit from the different qualities.

When my children were small they seemed to fall off their bicycles or other people's ponies with great frequency, often injuring themselves and needing stitches. I am very squeamish and panic at the sight of blood. I struggled not to show the children this, but my efforts were only skin-deep and children pick these things up. I would bundle them into the car and rush off to the casualty department of the local hospital, always relieved if their father happened to be around because he coped much better in these circumstances and would sit holding their hands to reassure them while they were going through the painful stitching process. My strengths consisted of being able to listen endlessly to their own and their friends' emotional problems in those painful teenage years. So my husband and I quite effectively complemented each other.

How to survive teenagers

Harriet's daughter went to America for a few months in the year between school and university. A few days before she returned home, Harriet rang to make last-minute arrangements about meeting her at the airport. Just at the end of the conversation her daughter said, 'By the way, Mum, you may be rather surprised when you meet me at the airport.' Then she rang off. Harriet spent the next few days worrying about what her daughter had meant. Had she got a totally unsavoury boyfriend in tow? Would she be puffing cannabis? What colour would her hair be? Would she indeed have any hair? Oh, surely not a tattoo?

As she leaned on the railings at the airport, staring intently at all the new arrivals, she suddenly saw her daughter waving and smiling at her. There she was with pink hair. Not too bad . . . and – oh, no – a ring through her nose! Harriet said to me, 'I felt such a mixture of emotions: a sense of shock because I thought the ring looked dreadful, anger because of the three rotten days of worry I had had, but also a sense of great relief because it could have been so much worse. But most of all I was just so pleased to have her safely home, and to hear how much she had enjoyed herself.'

I think this sums up what it's like being the parent of an adolescent. Because you love them and care about them they are constantly pulling you in all directions, causing you to experience every emotion in the book.

If you are not very careful or very lucky these adolescent years can be a period of high conflict in the family, either because you are falling out with your teenage children or because they are sparking off arguments between their parents. The teens are a period when the young, half-child, half-adult, are moving away from you and beginning to create their own independent lives. They are testing themselves out with you, each other and the world generally. You love them, and you try to do your best. But living with them is not always easy and they would probably say the same about you. You frequently feel they are pushing you to your limit, and at times beyond. You might be tempted to think back with longing to their early years. After a long hard day you could at least put them to bed, tuck them up safe and sound and know where they were. I am sure most parents of teenagers would agree at times that it would be nice to be able to do the same again.

Fathers' worst problems with teenagers

These are the things that men seem to find most difficult when coping with their adolescent sons and daughters.

- Like Gigi, she is no longer a little girl. Suddenly fathers find that their pretty, loving, amiable little daughter has disappeared. A frequently temperamental young woman has taken her place. She no longer thinks you are wonderful. She is embarrassed by what you say, do, think and wear.
- She is over-emotional and unpredictable. One moment she is arguing with her mother and you step in as peacemaker, the next it is you who have got it all wrong. She bursts into tears, rushes upstairs locks herself in her room, turns on the music at deafening decibels and refuses to come out for hours. Surely it can't be something that you, her father, said?
- Accepting her as a sexual human being. When she reaches fifteen, sixteen or seventeen and it's the end of the world if she hasn't got a date or party to go to on Saturday night, you don't really understand this tragedy. Or she is going out with someone who in your opinion is thoroughly unsuitable. One father who could not stand his seventeen-year-old daughter's boyfriend, called Hank, repeatedly referred to him as Wank. This understandably infuriated his daughter. But boyfriends generally seem to bring out the worst 'Victorian' attitudes in fathers – perhaps because they remember themselves at that age. Then their main aim was to score – to get the girl into bed and saying yes to sex. And now here are their daughters

likely to fall prey to all these young men who probably feel the same way.

- Father's ambitions are projected on to his son. Sons, he thinks, are far less complicated than daughters and wives, and can be his mate. But they can also be a repository for a father's past successes or his unfulfilled dreams. So if you never quite made it to the first eleven you may desperately want your son to. Or if you were captain of cricket you may put pressure on your son to do the same, and cut up rough if he is not interested in the game or feels he cannot compete.

- Coming to terms with your fading youth. As a father you have to accept that your son can now outrun you, beat you at squash, and is telling you that you are too old to risk life and limb on the rugger field.

- He is moving away from you. Maybe you are confronted with the fact that your chatty, outgoing son, who a year or two ago wanted to do things with you, would now much rather be with his friends. Added to which, despite a good education your son has suddenly become monosyllabic.

  'Where are you going?' you enquire.

  'Out,' replies your son.

  'Did you have a good time,' you ask on his return, hoping for a conversation.

  'Yeah, it was all right,' mumbles your son, yawning and turning away.

Mothers' worst problems with teenagers

And here's a typical mother's list of what drives them up the wall when there are teenagers in the house.

- Contrary to what they seem to believe, you are not running a hotel. You are less than ecstatic about the state of their bedrooms and of the bathroom – if you can ever get into it, that is. When you ask them to do the washing up, ironing, shopping or cooking they may say they will, if you are lucky – but it is in their own good time and certainly not in yours. Then there is what they are wearing, the colour of their hair, what time they go to bed at night and what time they eventually get up in the morning.

- What you see as responsible care and concern they see as interference. If your daughters are going out, particularly at night, you want to know where and with whom and to agree on how and when they are going to get back.

  'Oh! don't fuss so,' they storm, 'I'm old enough to look after myself. You'll show me up in front of my friends if you come and collect me.' Or 'Jane is allowed to stay out until two in the morning.' And there's also the worry of them getting hurt through unsatisfactory or unloving sexual relationships and the fear of unwanted pregnancies.

- Mothers can feel jealous of their daughters – not of physical prowess, as with fathers and sons, but because she may have good looks while yours are fading. If you had a fairly miserable adolescence, you may now be resenting the fact that your daughter is having a better time. If your own marriage or relationship is shaky you may be afraid of losing not only your man but your daughter as well.

- Cleanliness may not be next to godliness these days, but it's certainly close to a mother's heart. Mothers can no longer insist that their sons take daily baths or showers, or make sure they clean their teeth, wash their hair or have it cut – until the school starts to complain. So there are often ongoing rows. Mothers are wasting their time, of course. It takes another woman to bring about the changes. A girlfriend, or even the prospect of one, can achieve in days what a mother has failed to manage in years.

- Although girlfriends tend to have a civilizing effect on young men they give rise to ambivalent feelings in the mother. Has she done a good job as far as sex education goes? Is he going to be responsible sexually and not get his girlfriend pregnant? And, if he is sleeping around, what about AIDS?

- Experimentation is the name of the game. It is not easy having to cope with the three Ds – drinking, driving and drugs. Adolescent boys tend to drink too much or drive too fast, and are often tempted (as girls are, too) to experiment with drugs. Helping and guiding your children through this minefield is what makes those teenage years perhaps the most difficult of all.

The importance of teamwork

All these issues and more need to be discussed between you as parents, so that you have an understanding of how each of you thinks. If, as surely there must be, you have areas of disagreement, it is important to talk them through, to negotiate, and if you cannot agree to arrive at a reasonable compromise. This process enables you both to go on to talk things through with your children and to provide them with agreed guidelines and boundaries. For example, if you both agree on what is a reasonable amount of pocket money and what it should cover, if your child comes and asks for more because he or she has overspent it would undermine your partner if you said, 'Here you are. You can have another two pounds but don't tell your Dad.' It is much fairer to listen to why they have overspent and say, 'I'll discuss it with your father, then we'll see what we can do.' Being an adolescent involves being fairly self-centred, self-interested and often selfish. So it is easy for young people to achieve their own ends by playing one parent off against the other, particularly if you have an unhappy marriage or are separated or divorced. But you are not helping your children if you let them work on the divide-and-rule principle. They may get a feeling of satisfaction because they have got what they want, but it is fairly short-lived. It is much better for children and adolescents if you show them kindly and firmly that this does not work.

Supporting each other in the challenging role of parenting is very important, not only because it provides a secure and loving environment for the children but also because it contributes to the health and life of the marriage or relationship. In this chapter I have tried to show the importance of a loving relationship for the children and equally importantly for the couple. It makes sense to be realistic and accept that none of us will make a perfect job of parenting, whether we are married, living together, separated, divorced or single. 'Good enough' parenting is something that most of us have the chance of achieving, however, and this is what we should strive for and be content with. What is essential is to give our children love, encouragement, a belief in themselves and respect for themselves as well as others, so that they can grow up to live happy and fulfilling lives.

7

THE BALANCING TRICK

JUGGLING THE DEMANDS OF WORK AND HOME

One of the symptoms of approaching nervous breakdown
is the belief that one's work is terribly important, and to
take a holiday would bring all kinds of disaster.
Bertrand Russell, philosopher and mathematician,
The Conquest of Happiness, 1930

In Britain the workplace is not family-friendly, and I suggest it tends not to be very people-friendly either. We suffer from 'the long hours culture'. If you don't work a ten- or twelve-hour day, in some companies you are not seen to be fully committed. If you want to knock off at five and return to your family you are regarded as a clockwatcher or seen as not pulling your weight. Taking work home is par for the course, and weekends and holidays are not sacrosanct. Unless you can justify it as a working occasion, lunch, as the wheeler-dealer Gordon Gekko said in the movie *Wall Street*, is for wimps. Credit goes to those who eat their sandwich while glued to their desk or computer.

The recession has made this attitude worse because so many people have either experienced redundancy or live in fear of it. If you don't conform, there is always a risk that you will be shown the door. Women, and particularly mothers, are much more likely than men to rebel against this culture; most men, indeed, find it almost impossible. This may be why there are far fewer women than men in top jobs; and why men, having got to the top, feel they have to put their younger colleagues through the same hoops.

The other great mistake in British management, from the board room to the shop floor, is that people are managed by punishment rather than by praise. People are rarely told when they have done a good job, but if they make a mistake or something goes wrong they are told without delay. Working in this sort of environment makes people miserable and probably does nothing for their performance at work. And people take their unhappiness or discontent home. There it is easy to take the problems out on your partner, or to be so stressed out you have little left over for them or your children. When you have no outlet at work to resolve these issues, home often becomes the battleground. You know you shouldn't do it, but it's the only safe place in which you can.

In this chapter I want to look at how men and women can successfully combine the demands of work and home; why some men have more problems with their wife returning to work than they had anticipated; how having children can change a woman's attitude to work; and why absolute equality in the workplace still seems so difficult to achieve. I have also highlighted the very different expectations men and women have from their relationships when they get together at the end of the working day.

Support in the home

'When the children were little,' Jill said, 'much as I loved them, I also wanted a break from them. And I wanted to do some further training so that when I returned to work I would be more qualified and could get a better teaching job. My husband was very supportive of the whole idea and he was a very loving and involved father, so I had no worries about leaving the children with him.'

She sighed deeply. 'But men! I would tell him when my evening classes were, and if he was free he would agree to babysit. Then suddenly something would come up at work and he would just forget – his work just took over and my needs were pushed aside. I would just see red and find myself screaming at him like a fishwife. He would take this very calmly and say, "Don't worry, darling, we'll find a babysitter." This drove me into even more fury because what he meant was that *I* was to find the babysitter.

It was left to me to telephone and beg her to manage yet another evening.'

'What did you do?' I asked.

'Well, I continued with my fishwife act for a bit and scurried around at the last minute looking for someone to babysit. Then I realized that I was dealing with conflicting emotions within me. First, how much I resented my needs yet again taking second place to his job, and second, that I was clinging on to what I saw as my role, as needing to prove to myself, my husband and the world that I was a good and responsible wife and mother. And it was up to me to pick up the pieces. I also realized that the more I continued to let him off the hook by finding a sitter the more he would forget about his commitments.

'So I confronted him, and we agreed that if he really couldn't get away from work – which, since he's a vicar, tends to encroach endlessly on family life – then he would take the responsibility of finding the babysitter. He saw how important this was to me and he kept his promise. He also realized that having a working wife meant he had to adjust his life a lot more than he had bargained for, because I need not only encouragement but practical help as well.'

What Jill and her husband had also discovered, and still works very well for them today, is that if you have children and you are both going to work it is very important to support each other. If the man thinks his partner can work and do everything else without help, or if the woman makes the mistake of feeling she has to be superwoman, it's bound to lead to conflict, resentment, rows and chronic exhaustion for the woman.

As a society we are still not truly into joint parenting. For example, Britain is lagging far behind much of Europe in terms of paternity leave and allowing fathers time off if their child is ill. In Australia they don't have mother-and-baby rooms where women can go and change the baby's nappy, but parents' rooms. In this country the poor man has to settle for the gents' loo if he has care of the baby.

Some men find it very difficult to adapt to their wife or partner returning to work. Sometimes it's because they are insecure and feel threatened by the idea of you having more independence and more spending power. If there are real problems in the marriage they might fear that, if you become financially independent and things continue to be difficult, you might up and leave. It may be that you have returned to work and are making quite a success of it; rather than feeling that he can share that success, your husband may resent it. Some men find it particularly difficult if this happens at a time when they are not having much success or job satisfaction themselves, or when they have been made redundant. They feel that, even though you both need the money, you are undermining their firmly perceived role as breadwinner. There are some men who, because of their insecurity or jealousy, worry about your new opportunities to meet other men. Any or all of these things can make a man unsupportive – he may continually complain about you being out at work, or sabotage the practical arrangements you have made. If this happens, try to talk it through together to see if it's possible to deal with the fears and resentments and to give reassurance and time for adjustment.

A family discussion is also very necessary so that the children can express their views and opinions, and all of you can see which task each of you is going to take responsibility for. Going back to work should not mean that you as a woman are left doing everything while the rest of the family enjoys the greater spending power they now have.

Virginia had a good job that she very much enjoyed, and one of the things she really wanted to do was go on some of the conferences that the other staff attended. But they were often held in the evenings or at weekends, which encroached on family life, so she had always turned them down. When one particularly interesting conference came up, however, she discussed it with her partner and they both agreed that she should go.

She usually did the weekly shopping after work on Thursdays, as that was the day the supermarket stayed open late. Because of the conference she would not be able to do so that week. She explained this to her husband, who replied, 'Don't worry, darling. I'll go with you on Saturday morning.'

Now men reading this might think what a nice, caring man he was, offering to help her out on Saturday. Most women would probably react as Virginia did, by thinking, 'But that doesn't solve anything. There won't be any food in the house. I'll have been away for two days. There will be quite enough to do when I get back without having to go to the supermarket on Saturday morning. Nice as it might be to have your company, darling, it doesn't really help very much.' Because she felt angry and hurt by her husband's reaction she snapped: 'I'll cancel the conference, then.'

'Oh, don't be so unreasonable,' he replied. 'Why do you always over-react?' He was confused by her angry response – he thought he had offered to help her and could not understand why she was cross. It was only later, when they had both cooled down, that Virginia was able to say what she wanted – which was for him to do the shopping on Thursday evening after work. He agreed, if a little reluctantly, and they were able to sort things out.

This story not only highlights men's and women's differences in their expectations of each other but also shows what happens in the majority of households – this area of a couple's life is not shared equally. If a man wanted to go away on a conference he would be unlikely to feel he would have to negotiate anything first, and would be extremely unlikely to have to delegate the household tasks before he went. The fact is that men tend to help out – some a lot more than others – rather than take equal responsibility for childcare and housework. Social Trends survey 1995 shows that for example when it comes to looking after sick children women shoulder the great responsibility with – 60 per cent mainly woman, 1 per cent mainly man and 39 per cent a shared task.

Cinderellas of the workplace

The long working hours required of people in Britain mitigate particularly against women with children. At the back of many employers' minds is the idea that it's women rather than men who take time out to care for children, so they are not seen as a good investment. With this sort of attitude in the workplace it is not surprising that it still exists in the relationship between men and women in the home. If nature had devised a way for men to have babies I suspect they would solve the world population problem overnight and also change lingering male resistance to the concept of joint parenting. But without such a miracle, waiting for men to appreciate some of these factors is taking longer than most women want.

At a dinner party I was seated next to a banker, a large, confident man who talked a lot. His pretty and slightly tense wife was on the other side of the table. I noticed that if she was talking he would frequently interrupt her. She would immediately stop and let him say what he wanted, or finish the story she was telling. This had obviously become such a habit in the marriage that she was quite unable to stand up for herself. The conversation turned to work, and I asked how they had decided that his wife should stay at home and look after the children.

'Well,' he said, 'it didn't really need any discussion. I was earning more than she could ever hope to do, so there was no choice – not if she wanted the lifestyle that my salary provides.'

I wondered if his wife was going to say anything at that point, but just as she was about to speak he glared at her and changed the conversation to the stockmarket prices. She said nothing.

Although nowadays many more women are returning to work after the birth of a baby, it is still very common for them to take a few years out before returning to work. It is very important – unlike the banker and his wife – to discuss what you both want to do and what your financial needs are. When the woman does return to work it marks a major change in a couple's life and requires lots of negotiation.

Staying at home and being a full-time mother is a very important job that is grossly under-rated by society. If that is what you want and it's possible to manage financially, or at least to delay returning to work until the children are much older, that should be an acceptable and valued option. But going back to work after some time away is not always easy, for several reasons. The experience that women accumulate from bringing up a family is not seen to be very marketable when they try to re-establish themselves at work. Technology races ahead of her, and she will have to learn new skills. And a woman's confidence decreases in relation to length of time she spends away from work.

It is often lack of confidence, as much as the need to retrain or polish up their skills, that makes it so hard for women to re-enter the job market. Research undertaken by the Industrial Society showed that a man would be quite happy to apply for a job if he had only three or four out of a list of ten requirements specified. Women, however, would not apply unless they had at least eight or nine of the ten required. Though there has been a major change in this direction, many girls are still brought up to expect less of themselves than boys are. As a consequence, many women tend to set themselves lower standards of achievement or are less confident in their own abilities than men are.

A survey by MORI for Hays Personal Services questioned people working in the areas of law, banking, accountancy, construction and information technology on men and women and work. A not very encouraging picture emerged. While two-thirds of the men surveyed thought they would make it to the top, only half the women thought they would. Only two out of five women rated themselves in the top third of their peer group, whereas with men it was three out of five. On the crunch issue of children the survey found that men pay no more than lip service to equally shared childcare.

I continually see this lack of confidence in many women who come to me for counselling, as well as those I meet in everyday life. I am not, of course, suggesting that all men out there are thoroughly confident or that all women lack confidence – far from it. But it does seem that men find the acquiring of confidence less of an uphill battle than women. A shortage of confidence often makes women lack assertiveness; in men it often makes them turn to aggression by way of compensation.

Men's attitude to women and work

I mentioned earlier in this chapter why some men have difficulty making the adjustment to their wives and partners working. But most men are in favour of it and feel that both sexes have an equal right to work. One thing that men very much enjoy about being in a partnership or marriage with a working woman is the fact that she contributes to the family budget, which in the past has often been a heavy burden for men to shoulder on their own. For some families, it is essential. At the other end of the financial scale, it may mean that the family can enjoy a better lifestyle, with more luxuries, better holidays and so on. And it also makes the relationship between men and women on the home front more evenly based, which feels good to women as well – it is something she often misses out on when she gives up an independent income to stay at home to look after the children.

The other thing that men appreciate in a working partner is that she is often happier, more fulfilled and not so reliant on him at the end of the day to fulfil her needs. But here I want to look at a striking difference between men and women that I have observed over many years of counselling.

Men opt out, women opt in

At the end of the working day men and women want different things from a relationship, and this causes tremendous friction. When a man comes home he wants to switch off from the hassles and problems of dealing with people, and be looked after and cared for. That requires a totally undemanding and unpressurizing wife or partner, and children with whom he may play for half an hour before they go to bed, their homework done so he doesn't have to help them with it. He just wants to switch off and recharge his batteries. Most of all he wants time on his own, or to do his own thing.

The woman would not deny that some of the looking after would be extremely agreeable, and would value time to unwind and to devote to herself. But she wants something more from the man – she wants to opt into the relationship, to connect to her partner.

When she asks this of him, it seems like just one more pressure when all he wanted to do was unwind. As he sits and watches television, or reads the paper, it seems to her that he has withdrawn from her or is even rejecting her. 'Do you know,' said Kay with frustration, 'he thinks being in the sitting room with me, saying nothing all evening because he's reading the paper or watching television or making one of his models, is being companionable! I could scream. The fact that he hardly utters a word drives me crazy.'

So if a woman wants to talk in any depth or at any length to the man in her life, he feels this is unreasonably demanding. The woman's response to this is to find him unreasonable, selfish and self-centred. Deep resentments can build up. This is the collision course that so many couples are headed on at the end of their day.

Charles worked long hours, leaving home at seven in the morning and arriving home at eight at night or even later. Despite being absent so much during the week, at weekends he was a super father and very involved with his children. Nevertheless by the time they came for counselling Chloe, his wife, was very angry. She had a part-time job and looked after their three young boys aged from six to ten. She had made a close circle of friends and she was always ready to listen and discuss their problems with them. Although she loved Charles, he was driving her wild.

'I know just what is wrong,' she said. 'I love him very much, and both of us are very committed to the marriage, but he is so withdrawn when he comes home from work that I just don't feel he has time for me or the children.'

'It's not that,' said Charles, looking at her intently. 'It's just that I'm worn out. The trouble with you is that you just don't seem to understand.'

'Well, I'm tired too. After all, I have a demanding job and three children, but I don't sink into silence and become practically monosyllabic every evening as you do.'

'Oh, come on. That's not fair,' said Charles. 'We do talk. You know we do.'

'Well, it's not what I'd call talk,' Chloe snapped back at him.

As they continued arguing it became clear that they both had very different expectations of what talking actually meant. For Charles it was sharing some of what had been going on during the day, but not very much as he had had enough of it by the time he got home. He wanted to put it behind him and relax. Chloe, on the other hand, wanted a blow-by-blow account of what he had been doing and felt that his failure to do so meant that he didn't value her thoughts and opinions. What she wanted for herself was to talk at length about her ups and downs at work. She and her friends would often spend afternoons around her large kitchen table discussing their lives, while the children played around them. She wanted to share some of this with Charles, and was very frustrated at finding him such an unresponsive audience.

Chloe came from a large family, mostly of women. She had a very eccentric, beautiful and volatile mother and four talkative sisters who loved nothing better than all being together and talking about each other's lives. 'They don't so much solve problems as create them,' said Charles with obvious irritation. Chloe's father, who was seen as a rather distant head of this household of women, had opted out by having numerous affairs. Charles came from a family of boys and had gone away to boarding school at the age of eight. His parents adored him, but were very involved in work and their own socially demanding lives. So as a child he had learnt to be very self-contained and not to show his feelings very much. Their conflicting childhood backgrounds were manifesting themselves as conflict in their adult relationship.

What they had to learn to adjust to was the fact that Charles needed time and space at the end of the day, and that endless detailed talk was driving him into the ground. So, during the week at least, the talking had to be less intense and take less time. Charles could in return be more talkative and give more, because he would not feel he was about to embark on Wagner's Ring Cycle as soon as he stepped through the door. Neither found this adjustment easy, particularly Chloe. But Charles also agreed to put work aside completely at the weekends and that he would do some more real talking, as Chloe called it, when he was not so tired.

Equality is improving in the workplace – or is it?

Recent surveys of eighteen- to twenty-five-year-olds have shown that we are now achieving greater equality between the sexes in the workplace. Maybe they do, but I'm not sure that is the whole picture. During counselling sessions I am seeing two interesting things. The career women in their late twenties and early to mid-thirties are saying, 'I'm going to combine the two, no problem.' But once they have a baby many are not quite so sure. They are actually questioning what the previous generations have fought so hard for – the right for equal opportunities in the workplace. I don't mean they don't want them to exist; they do very much. But they don't necessarily want to take advantage of them. They are opting out of the fast track and wanting to spend time, and that often means all the time, with their children. They are saying, 'What is the point of having children and then missing out by farming them out to a nanny or au pair all day? Especially if that day lasts from eight in the morning until seven at night.'

Fiona, a brilliant and successful lawyer, gave up her job and a hefty salary to participate more in her children's life. Nina went back to work after maternity leave for a couple of months before she did what had never before crossed her mind, which was to ditch it and become a full-time mother. Of course, many women are not in the position to make such choices, but it is interesting that those who can are increasingly coming down on the side of motherhood. This trend may well continue if substantial changes are not made in the working patterns in this country:

Differences between the sexes at work and play

At work

I cannot let a chapter that is mainly concerned with women and work go by without saying of working mothers, 'Show me one and, if you scratch the surface just a little, guilt will be written across her heart. For some women it will be in great big letters, for others fairly small ones, but few escape.' Most of the time it's under control. But when you have to choose between the needs of your child and the demands of your job, and because you are a serious working woman you have to put your child second, you are right into that good old guilt trip. Few men find themselves in this situation.

James combined looking after his two children, aged ten and eleven, with a fairly demanding job. He shared a nanny with another family. When he got home in the evening she had fed them before she left for the day, and he would then spend time playing with them and helping them with their homework before they went to bed. He could often not be bothered to cook for himself, so he would go to the restaurant round the corner for a quick meal. The children had the number of his mobile phone, so he could be back in five minutes if necessary. Financially that is not an option for many people, but emotionally most women would find it very difficult to do.

At play

More men than women who work outside the home feel entitled
to take time out to play, whether this is sport or hobbies or a
Sunday lunchtime drink. And just in case you think I am being a
little unfair to men, statistics on how much time men and women
spend on leisure bear this out. Women in full-time employment
have ten hours less free time a week than men (Social Trends
1992). In counselling I see a lot of women who are complaining
that they are golfing or football widows, or that their partner is
always out with his mates. But it is more unusual for men, though
not unknown, to feel cheated of their wife's company because she
is always playing tennis, or is at the pub playing darts with her
friends. This especially applies if there are children in the family.
If they do a hard week's work, men, more than women, feel they
are entitled to their leisure time and though women may also feel
this they are more likely than men to let children, household tasks,
visiting the sick or looking after an elderly parent encroach on it.
This is maybe the reason why women on reaching mid-life with
their child rearing behind them, think now is the time to do her
own thing, or to find herself. This was rather delightfully portrayed
by Pauline Collins in the film *Shirley Valentine* where Shirley left
her rather dull, boring husband and her everyday responsibilities
to go for a holiday to a Greek Island.

Confidence and criticism

Women often have more difficulty than men in coping with
criticism in the workplace. Possibly they take it more personally
and are less able to distance themselves from it. Most women,
however, would agree that there are two areas of men's lives in
which they react very badly to criticism. They both, unsurprisingly,
have phallic implications. The first is a man's ability to drive a car.
It's rare indeed to find a man who does not consider that he is not
a far better driver than his wife, partner or indeed the entire female
sex. Joke about it as he may, he really does believe that he is better
behind the wheel than the average woman. Maybe he is right? Try

a little private survey between the two of you, then introduce the idea to a group of friends and see what the results are. He may or may not be better, but I am sure the survey will say that he thinks he is! The other area where men can be devastated by criticism is sexual. As a woman, never under-rate a man's often fairly fragile sexual ego. However great he is in bed, he still likes you to tell him so and is likely to feel easily hurt by disparaging remarks.

But at work the boot is on the other foot. I was having lunch with a group of men and women, and the women were talking about the difficulty they experienced in coping with criticism at work. Fran, a very experienced and talented radio producer, said: 'If I made a programme that I thought was good and then one or two people criticized it, I would feel totally decimated.'

Steve, one of her colleagues, thought differently: 'If I felt the programme I had made was good, a few critical comments wouldn't affect me.'

Another man added, 'If I thought I'd done a really good job, I'd think what a bloody fool the person was who criticized me. He obviously doesn't know what he's talking about. What I've done is a good piece of work. If, on the other hand, it was a whole lot of people making unfavourable comments then of course I would take that seriously.'

Maybe women's attitude to work and criticism is a legacy of the struggle to get there in the first place, and feeling that you had to be better than men to get the job. (Another part of me thinks that men are just a little more rational about these things . . . but perish the thought!)

One of the fundamental differences between men and women when it comes to combining the demands of a job with the needs of looking after the children and a home is that men expect to have it all – marriage, a wife, a career and children. Whereas women, who for centuries have been conditioned to see themselves as primarily carer of husband, children and home, spend a lot of time and energy working out how on earth they can combine all these tasks with work or a career. Most women, though they would like household tasks and childcare shared equally, still feel deep down that it is more their responsibility than that of their partners, and most men take advantage of this attitude. But we also need to recognize that the working life of most men today is more stressful than it has ever been – as it is for women in demanding jobs. But more women than men are working part-time, and many do so through choice because it allows them to combine work and children without suffering major exhaustion and pangs of guilt, especially when the children are very small.

In Chapter 8 I want to tackle the tricky issue of money and relationships. In nearly all surveys that I have read money comes near the top of the list of topics that couples argue about most, but as with so much in life I don't think it is quite as straightforward as it seems.

8

BANKING ON EACH OTHER

BETTER WAYS OF HANDLING MONEY IN A RELATIONSHIP

A woman who has no way of expressing herself and of realizing herself as a full human has nothing else to turn to but the owning of material things.

Enriqueta Longauex y Vasquez,
American civil rights activist, 1960

In the 1950s the singer Eartha Kitt was far less high-minded in her approach to money and material things:

I like Chopin and Bizet, and the voice of Doris Day,
Gershwin songs and old forgotten carols,
But the music that excels is the sound of oil wells
As they slurp, slurp, slurp into the barrels.
My little home will be quaint as an old parasol,
Instead of fitted carpets I'll have money wall to wall,
I want an old-fashioned house,
With an old-fashioned fence
And an old-fashioned millionaire.

A taboo subject

Money is still one area that couples spend too little time talking about – until they are married or co-habiting. Then they spend too much time arguing about it. Nowadays many people embark on sex surprisingly soon after meeting each other; sexual intercourse has replaced social intercourse in the getting-to-know-you stage of a relationship.

It is much easier for a woman to gain access to a man's bed than to his bank account. By gaining access I don't mean having the chance to spend it – no such luck. I mean knowing how much he's got available, or the size of his overdraft. To him his money is more private and personal than sex, and he talks about it a lot less.

Talking about money is often avoided even in relationships where couples know each other well, or are planning to put their relationship on a more formal footing. They still skirt round this delicate matter. It seems too intrusive to enquire too far, too calculating, too unromantic. There are plenty of excuses to avoid such conversations, which makes finding out the truth all the more surprising when you do settle down. You had probably made assumptions about the way your partner handles money – and probably based them on your own methods. Then suddenly, you discover that your approach to the issue of money is worlds apart.

When the statement of their joint bank account arrived and Irene discovered that she and Jack were overdrawn she was outraged. She screamed at him: 'How has this happened? It's totally irresponsible. We'll cancel the holiday, stop eating, turn off the heating. This must stop.' She was in a complete panic.

Jack, however, was very calm about it all. 'It's only a cash flow problem. Don't worry, if we cut back a little it will soon be sorted out,' he said with obvious irritation.

A quick look at their childhood backgrounds soon revealed their differences. Irene's parents, particularly her father, had always taken a very firm view on money. 'Never a borrower or a lender be' was his favourite motto. If you did not have the money for something, you saved up or went without. Jack, on the other hand, had had parents with a very free-and-easy approach to money. There was never a lot of it around, but nor were there huge debts. His father's attitude went along the lines of 'Spend now, pay later.' So Jack's idea of an overdraft that you needed to worry about was a few thousand pounds or more. Irene was creating uproar over a mere hundred, and he could not see what all the fuss was about.

When there are arguments about money, and particularly where different views are involved, it is often very useful to talk about the prevailing attitudes in the family you grew up in. These attitudes, as Irene and Jack discovered, are likely to influence the way you yourself behave. In this chapter I also look at various other money-related issues: at how arguments about money can often mask deeper conflicts in the relationship; the different attitudes toward spending, ranging from the spendthrift to the tight and mean; the need for honesty and shared responsibility in handling the household budget; and how, if there is only one salary coming in, whether that feels like his or hers or is seen as joint. Another major topic is how men feel if the woman is the main breadwinner, and how women feel when they give up or lose the independence of an income of their own.

Before you settle into marriage or living together certain tell-tale signs indicate a person's attitude to money, but we often fail to see them or choose not to. A man who goes in for wonderfully extravagant gestures when you are newly in love, by sending you a hundred red roses when you know he had not a bean to his name may seem wonderfully romantic. But five years on, with two children to clothe and feed on a tight budget, those gestures may drive you mad.

A woman may look a million dollars when you first start dating her and you never see her in the same dress twice. This seems great, but five years into the marriage her immaculate taste and shopping habits may have extended to dressing your three children in designer clothes and redecorating and recarpeting the house three times in three years. Has she become a luxury you can no longer afford?

A man who is very slow to put his hand in his pocket to buy a round of drinks may turn out to be equally mean with the housekeeping. A woman who never offers to go Dutch or pay for the both of you, despite the fact that she is earning as much as you or more, may turn out to believe that your salary is joint, but hers is hers.

Hello poverty, goodbye love

If there is just not enough money to cover even the basics of life, that can cripple many relationships. If you have to choose whether to heat or eat, if you cannot afford the children's shoes and clothes, if Christmas is just an expensive nightmare that brings nothing but fear, the daily grind and worry can undermine the best of marriages.

If you do get into debt, don't be tempted to take out loans with high interest repayments. Such short-term solutions only result in worse debts being built up as you struggle to make the repayments. Go to your local Citizens' Advice Bureau, who can if necessary refer you to a debt counsellor who can help you prioritize your debts and make arrangements to repay them in instalments over an agreed period. A debt counsellor can also help you with money management for the future.

But arguments about money are not confined to the very poor. They stretch across all income groups, age groups and socio-economic backgrounds, from the unemployed via a young couple starting off on their relationship to the well-heeled and comfortably off.

Negotiation, joint responsibility and compromise

As Irene and Jack discovered attitudes to which you were exposed as a child influence your approach to money as an adult. But it is essential not to impose your way of doing things on your partner. You must develop and agree a system that works for both of you. That means being honest, open and able to negotiate as circumstances change, and, perhaps most importantly, agreeing to take joint responsibility for all the decisions you make.

What can be really disastrous in a relationship is if one of you says, 'I'm hopeless with money, and you're much better. You do it all.' Firstly, that is abdicating responsibility, and the person who makes this statement is probably doing it in other areas of the relationship as well. Secondly, if one of you takes on the whole responsibility that can in time lead to resentment, because organizing family finances involves a lot of work. It can also mean that if anything goes wrong the person responsible is jumped on heavily by the other in a critical and blaming way. And if the relationship subsequently breaks up you may find yourself totally at sea, or even disadvantaged, if you are the one who has had nothing to do with the money side.

If your money just runs through your fingers it is important to have joint discussions and agreements about it. It is sensible to let the more responsible one take on the role of organizer, paying bills and handling cash transactions but it is important that all money matters are discussed and agreed jointly before any money is spent. In return you can organize and take the responsibility for another part of your lives together.

It's all too easy for debts to creep up, overdrafts to increase and for catalogue shopping or hire purchase to catch up with you. This is especially so if the man thinks to himself 'I don't want to worry her about how tight money is.' Or she thinks 'If I buy something on credit I needn't tell or worry him about it.' As time goes by, the truth will out and by then it tends to be along with a really nasty surprise for the one who has been kept in the dark. That's when the bills hit the mat in the grey light of dawn. Arguments will inevitably follow.

Money management

A considerable amount of research has been done by Jan Pahl on the methods that couples use to handle their money. He classified them into four different systems.

1. *The whole wage system*. One partner, usually the wife, is responsible for managing all the household finances, except possibly the personal spending money of the other partner. This system is typically associated with low incomes.
2. *The allowance system*. Typically, the husband gives his wife a set amount of money and she is responsible for housekeeping,

while the rest of the money remains in his control and he pays for all other items.

3. *The pooling system.* Both partners have access to all household money and both are responsible for managing the common pool and for expenditure. Pooling is more likely to occur as income rises, and when the wife is in employment.

4. *The independent management system.* Both partners have an income which they maintain separately, neither having access to all the financial resources of the household. In this system each partner is responsible for specific items of expenditure; these responsibilities may change over time, but the principle of keeping flows of money separate within the household is maintained.

Two surveys, one by Pahl and the other carried out by the University of Surrey, showed that just under a quarter of all husbands gave their wives an allowance, retaining the rest of their earnings; over half use a pooling system; the remaining quarter use either the whole or the independent management system.

In my experience, for most people the pooling system works best. It is essential to agree together which system is right for you or to develop a system of your own that you are both happy with. If circumstances change, for example if the woman stops work to have a baby, you must both review the system and see if it is desirable or necessary to make any changes.

Balancing the books

It is essential to be totally honest with each other about your earnings and other money, so that you can see what disposable income you have and where it has to go. Having agreed what the total income is, then work out your outlay. The following lists are not definitive, but are intended as a guide.

Essentials

- Mortgage or rent
- Heating
- Lighting and other electricity/gas uses

- Telephone
- Insurance, pensions, school fees
- Food

Other major items

- Car, travel to work
- Clothes
- Holidays
- Replacement of equipment
- Christmas, birthdays

Individual spending money (very variable)

- Subscriptions and fees to gym, golf club, health club etc.
- Books, records, magazines
- Hairdresser, make-up
- A round at the pub, lunch with a friend, a visit to an art gallery

It is very important to see how much of your budget has to go on essentials, and then to decide on the next most important things for you as a couple. All this has to be negotiated, with give-and-take on both sides. The problem is that there is often not enough money to go round in these categories, let alone any left over for individual spending money.

One of the many points that Alice and Eddy frequently argued about was the fact that somehow Eddy seemed to spend about £100 a month more on his drinking and fishing than Alice spent on herself. When she protested, Eddy said, 'I'm quite happy for you to spend the same.'

'But I can't,' complained Alice. 'The money just isn't there.'

'That's rubbish!' responded Eddy.

It was only when they were able to break down their finances and see the facts that Eddy saw how right Alice was. So he had to cut back a little. Alice was not demanding a fifty-fifty split, as it turned out, but she did want things a little more evenly distributed.

Alice is fairly representative of women generally. Many research findings on different spending patterns between the sexes demonstrate a characteristic female spending pattern known as maternal altruism: the needs of the family and children are always treated as paramount, and come before those of wife and mother. The male pattern, on the other hand, is much more concerned with personal spending power.

Arguments over money can be reduced if you negotiate which system you are going to use, and then agree how you are going to pay the bills. Will you have a joint account at the bank or building society, or separate accounts, or both? What methods are you going to use to pay – banker's order in instalments or outright? And who is going to take responsibility for making sure it is paid? All these things should be agreed together.

Are money arguments a smokescreen?

If you are constantly having long, bitter arguments about money and never seem to be getting anywhere, the real source of the argument may lie elsewhere. When Rosie and Bill came for counselling they were in just such a situation. Rosie had given up a good job to stay at home looking after their eighteen-month-old son, Harry. And although money was extremely tight she was now very happy. Her main complaint was that Bill saw his salary as his own. She, on the other hand, felt that, although he was the one out there earning the money it should now be seen as their joint salary, as it was their joint baby that she was staying at home to look after.

Bill said: 'Of course it's our joint salary. But look, we agreed that I would handle the money and the paying of the bills, because this past year you've been so busy looking after Harry. I've been trying to help by taking some of the burden off you. I don't understand why you're so angry. I just can't seem to get anything right.'

Rosie turned to him and said, 'Just giving me the housekeeping every month makes me feel you're feeding your need to control, and this is giving you the perfect excuse to take away my independence.'

Bill said, looking at her angrily: 'That's ridiculous! It's not the housekeeping, it's a monthly allowance that we agreed. It gives you control over buying the food and whatever you and Harry need.'

'But there's never enough left over. It all goes on food, so I never have any money of my own. I have to ask for everything.

It's so humiliating. What's happening to the rest of the money? Why are we always so short?'

'We're not short of money,' shouted Bill. 'There's just less coming in with only me working. Why do you always blame me for everything?'

'I'm not,' yelled Rosie. 'You're blaming me because I'm not working. That's unfair.' By this stage both were so angry that neither was capable of making sensible financial decisions.

But finding a practical solution was not very difficult. Instead of Bill handling everything on his own they set up monthly discussions and looked at all the bills together. That way Rosie knew what money was coming in and going out, so it no longer felt out of sight and out of control. Then, instead of Bill handing over cash each month, Rosie used her own cash card to withdraw money out of their joint account. She took an agreed amount for household items, and another amount for personal spending. She had to take personal responsibility for not spending her own money on food and then complaining that she had no money for herself. The reasons they had not really managed to do so earlier was that any discussion about money rapidly became a battle scene. They were each projecting on to the money issue their fear that the other was trying to control and bully them. As this was what the real arguments were all about, it made the simpler question of working out how to handle the budget virtually impossible.

When they began to look back into their past they were better able to identify the causes of their arguments. Bill's father was an aggressive and domineering man whom Rosie disliked intensely. Bill's mother was just pushed around by him, and Rosie was very sure she was not going to play the downtrodden wife to Bill. Rosie, on the other hand, had been brought up by her mother, who had never really got over the fact that her husband had walked out leaving her with three small children. Rosie remembers always being in debt, having to move from one miserable, dingy house to another. There was so little money that she often went hungry. By the time she was thirteen or fourteen her mother was relying on her more and more to look after the younger children, handle the money and do most of the housework – a lot of responsibility for such a young person. So she missed out on the fun, irresponsible teenage years. She was far too busy looking after her inadequate mother and younger brothers and sisters and trying to cope despite the never-ending shortage of cash. So when she became a mother it was lovely to hear Bill say he would look after her and Harry and she could take time out to be at home. But the other part of her – because of her childhood experiences – found this very difficult to accept. Her experience was that being at home looking after a child meant chaos. So part of her felt she had to stay in control.

Bill also recognized that, if he felt Rosie was trying to control him, he immediately came down on her like a ton of bricks. His experience was that, if you didn't, you got pushed around like his mother had been. Bill hated the way his father treated his mother, and when he saw shades of this in himself he found it so appalling that he at once denied to himself and Rosie that he was behaving in the same way. It was only when the two of them were able to unravel these deeper issues and realize why they were behaving like this that they were able to do things differently and learn to trust each other.

Whose income is it really?

This is a thorny question and there are no simple answers. When you are both working and there are two incomes coming in, it is not a problem. But when there is only one – if the man is made redundant or the woman gives up work to stay at home and look after the children – difficulties can arise.

In the past, men traditionally controlled all family money. On marrying, any money and property belonging to the woman became her husband's by law. Until quite recently there were also still families where the husband put his unopened pay packet on the mantelpiece every Friday night. His wife then took possession of the money and gave him his beer and skittles allowance while she controlled the family finances. Most couples, as research shows, have moved away from these systems. But it is important to recognize that whoever is not earning, for whatever reason, is going to feel sensitive about their lack of earning power or lack of independence. Therefore, though only one of you may be out there earning, the salary or wages should be seen as joint, just as the spending of it should be by joint discussion and agreement. Many unemployed men are delighted that their partner is earning, but others find no longer being the main breadwinner very painful. The women should therefore handle this situation extremely sensitively and never put him down because of it. Any idea held by either sex that because I am the one earning, or because I earn more than you, I have the right to a greater say, or am more entitled than you to make the major decisions, should not be given the time of day in today's relationships.

Men's and women's different attitudes to money

As in most areas of life, different attitudes and behaviour patterns determine the ways men and women handle money.

- *Men set more store than women do on the amount they earn*. Their identity and evaluation of themselves are closely linked with the job they do and the salary they earn. This is particularly noticeable the further up the ladder a man gets. One very talented and successful man said to me, 'If I'm doing consultancy work for a company, it costs that company £xxx. That's how much I'm worth, and it's £x more than any other consultant can charge within my firm.'
- *Women, more than men, marry for money*. Men perhaps set greater store on looks than women do. This may be because until recently women did not have the same job opportunities or earn money at the same level as men. But I do not think that tells all the story. At a charity luncheon a pretty, slim blonde woman in her thirties was holding on to the arm of a very elderly man. He was repeatedly trying to give his glass to a very elegant woman standing next to me.

   The blonde was saying to the old man, 'No, darling, that is not the waitress, that is Lady X.'

   After a while the blonde woman and the old man moved

away. I said to the elegant woman: 'That's really nice of her, to bring her father to the luncheon.'

She smiled. 'It's not her father, my dear, that's her husband. They were married a year ago.'

* *Economy with the truth*. Men are more likely to be economical with the truth over the size of their overdraft or what they have invested in stocks and shares, women over the price of that little black number they bought in the sales.
* *Handling money*. Men are more likely than women to handle the family budget and to organize the standing orders and payment of bills.

A survey undertaken by the Financial Forum for Women, an organization set up not only to change attitudes but also to educate women in financial matters, found the following slightly worrying facts.

* 17 per cent of women leave all major financial decisions to their partner. Marriage and age increased the likelihood of leaving decisions to a partner.
* 30 per cent of women feel that women who have a good grasp of financial matters are often too dominant. This belief is particularly held by older women and those who are widowed, separated or divorced.
* 39 per cent of women admit to finding financial matters boring.
* 15 per cent of women profess to believe that, on the whole, men have a better head for financial affairs.

And here are some further differences, concerning the way money gets spent.

* Men are more likely than women to pay for the meal either on a date, or when they are married or co-habiting and go out as a couple.
* Women are more likely than men to go without so that their children can have something, whether it is better food or an expensive Christmas present.
* Women are more likely to use shopping for clothes, shoes and personal items as a way out of unhappiness (comfort shopping) than men are.

- Women are more likely than men to want to spend money on a new kitchen, new carpets or redecorating the house. Men would prefer to spend their money on an expensive and powerful car, a boat, the latest CD player, a video camera or a computer.

9

WHO RULES THE ROOST

IN-LAWS – FRIEND OR FOE

The family – that dear octopus from whose tentacles we never quite escape.

Dodie Smith, novelist and playwright,
Dear Octopus, 1938

It was Christmas Day, and Pat and Tom had been married for five years. Tom's mother was staying with them and so were Pat's parents. Christmas had been fun, but quite a lot of work, and after lunch Pat was glad to be relaxing in front of a lovely roaring fire. Tom's mother was sitting on the sofa busy knitting what looked like baby clothes.

'Who are those for?' Tom asked, stretching out sleepily.

His mother looking hard at Pat said: 'They are for my grand-children.'

'But Mum,' protested Tom, 'you haven't got any grand-children.'

'I know,' responded his mother, 'and that's the problem. But it's about time I had some. You two are not getting any younger.'

Pat was so shocked and upset at this outburst that she just sat there, not knowing what to say.

Tom got up and went to sit beside his mother on the sofa. He looked at her and said, very kindly and gently, 'Look, I know you want grandchildren, but sitting there knitting is not fair and it's deeply upsetting to Pat and to me. We're planning to have them in another couple of years, but not just yet. So please put away your knitting.'

Pat felt very supported by Tom, and that was very important

to her and to their relationship. Her mother-in-law did nothing for a few minutes, then she picked up her knitting and put it away. 'I'm sorry,' she said, hugging Tom.

When Rupert's mother came to stay, she marched up the garden path clutching brooms and brushes and dusters. Julia, her daughter-in-law, looked rather surprised. As her mother-in-law put them down in the hall she said: 'Well, I know with three children you find it quite impossible to keep the house clean and tidy, so I thought a thorough spring-clean would be a good idea.'

Julia caught her breath and was just about to reply when her husband said, 'That's really kind of you mother. It will be nice to come home to a clean house at the end of the day.'

Julia was furious. She felt that Rupert had been thoroughly disloyal, and her mother-in-law's look of triumph did not improve matters. Over the weekend her mother-in-law dropped a number of critical hints, from Julia's cooking to how she was bringing up the children. When Julia complained to Rupert, he said: 'Don't be hard on her, she's only trying to help.'

So when Julia wasn't coping with the children or her mother-in-law she and Rupert were having rather noisy rows behind closed bedroom doors, because, unlike Pat, she felt very unsupported and ganged up on. If that happens it is always detrimental to the relationship. When you marry or settle down into a committed relationship your first loyalty should always be to your partner. If not, arguments and deep resentments can ensue and may even drive you apart. Just as arguments over money are frequent between many couples, problems with in-laws are also very common.

As well as looking at how to handle difficult in-laws, I shall also be touching on difficult daughters-in-law and sons-in-law, because the situation is far from one-sided.

In-laws or outlaws?

When you marry or decide to live with someone you don't just marry the person you love, you also marry into their family. You may be lucky and your new in-laws may think you are lovely and just right for their offspring. On the other hand they may be ambivalent or even downright hostile.

Even the royal family are not immune to marriage problems. One moment it is reported that the Queen supports and likes the Duchess of York, then the next moment she is said to be an embarrassment to the royal family and they want her out. Or her father claims that part of the reason for the breakdown of his daughter's marriage was that she was so unsupported by the royal family and royal household. Similarly it is reported that the Princess of Wales goes in and out of favour. The Princess herself is claimed to have said: 'How could they treat me like this after all I have done for that family?' Rows happen in all families, but what must be so painful for the royals is that theirs happen in the glare of publicity.

Standing in a bus queue a couple of months ago I overheard a conversation between two women in their late twenties to early thirties. One said. 'My in-laws are coming to stay for the weekend.'

'Oh,' said the other woman. 'Is that difficult?'

'Not at all. They're lovely and such fun. My father-in-law loves his grandchildren and plays with them for hours, and so does my mother-in-law. She even helps with the decorating – she's really good at it. And she's so easy to talk to. We really enjoy having them. The best is that they are both always willing to help out yet never interfere or tell us what to do unless we ask them for advice.'

There we have a pair of in-laws who have really got it right. And there are many that do. But a good relationship with your son-in-law or daughter-in-law, and vice versa, does not automatically happen, and even then it still has to be maintained, just like any important relationship. But what does seem very important is finding that very fine balancing line between being there when they need you and interfering.

Perhaps the most difficult part of being an in-law is seeing how your son's or daughter's partner behaves towards them. Next is the way they are bringing up their children – your grandchildren. Because of the generation gap, it is very likely that you will have done things quite differently, and accepting that it is their way rather than the wrong way is not always easy. Nowadays you may think discipline seems to be minimal, table manners worse, and the baby often stays in the parents' bed or bedroom up to the age of two or three and sometimes longer. Seeing your grandchild being looked after by an au pair or babyminder all day while their parents are at work might worry you. The amount of freedom that teenagers have might feel far too lax to you.

But you must never deprecate the person your child has chosen as a partner, because that can undermine the relationship. It also risks the possibility of alienating you not only from your son-in-law or daughter-in-law but also from your own child.

Mothers-in-law seem worse

In my experience there is more conflict between mothers-in-law and the younger generation than there is with fathers-in-law, who are often happy to go off to the pub with their son or son-in-law in a supportive man-to-man role. With the two couples I mentioned at the beginning of the chapter, Tom was able to support Pat whereas Rupert sided with his mother, which immediately caused rows between Rupert and his wife. If this is occurring in your relationship, you need to find out why. When a grown man finds it difficult to stand up to his mother it is because as a child he was constantly bullied or controlled by her. One senior civil servant, married with four grown-up children of his own, admitted that when he goes to stay with his mother he cannot bring himself to ask for a second cup of coffee at breakfast unless she offers it to him. He is married to a woman who in many ways is very delightful, but there is a part of her that behaves like a spoilt child, with whims and fancies which she feels must be fulfilled. He copes with that by going along with them, hoping that before he has to put his foot down and say, 'We really cannot afford that house in France,' she will have moved on to another fantasy. Then the whole procedure starts all over again. Consequently she has never learnt to grow up, and he continues to bend over backwards to keep her happy. It's just a vicious circle.

A man whose mother was dominating when he was a child either re-enacts that behaviour as an adult or finds that he has never really been able to move away from her controlling influence. As a result he finds confrontation almost impossible. Another crueller but perhaps subtler way that over-domineering mothers use to exercise power is to threaten that his behaviour is making her ill, or words to that effect. So he learns as a child that it is either not safe or not possible to confront her because his behaviour might cause her to do something terrible. Once this pattern is learnt, it is not easy to unlearn.

That is where counselling can help. If a parent is playing too controlling a role in the lives of their grown-up sons or daughters, and disrupting their adult relationships, an objective third person can help. What often makes it particularly difficult for a couple to sort out on their own is that the domineering parent sees the new wife or husband as competition, coming between her and her child. So their existing overbearing behaviour often gets worse at this point and, consciously or unconsciously, they may try to destroy the relationship. The 'good enough' parent, on the other hand, will be pleased to see the child she loves meet and fall in love with someone.

Bronwen, a lovely bubbly Welsh woman, said that her mother-in-law was driving her mad and causing endless rows. At her insistence both her sons called in every day after work, ostensibly to see if she was all right, despite the fact that she was extremely hale and hearty. She then wanted to know all there was to know about their day. So by the time her husband had told his mother about it and got home Bronwen found that he didn't want to go through it all over again – all he wanted was peace and quiet and his supper. She felt rejected, and in her mind wanted to murder her mother-in-law.

Her husband, however, said, 'Don't be so unreasonable. She's a lonely woman – she needs cheering up.'

Yes indeed, and now she had her two sons exactly where she wanted them. When Bronwen and her husband went to Italy on holiday they were shown up to their hotel room and Bronwen went out on to the balcony to find it had an exquisite view. She came back into the room to share her pleasure and excitement with her husband, only to find him on the phone to Wales, saying: 'Yes, we are here now, mother. Yes, I miss you too. Don't worry, two weeks will soon pass.' She felt her happiness just ebbing away, because there she was with this tough Welsh rugby player and, like the song said, 'mother came too'.

Unfair to daughters

Alan found his mother-in-law very difficult. She constantly gave him the impression that he was not good enough for her daughter, Beth. She would compare everything he did with her husband. If he put up a shelf she would say, 'I wish you'd let Jim do that for you, he's so good at carpentry.' Or, 'Of course, Beth's father is such a good provider that she's used to a very good standard of living.'

When he complained to Beth about her mother's put-downs she would say, 'Don't be so stupid! You're imagining it.' And then she would tell him what a wonderful man her father was. In fact, her father hardly uttered a word. He was a very silent man who had long since withdrawn from his bossy and domineering wife in favour of work, fishing or going down to the pub for a bit of peace.

What really enraged Alan was that, for the third Christmas running, his mother-in-law knitted him a green cardigan, a colour he hated – and anyway, he never wore cardigans. When he pointed this out to her as nicely and kindly as he could (for the third year running), she looked surprised and hurt. Beth flew at him, making him feel that the two women were ganging up on him. Every time he tried to have it out with Beth she threatened to pack her bags and go back to her parents' home. In the end the marriage broke up because she was quite unable to move out of her mother's clutches.

Women with overpowering and dominating mothers often play the little girl role in marriage when they become wives. That way they avoid having to grow up and take responsibility for their own actions. As soon as anything gets difficult, instead of trying to sort it out with their partner they leave – usually to return to be with their mother.

These more deep-seated problems are quite difficult to sort out without help. But sometimes exploring what has caused someone to behave in the way they do provides the understanding which in turn can help a person change their own behaviour. But in the main, if there are differences with other family members try talking it out first as a couple and support each other. Then firmly and kindly try to talk it through with the other relevant members of the family.

Love me, love my hobby

A workbench or a rugby ball are not quite the same as a mother-in-law, but they can have the same effect. Hobbies and outside interests are fine as long as they don't intrude too far into your all-important relationship as a couple. There is an apocryphal story of a man who collected reptiles of every shape, sort and size. Despite his wife's pleadings he continued building up his collection so that they took over every bit of space in the house and garden. She even had to share the bedroom with a number of the scaly creatures. One day, at the end of her tether, she faced him with an ultimatum:

'Either they go or I do,' she said.

Hardly turning from feeding one of his favourites, he replied: 'You go, then.'

For most people things are not as extreme as that. But if hobbies are taking more and more time and one of you is finding them more interesting than your partner, it could well be because they are being used as an escape from a difficult relationship. One man's wife caused such a fuss about the time he spent away from home playing the trombone in a jazz band that he gave it up – he became a sub-aqua diving fanatic instead. If a relationship has become mundane and boring, or you are both out of love with each other, hobbies provide a welcome alternative. If any of this rings bells, have a frank discussion with your partner. If your partner refuses to listen, or denies that it is happening, that is confirmation that they possibly no longer care enough to do anything about it.

In new marriages and relationships it can be difficult to adjust to being a couple and to recognize that you can no longer please yourself most of the time. There is now someone else to think about, someone else's needs to take into consideration. Too much sport can be very intrusive. If you are at work all day and then spending nearly every evening and weekend pursuing one sport or another, perhaps you are trying to have your cake and eat it – feeling you can have the benefits of married life as well as the freedom of your bachelor days (it tends to be men rather than women who fall into this category). But it won't work – the relationship is bound to suffer. Neither should you feel you have to give it all up. That road only leads to resentment. You need to find somewhere in between that is a compromise for you both: maybe you settle for playing sport a couple of nights a week and Saturday afternoons.

Although it is important to have individual interests as well as shared ones, it is equally important not to end up excluding each other. Frequently, when people first come to counselling, I discover that they have slipped into spending very little time together and have become strangers under the same roof. If that happens the chances are that someone else will come along and fill that gap, or the marriage will break down, or both.

In this chapter I have looked at the difficult relationships that many people experience, either with their parents or their in-laws, and have acknowledged that it's not always the older generation which can cause problems. I have also stressed the importance of making time for each other. Spending time together is, after all, one of the reasons you chose to marry or be with each other in the first place, and it is important if you want to keep your love alive, as I shall be describing in Chapter 10.

10

MAKING LOVE WORK

GETTING THE BEST FROM YOUR RELATIONSHIP – FOR LIFE

It was the generosity of delight
that first we learned in a sparsely-furnished flat
clothed in our lovers' nakedness. By night
we timidly entered what we marvelled at,

ranging the flesh's compass. But by day
we fell together, fierce with awkwardness
the window-light and scattered clothing lay
impassive round such urgent happiness.

Now, children, years and many rooms away,
and tired with experience, we climb the stairs
to our well-furnished room; undress and say
familiar words for love, and from the cares

that back us, turn together and once more seek
the warmth of wonder each to the other meant
so strong ago, and with known bodies speak
the unutterable language of content.

Maurice Lindsay, 1964

It was their fifth wedding anniversary. As a celebration Fleur's husband Charlie said he was planning to take her away for the weekend and asked if she could arrange to have the Friday and Monday off work. He said the destination was a surprise.

'How will I know what to pack?' asked Fleur, guessing that it was probably Scotland as they had been talking about going there.

It was June. Charlie said, 'Well, you won't need clothes for very cold weather, so take some light clothes as well.' Fleur thought now that perhaps it would be Jersey. Scotland was unreliable in June and they had talked about going there as well.

Early on the Friday morning they set off for Heathrow. Charlie parked in the long-stay car park and they climbed aboard the airport bus. At the first stop Charlie got up to get out. 'Internal Flights,' thought Fleur, 'so it is Jersey.' Then, just as Fleur was about to follow him, he sat down again. At the next terminal stop Charlie gathered the cases up. 'Perhaps Paris or Prague,' thought Fleur as she started to leave the bus. 'Have I packed the right clothes?' But there was Charlie, laughing and sitting down again. Then, as she sat down beside him, he turned to her and said, 'Happy anniversary, darling,' and gave her the *Berlitz Guide to New York* and two airline tickets.

It was a lovely, total and utter surprise – the one place she most certainly had not thought of. It was somewhere she had always wanted to go to, but it had also been somewhere they had always thought was too expensive. Of course, not everyone can afford New York for the weekend, even if they do save up for it. But an unexpected gift, going out to dinner or tickets for a show you know your partner would really like to see are all small but important ways of showing them you love them and have thought about them.

One 14 February Liz prepared a Valentine's Day meal for her husband, Peter. 'I know it sounds silly,' she said, 'but it was lovely and he thought it was great. Everything was pink – the lighting, the candles, the tablecloth, the food, my dress and even the champagne. We sat and talked, drank the champagne and made love. It was a wonderfully romantic evening. That was over thirty years ago,' she said, smiling. 'Thirty years and one daughter later, and I'm still just as much in love with him today as then – perhaps even more so because now we've shared so much. We still just love being with each other.' This year it was he who surprised her. He knew she really wanted to travel through the newly opened Channel Tunnel, so he booked tickets for New Year's Eve. They arrived in Paris on a lovely winter's day just in time for lunch. They celebrated with a delicious meal for two in a charming little restaurant and spent the night in Paris before returning home the next day.

In this final chapter I want to touch once more on that all-important element in any relationship – communication. Keeping love alive is about talking, being open with each other, supporting your partner and making them feel loved and special. Enjoy the differences, but also have lots in common. A good relationship combines love, intimacy, respect, sexual attraction, laughter and fun. Coping with difficult and painful experiences can give greater maturity to the individual and greater depth to the marriage or relationship. A true partnership is one which not only brings joy in its own right, but gives people a chance to repair some of the damage that all children experience while growing up.

Romantic love

Another very important ingredient in a marriage or committed relationship is romantic love. I think there is a place for it alongside all the other things mentioned above. It is so important not to slide into taking each other for granted and thinking that because you are married there is no need to show and tell each other that you love them. Of course you cannot spend every weekend on romantic journeys or every evening sharing an intimate dinner for two. The day-to-day process of living, looking after the children, paying the bills and dealing with all that life throws at you gets in the way. But relationships in which the time and attention you gave each other when you first met have dwindled to nothing very often come to grief. If you are feeling neglected and unloved, and suspect that your partner has no time for you, is it really surprising that your marriage or relationship breaks up?

Don't make assumptions

If you assume that, because you love someone, you always know what they are thinking and feeling and they in turn understand all your needs, you could be in very dangerous waters. Penelope assumed that on Zoe's first birthday her husband would want to make it a very special day for both her and their daughter. She had wanted him to buy little presents to show he was thinking of them, and to tell her how clever and lovely she was for having their baby.

There was, of course, more going on at a deeper level. She had little good mothering as a child and had wanted to be made to feel very special on that day, as he had made her feel a year ago at the time of the birth. Part of her had assumed he would know all this, and the other part wanted him to know it without her having to say anything.

There was no question of him not remembering the day – it had in fact started by him bringing her lovely fresh coffee in bed and insisting that he would prepare the breakfast. But it was not until she explained to him how very important the day was that he realized the depths of her needs. There had been a minor argument because she had felt disappointed that he had not automatically recognized her needs, but instead of getting angry and feeling rejected she had explained how she felt. He had very quickly cottoned on and made a note that next year he would meet her needs, and not assume that his way of celebrating the day was necessarily the same as hers.

Though women on the whole may be more emotionally literate than men, they don't have the monopoly in the sensitivity stakes. In my time I have come across some extremely insensitive women. I am also aware that, in their impatience and exasperation over men's apparent inability to express their feelings, women often fall into the trap of telling them how the men feel. They may or may not be right; whether or not, the woman is pretty sure to get a defensive reply, a put-down or a denial. This stops any exploration on his part or hers of how he really was feeling. Being asked how you feel and being given time to explore your feelings at your pace is very important in intimate relationships.

But being aware, being more in touch with how others feel, being empathic and sympathetic, less inclined to tell someone in trouble to snap out of it or wondering what all the fuss is, does seem to be more common in women than in men. This is perhaps not only the result of society's expectations of women but also because women tend to play the nurturing role in families. So listening to others' problems is traditionally seen as women's work, just as problem-solving is seen as men's.

Understanding yourself

Sometimes people find it very difficult to cope with strong feelings, because they make them feel uncomfortable or vulnerable. So they project what they are feeling on to the other person and then attribute their feelings to them. Then, because they find them unacceptable in themselves, they criticize or blame their partner for the way they are behaving.

When Nina and Simon came into counselling they both had several marriages and broken relationships behind them. What they had in common was a tremendous commitment to try to make the present relationship work, and intense fear that it was going wrong as their past relationships had done. Both of them had great problems trusting each other, as they had both been badly let down in the past: Simon by his alcoholic father and suicidal mother, and Nina by a father who had walked out when she was ten.

Both of them were very quick to anger, but in quite different ways. Simon's anger was very controlled and he would always deny it: this was his way of dealing with it. So he would unconsciously try to make Nina express it for him, by saying something to which she would be likely to react adversely. He then criticized her for being unreasonable, by which time Nina would be reacting not only to her own feelings of anger but to his as well.

Once, when they were well into one of these arguments, Simon said quietly: 'If you weren't so totally unreasonable we could resolve these disagreements much more easily.'

Nina, by then thoroughly wound up, shouted: 'How can you say that? It's absolutely not true – what you've just said makes me feel totally destroyed.'

Then Simon, with a look of satisfaction on his face and using a patient, teacher-like tone of voice, said even more calmly, 'If you're set on being so uncontrollable, there's little point in me saying anything.'

This infuriated her even more, as it was designed to do. She came back at him with a whole cartload of complaints and threatened to leave him.

So yet again nothing was resolved and Nina had one more

grievance to add to her list. It was only when Simon was able to understand that his real anger lay with his father over his drinking and his mother's attempted suicide, but that as a boy he had never been able to express these feelings for fear of things getting even worse, that he was able to see that he was getting Nina to express his anger because for him to do so felt too dangerous.

Who talks more?

When asked who talks more, men or women, most people will answer: 'Oh, women, of course.' But when you look at this more closely, as many researchers have done, what you actually find is that it depends on the context. In the home and in intimate relationships it is women who talk more, but in public meetings, conferences and work situations it is men who are more likely to dominate and to speak more often and at greater length.

In her book *You Just Don't Understand Me* Deborah Tannen highlights the difference by describing men as being more comfortable with what she calls 'report talk' and women with 'rapport talk'. By this she means that most women use the language of conversation as a language of rapport, to make connections and reinforce intimacy. For most men, however, talk is primarily a means of preserving independence and negotiating status in a hierarchical social order. This is done by exhibiting knowledge and skill, and by holding centre stage through verbal performance such as parliamentary question time, storytelling, joking or imparting information. From childhood, men learn to use talking as a way to get and keep other people's attention. She suggests that men are therefore more comfortable speaking in larger groups made up of people they know less well. If men transfer this use of language into their intimate relationships, women can feel that they are on the receiving end of a lecture. What they want, of course, is intimacy through talking together. And whereas men seem to do a lot of talking in work situations, when they come home at the end of the day to a domestic intimate situation they often appear to have taken a vow of silence and hardly utter a word. The result is often frustration and confusion.

Men hold conversations, women gossip

Some people believe this statement, but as a woman I am hardly likely to agree. There are however differences in the way men and women talk not only to each other but also to their friends of the same sex. Women try to create intimacy through talking and sharing their thoughts and feelings and by being open about their problems. They get a lot of reassurance from their friends' networks, and it is very important to them to have female friends whose company they enjoy and who, they feel, understand them. Women often talk to their female friends much more openly than men would perhaps like them to. They don't see it as running the man down, but more as a relief of tension and frustration and in order to be heard, which is something they don't always get from their partners. But men hate being talked about in this way and see it as a form of betrayal which belittles them.

In male friendships, men's talk is often an exchange of ideas and information rather than an exchange of feeling. To them this creates bonding and friendship. They do talk about feelings and difficulties in relationships, but in a much more limited way.

A man meeting a good friend for a drink in a pub is more likely to talk about work, sport or women than admit to his male companion that he has a problem, especially if it's a sexual one. He is unlikely to say, 'I feel bloody awful, I haven't been able to make love to my wife for several weeks now. Every time we make love I lose my erection. I don't know what to do.' He'd be afraid of being laughed at or thought a wimp. But two close women friends talking would be more likely to be able to say, 'Since Vicky was born I've just lost all interest in sex. We haven't made love for over six months. Do you think I'll ever feel sexy again?'

I believe men do not necessarily need intimacy and disclosure to deepen a friendship. They are more likely to be looking for a sense of comradeship, a fun companion to play squash or golf with, someone they can trust – in fact a nice uncomplicated relationship in which you can say what you think without reducing the other fellow to tears.

Many women seem to be better at basic conversational skills than men, either by using small talk as an ice-breaker in the early stages of the getting-to-know-you process, or, more importantly, by being supportive and co-operative. A woman is more likely to end what she is saying with, 'isn't it' or 'what do you think', inviting the other person to respond. This minimally aggressive or assertive way is likely to get a similar response. But in conversation socially and at work many men try to dominate. So they are blunter, interrupt each other more and jostle for the high ground.

If these different conversational styles are taken into men and women's relationships at home, women soon resent it and will probably respond by withdrawing their support. At one time it was a wife's duty to make the man feel good by humouring him, agreeing with him and introducing a new subject if he got bored with the one under discussion. But modern women have an entirely different script. They want equal understanding to that which they give.

So as a rule in relationships, men tend to be more hooked into the need to maintain their independence than women. And women are more likely to be seeking intimacy than independence in their relationships with men. These different goals, if not understood and negotiated, can become a constant struggle and balancing act between the couple.

Why do we want loving relationships?

When the writer Jeannette Kupfermann's husband was dying of cancer, she wrote: 'I weep for this man I love above everything and everyone else: who has been my mother, father, friend, lover, comforter and mentor – my constant companion and ally.' She is describing so poignantly what women seek in relationships, because to be so loved and to love in return is perhaps the greatest gift that life can offer.

All of us, when we choose our partners in marriage and in relationships, are seeking among other things someone who can make up for some of the things we did not get from our parents. Or we are trying to find another adult who can repair some of the hurts that lie buried but still unresolved deep down within us. When we find such a person, it is emotionally very satisfying.

Someone who has been very emotionally deprived as a child will probably be the neediest adult of all. Their 'inner child' (unresolved childhood needs) will be in search of constant love, affirmation and reassurance from their partner. If they then marry someone with equal needs, frequently neither of them has the emotional maturity to fulfil the demands on them. Even if they have, being continually asked to fill up those big empty spaces in another human being can drain you of all your emotional resources.

That is not to deny that all of us want love and reassurance, but those who believe they are lovable human beings, and who have a good degree of self-value and self-worth, are the people most equipped to give love to others. Self-love, which is quite different from self-centredness, enables you to be more loving to others. Often when people come for counselling it emerges that they have little self-love or belief in themselves. It is necessary to work with them individually so they can establish some self-worth before working with them on the couple relationship.

Talking it through

In this book I have tried to highlight the differences between men and women because it is only when we are really able to understand them that men and women can learn to form better and more fulfilling relationships. As I have constantly made clear, I believe the key to unlocking the secret of a fulfilling relationship is communication.

As well as loving women, men find them at times complex, emotional and unpredictable. They are often quite baffled by how much and for how long women need to talk issues and problems through. Or men think they have had that conversation before – and indeed they might have done – so they wonder why she wants to go over it all again and again.

Similarly, women often find men frustrating because in their opinion many of them are not able to articulate their feelings or understand the woman properly – and doing so does not seem important to them anyway. Women can also find the tendency to adopt the male-orientated, solution-focused approach to problems infuriating because it ignores the fact that they as women don't want to be told what to do, but rather to talk it through carefully and then come up with a solution. The typical male approach makes them angry. This feels like rejection to the man, when after all he was only trying to help. And it also confirms him in his belief that women can be impossible and he will never learn to understand them.

Men need to learn to understand their partner's need to talk things through more, and to appreciate that for her talking is not just about sharing information and discussing solutions but also to do with feeling understood and supported. And women need to learn to understand that men often find female reactions to problems emotionally over-charged, and that in the main they need less talking time than women do, then the differences might not alienate the sexes so much. And if each could try to meet the other 50 per cent of the way they might achieve greater mutual understanding.

As a counsellor I have shared in people's lives at times of great unhappiness and despair, but have also seen their amazing courage and determination to resolve their problems and to make those relationships work. I frequently see couples who are able to strengthen and renew their relationships for the benefit of themselves and their children. I also see couples who have been to the brink of divorce but have found loving and positive ways of understanding and overcoming their difficulties. Other couples find that this is not possible and break up, but they can go on to build fulfilling, happy and successful new lives and embark on new marriages and relationships which can bring happiness for themselves and their children.

Having someone to love and be loved by is, I believe, a fundamental need for almost everyone. When we come into this world our first experience is being loved and cared for, and that feels good. Most of us want to recapture and experience those early feelings, which is why people are constantly seeking and searching for love. If it goes wrong, the majority of people continue that search. There are others who feel they have been so hurt by their experience that they try to avoid further intimate relationships, but after a while they too usually want to pick up the search for someone to love who will love them in return.

The trouble with you

When social historians look back over the last fifty to a hundred years I am sure they will be struck by the degree of change that marriage has undergone in that period. They will perhaps wonder not why the divorce rate increased so much, but how so many couples were able to adapt to these changes and make their relationships work. The period in question encompasses the emancipation of women, the impact of two world wars on the lives of both sexes, the feminist movement and the search for equality in relationships as well as at work and life generally. They will see how the changing role of women has had a major impact on their lives and those of men both at home and at work. This is also reflected in changing moral values and the increase in one-parent families through separation and divorce as well as the never-married single parent. There have been huge changes in sexual freedom, within marriage and outside. A wide choice of contraception has resulted in much smaller families among other things. And the majority of women now have jobs and careers outside the home. All of this has greatly influenced the very different expectations that men and women have concerning marriage and relationships when compared with those of previous generations. If we compare marriage in the past to what it is nowadays, we cannot fail to recognize that couples' expectations of each other in marriage and relationships have never been higher.

The companionate marriage which I talked about in Chapter 1, and which is what we have in this last part of the twentieth century, embodies among other things the expectation that husband and wife will be faithful partners, lovers and best friends. Many people go into marriage expecting that it will fulfil their needs, but this is often unrealistic since no two people can fulfil each other's needs all of the time. It is quite appropriate that some of these needs are satisfied outside the central relationship – in work, interests and hobbies, friendships and experiences. These outside interests can be brought back into the marriage and can enrich and strengthen the couple's relationship.

Never before have marriage or committed relationships offered such opportunities for fulfilment and happiness, but to achieve this state men and women must continue to struggle with the changes and learn how to understand each other better. The trouble with women, to quote Professor Higgins in *My Fair Lady*, is this:

> *Let a woman in your life and your serenity is through,*
> *She will redecorate your home, from the cellar to the dome,*
> *Then go on to the enthralling fun of overhauling you.*

And the trouble with men – women would say – is that they are rather resistant to change.

But I would like to leave the last word to Sigmund Freud, writing to Marie Bonaparte in 1856: 'The great question that has never been answered, and which I have not yet been able to answer despite my thirty years' research into the feminine soul is – what does a woman want.' I hope this book has gone a little way in helping to answer that question.

SURVEYS

Financial Forum for Women Survey, founded by National Council of Women and National & Provincial's Financial Services, London, October 1993

What Men Really Think About Women, GQ Magazine, Conde Nast Publications Ltd, London, January 1995

The Hidden Figure Survey, Domestic Violence in North London, Borough of Islington, 1994

Mintel *Women 2000* Survey, Mintel International Group Ltd, London, January 1995

MORI Survey, Hays Personal Services, London, 1994

Office of Population Censuses and Surveys (OPCS), Government Central Statistical Office

Social Trends, Edition 25, Government Central Statistical Office, London, 1995

Wilson G.D. Survey, The Secrets of Sexual Fantasy

Zero Tolerance Campaign, Association of London Authorities, 1990

BIBLIOGRAPHY

Belsky, Professor Jay, *The Transition to Parenthood*, Vermilion, London, 1994

Bowlby, Dr John, *Attachment and Loss*, Penguin Books, London, 1991

Briggs Myers, Isobel, *Gifts Differing*, CPP Books, California, 1993

Brown, G.W. and Harris, T., *Social Origins of Depression*, Tavistock Publications, London, 1978

Gilligan, Carol, *In a Different Voice*, Harvard University Press, USA, 1982

Hawton, Dr Keith, *Sex Therapy – A Practical Guide*, Oxford University Press, Oxford, 1991

Hochschild, Dr Arlie, *The Second Shift*, Piatkus, London, 1990

Jung, C.G., *Psychological Types*, Harcourt University Press, New York, 1923

Lawson, Annette, *Adultery*, Basil Blackwell, Oxford, 1989

Longauex y Vasquez, Enriqueta, *Sisterhood is Powerful*, Robin Morgan, USA, 1970

Lurie, Alison, *The War Between the Tates*, Heinemann and Random House, London, 1974

Pahl, Jan, *Patterns of Money Management within Marriage*, Journal of Social Policy 9, 1980

Russell, Bertrand, *The Conquest of Happiness*, first published 1930, Routledge, London, 1992

Smith, Dodie, *Dear Octopus*, Heinemann, London, 1938

Stassinopoulos, Arianna, *The Female Woman*, Davis Poynter, London, 1973

Tannen, Deborah, *You Just Don't Understand Me*, Virago Press, London, 1991

Thomas Ellis, Alice, *The Other Side of the Fire*, Penguin Books, London, 1983

Weiss, R., *The Fund of Sociability, Transactions*, The Journal of Sexual and Marital Therapy, vol 8, no. 3, 1993

Whitton, Charlotte, *Canada Month*, Ottawa, 1963

INDEX